W9-DDE-339

Edith Head

The Life and Times of Hollywood's
Celebrated Costume Designer

DAVID CHIERICHETTI

HarperCollins*Publishers*

Photograph opposite title page: *Edith sketching*

HarperCollins books may be purchased for educational, business, or sales promotional use. For information, please write: Special Markets Department, HarperCollins Publishers Inc., 10 East 53rd Street, New York, NY 10022.

All photographs were provided courtesy of Photofest unless otherwise credited. Tom Culver, Jay Jorgenson, and the author supplied the sketches.

FIRST EDITION

Designed by Jessica Shatan

Printed on acid-free paper

Library of Congress Cataloging-in-Publication Data

Chierichetti, David.
Edith Head / David Chierichetti.—1st ed.
p. cm.
Includes index.
ISBN 0-06-019428-6 (hardcover : alk. paper)
1. Head, Edith. 2. Costume designers—California—Los Angeles—Biography. 3. Motion picture actors and actresses—California—Los Angeles. I. Head, Edith. II. Title.
TT505.H4 C455 2002
746.9'2'092—dc21
[B] 2002024677

02 03 04 05 06 ❖/RRD 10 9 8 7 6 5 4 3 2 1

For my brother,
Paul Chierichetti,
and his family

Edith Head, her husband Wiard Ihnen, and their ten Oscars

Contents

Acknowledgments

Many people helped me with information about Edith Head over the past thirty years; they are too numerous to mention here but are cited in the text. I would also like to thank my editor, Susan Friedland, her assistant Monica Meline, Victoria Wilson, and my friend Howard Mandelbaum of Photofest, who supplied many of the illustrations, read the manuscript, and gave much encouragement over a long process, as well as Amy Fine Collins of *Vanity Fair*. For other illustrations, I am indebted to Jay Jorgenson, Tom Culver, and the Margaret Herrick Library of the Academy of Motion Picture Arts and Sciences. Several of their librarians also helped with the research: most important, Robert Cushman, Barbara Hall, and Stacy Behlmer. Last, James Kaumpf sent me much published research, which was very helpful too.

Introduction

Edith outfitted Hollywood's most memorable stars for over four decades, winning eight Academy Awards for costume design. She worked across genres, from screwball comedies like Preston Sturges's *Miracle of Morgan's Creek* to noir thrillers like Alfred Hitchcock's *Notorious.* She worked with legendary screen actresses—Bette Davis, Ginger Rogers, Barbara Stanwyck, Marlene Dietrich, Ingrid Bergman, Joan Crawford, Audrey Hepburn. Head was a master of understated style, but throughout her career she had moments to shine. It's impossible to imagine Hitchcock's films without the clean lines and understated feminine vulnerability of Grace Kelly's wardrobe. Gloria Swanson's haunting depiction of lost youth and twisted ambition in *Sunset Boulevard* would not hold the same power without the faded, eccentric glamour of Norma Desmond's party dresses.

Edith Head was talented, ambitious, endlessly hardworking, adept at solving problems. She worked within the rigid structure and cruel maze of the studio system, where the whims of directors and actresses often collided with the practical world of the costume designer. Head's critics have suggested that she lacked artistic talent and creative flair. But if she lacked something in terms of a pure artistic gift, she made up for it with diligence and diplomacy. "She was not the best designer in Hollywood, but she knew how to work it," said celebrated designer Bob Mackie, who was briefly Head's assistant. Often Head didn't use a creative new design idea for fear it might get in the way of her main goals: keeping everybody happy and keeping herself permanently employed in a very unpredictable business.

Hollywood has always been a place of paradox, and while Head lived and designed in the midst of glamour, politics and hard work were never far behind. Keeping her career going meant absorbing disappointment and abuse, even as her fame and success grew. It meant decades of working seven days a week. It meant endlessly promoting herself as diplomatically as possible and protecting herself against other designers who might usurp her position. It was a lonely life. Of course she wanted friends, but friends required time she didn't have. And in Hollywood sometimes it's better not to get too close to a friend, for then it becomes harder to stab him in the back if he gets in the way. She had few close friends throughout the years, but she never gave up on her second husband, Wiard (Bill) Ihnen, a man who accepted her career and supported her emotionally through all its vicissitudes.

Careful observance of screen legends like Marlene Dietrich and Mae West taught her the importance of creating a unique personal image. Hers consisted of dark glasses, an unchanging hairstyle, and a blank "schoolmarm" expression she wore at the studio and on TV talk shows. The real Edith was anything but emotionless. She was jubilant when a dress turned out well or she got a favorable notice in the press. She was despondent when another designer got an assignment she wanted. She was anxious when she got a project she feared was beyond her abilities, yet deep down she knew she would manage somehow. She always did.

Her knowledge of all aspects of film production was impeccable. Tom Bronson, who worked as a costumer with her in the late 1960s, remembers, "I'd go to a production meeting with Edith and she had an instinct about just when she could make a suggestion about the hairdressing or the art direction and when she [should] keep quiet. When she walked onto a soundstage, literally all talking stopped, the respect for her in the business was that great. But she knew how to treat people. After she'd talked to all the important people, she'd go over and say something to the man who swept the sets."

Ultimately Head found that being famous made her position in work and life more secure than either hard work or sacrifice. Head was strong and wise, but there were also moments when she showed a childlike need for constant attention and approval. Although being famous didn't make her tremendously wealthy, it went a long way towards compensating for a miserable childhood.

When I began researching my book, *Hollywood Costume Design,* in the early 1970s, I approached Edith with trepidation. Rumors abounded that she didn't really do the work herself and couldn't even draw. Her subordinates in the wardrobe department were terrified of her. When I interviewed the other designers, some spent more time putting Edith down than extolling their own virtues. Nonetheless the Edith Head I knew was the personification of humor and kindness. At home she was witty and laughed often. (Once she pulled on my shoulder-length hair and cracked, "What's new, Goldilocks?") It wasn't hard to be her friend as long

A rare photo of Edith smiling, with her black-and-white dog Boppo (Boppo was Bill Ihnen's middle name)

as one accepted the basic premise that she was *the* Edith Head and always would be, no matter how much else in the world might change.

In the late 1970s, I worked as a costumer at Universal and other studios. Everywhere I went I asked my coworkers about their experiences with Edith. The two colleagues who both eventually became Edith's friends as well, and who helped me the most, were Sheila O'Brien and Yvonne Wood. O'Brien started as a seamstress at Paramount, later founded the Motion Picture Designers' Guild, IATSE Local 892, and served as its business agent. Wood, a talented artist and designer herself, was Edith's ghost on the film *The Life and Times of Judge Roy Bean* (1972).

Many people I've interviewed who worked alongside her for years could truthfully say they hardly knew her. Olivia de Havilland remarked, "I requested Edith many times for my costumes because I knew she would deliver what I needed to play the roles. Yet after thirty-some years, I could never penetrate her wall of reserve. Once I dropped by her house when Anne Baxter was there. In just a moment I could see her talking frankly to Anne about something and I thought, 'That's good. She has one friend.' "

In the twelve years I knew her, I had many conversations with Edith. I dined with the Ihnens almost every week and talked to her on the phone almost daily. She liked me because I knew enough about costume design to know what she was talking about, yet was unambitious enough to pose no threat to her. (She once remarked to my mother, "That kid of yours thinks he knows all about film history." Then she added, ruefully, "And he does.") As a friend, I had to respect her ground rules: she wouldn't talk about her miserable childhood and she would not tolerate any mention of her first husband, Charles Head. She never divulged anything a star had told her in confidence, even if that star had long since died. Other than quotable, cute little anecdotes, she was reluctant to say anything negative about anyone she had worked with, explaining: "I might have to dress her again."

Ultimately, however, she did share more with me as she realized her life was coming to an end. Hers is a remarkable story of a time and a place, and of a woman whose life and career will never be duplicated.

Edith
Head

1

Early Life

I didn't have what you would call an artistic or cultural background. We lived in the desert and we had burros and jackrabbits and things like that."

With those two sentences, Head dismissed her whole childhood the first time I interviewed her. Throughout her life, Head rarely revealed any details of her birth or childhood, though on a small table in her dressing room she kept studio portraits of both her parents. Jane Kesner Ardmore, who cowrote Head's autobiography *The Dress Doctor,* recalled, "Edith was strictly today and tomorrow. She didn't like thinking about yesterday. At first I insisted that she tell me something about her childhood, and she insisted she couldn't remember anything. So I said, 'At our next meeting, I want you to bring along all of your childhood photos.' Edith said she grew up in Mexico and they never took any. I said, 'I've lived in Mexico too, and I've seen peasants carry their children for miles to have them photographed.' So at the next meeting she came with a whole suitcase full of photos. She showed me a picture of one man and said, 'That was my father.' Then she showed me a picture of another man and said that one was her father. I told her they were obviously two different men. She finally admitted that the second man was her stepfather. She found it painful to admit that her mother remarried."

Edith Head was born Edith Claire Posener on October 28, 1897, in San Bernardino, California. Her biological father, Max Posener, was a naturalized American citizen who had come to the United States from Prussia in 1876, at the age of eighteen. Her mother was Anna E. Levy, born in St. Louis, Missouri, in 1874, to an Austrian father and a Bavarian mother. There is nothing to document how Max and Anna met, or if they moved to California together, or met after arriving there. Together they traveled around Southern California and lived in various cities. Shortly before Edith's birth, Max took out a $1,500 promissory note from the San Bernardino National Bank to set up a haberdashery on Third Street. It failed within a year, and the bank sued. Max's stock and fixtures were sold for a fraction of their worth, and he left town. The 1900 census found Max living in an El Paso boardinghouse and working as a merchant of millinery goods. He said he had been married for five years and listed "Annie" and Edith as fellow boarders. It is the last record of the three living together.

In *The Dress Doctor,* Edith makes only one mention of Max Posener, referring to a visit she paid him in El Paso after her mother had remarried, and describing him as a "slender man, with brown hair, thinking eyes and a moustache. He was a fine Latin scholar, my father, a man who read a great deal." Posener stayed in her life, however, as people at Paramount remembered him visiting her there when he was elderly. Edith's maid Myrtle City later described him as looking like "a little Jewish peddler man."

Was Anna Levy ever married to Max Posener? There is no record of a marriage or a subsequent divorce. In 1901, in San Bernardino, Levy married Frank Spare, a mining engineer born in Pennsylvania in 1856. At the time of their marriage, Levy said she had not been married before and had no children, though her daughter, Edith, was three years old at the time. The family moved around often as Spare's mining jobs changed locations. The only town Head remembered well enough to name was Searchlight, Nevada. Jane Ardmore remembered seeing a photo of Edith, perhaps five or six years old, sitting alone on the porch of Spare's cottage in Searchlight, without another person or even any vegetation to be seen for miles around.

COURTESY OF THE ACADEMY OF MOTION PICTURE ARTS AND SCIENCES

Edith, circa 1908 (photo taken during a trip to Chicago)

Frank and Anna Spare passed Edith off as their mutual child, and since Spare was a Catholic, Edith became one too, or at least she pretended she was. I wondered later if she ever officially converted herself to Catholicism after an exchange one night when she was joking about the fact that she and her second husband, Bill Ihnen, were "living in sin," since they had had a civil wedding and were never remarried in any church. It was the only time I ever saw Bill come close to losing his temper with Edith. He said, "I've told you before, Edith. Let's go see the priest and find out what I have to do and we'll get married again." She nervously jested, "Oh, I think it's much more fun to live in sin," and quickly changed the subject.

Maybe having to hide the fact that Spare was not her real father and that she was Jewish started Edith on a lifelong pattern of lying. Of course, dissembling would often be necessary at the studio, to be diplomatic; there were times when telling somebody they would look great in a costume (when obviously they wouldn't) was unavoidable. However, Edith's designing colleague Natalie Visart commented, "Edith lied when the truth would have served her better." These lies gave her the confidence that she was in control of the situation. This would become the aspect of her personality, even more than her blazing ambition, which turned people against her.

Frank Spare's mining activities seemed to bring him a measure of affluence, for he took his wife and daughter to Chicago when Edith was about five and to New York when Edith was eight. In New York she was fitted with glasses for the first time. Gradually his assignments were more and more often south of the border (something she could not bring herself to admit in *The Dress Doctor,* though she talked of visiting Juarez as a tourist). Shortly before her death, she asked me to be her biographer, and I gently reminded Edith that I would have to know more about her childhood. Very haltingly, almost like somebody admitting to a crime, she named several locales in Mexico where Spare's work took them, each more dismal than the last. In some cases, she and her mother were the only women in the camp, and it fell to them to cook for the miners over open fires. For several years, Edith received no education except what her mother could teach her.

Anna Spare had once known a comfortable life, and she was

COURTESY OF THE ACADEMY OF MOTION PICTURE ARTS AND SCIENCES

Edith, her mother, and playmates at a birthday party (Edith is about seven)

determined to get her daughter away from the rough miners. She took Edith to Los Angeles to live with her best friend, Mittie Morgan. After some intensive tutoring, Edith enrolled in Los Angeles High School, which was then at the corner of Sunset Boulevard and Grand Avenue in downtown Los Angeles. Mittie lived on Fourth and Grand, in the Zelda apartment building. There was a ballroom on the top floor. Edith arranged for the school to use it for a dance and plunged into both her studies and extracurricular activities with a vengeance. She took the lead in a school play and trained in sports, especially tennis. Also enrolled at Los Angeles High at that time was Harold Grieve, later an important art director for silent films. He and Edith became lifelong friends.

Edith's last two years at Los Angeles High were the equivalent of junior college. After graduating in 1917 at the age of twenty, she enrolled in the University of California at Berkeley. Frank Spare had kindly taken her aside and said, "Edith my girl, you're no beauty. If you're going to get anywhere in this world it will be with your brains." She was short and dark, bowlegged, and behind her thick glasses her right eye was slightly crossed. On June 4, 1919, she received her B.A. degree in Letters and Sciences with honors in French from the University of California at Berkeley. In 1920 she received a master's degree in Romance Languages from Stanford. The 1920 census listed Frank and Anna Spare as being back in San Bernardino where Frank was mining potash. Max Posener was still in El Paso, the proprietor of a Millinery department store.

Returning to Los Angeles in the summer of 1920, Edith moved back in with Mittie who now had a house near the fashionable Westlake Park. Virtually the only work open to educated women at the time was teaching school, and Edith unexpectedly got lucky.

COURTESY OF THE ACADEMY OF MOTION PICTURE ARTS AND SCIENCES

Edith with other teachers at the Bishop School, 1919

The prestigious Bishop School in La Jolla (just north of San Diego) suddenly needed a French teacher to replace a lady who had gone back to France on a family emergency. Although hardly older than the girls she was teaching, Edith already seemed matronly and fit in with her spinster colleagues. With them she chaperoned dances though she longed to dance herself.

This job ended, and in June Edith returned to Los Angeles where she secured another teaching job at the Hollywood School for Girls. This one she was less enthusiastic about since she would now be teaching French to students of all ages. Cecil B. De Mille was on the school's board of trustees and his two daughters, Cecilia and Katherine, were students there. Katherine didn't have Edith's class but her sister did. Although Edith told interviewers that she wasn't suited to teaching, Katherine told me that Cecilia thought she was a great teacher, full of energy and fun. The parents of most of the girls were involved in the movie business one way or another. When De Mille planned to shoot a spectacular scene at the Paramount studio, the school would close for the day to allow all the students to come and watch.

In order to get a slightly higher salary, Edith told the school that she could also teach art, though she had studied it only briefly in high school. Her high school friend Harold Grieve suggested that, in order to bone up on the subject and keep one step ahead of her students, she study evenings at the Chounard Art College, which was within walking distance of Mittie's new house.

One of her Chounard classmates, a girl named Betty Head, decided to play matchmaker for her brother Charles and Edith. She reasoned that both needed some outside help in getting "married off"—Edith because she wasn't pretty and Charles because he was irresponsible. Charles was already working as a traveling salesman for the Super Refined Metals Company, and showing signs of a drinking problem. He was, however, tall, handsome, charming, and well educated. Since he and Edith courted primarily through letters, it was easy for her to see all his good points and ignore the

COURTESY OF THE ACADEMY OF MOTION PICTURE ARTS AND SCIENCES

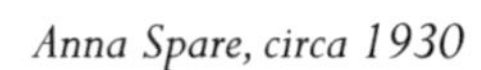

Anna Spare, circa 1930

bad ones. They were married on July 25, 1923, in Los Angeles and went on a honeymoon. Almost as soon as they were back in town, Charles left on a business trip and Edith resumed her summer school studies at Chounard.

As sporadic as their time together turned out to be, Edith was terribly in love with Charles. She prepared a lavish scrapbook of their honeymoon, which she would keep for the rest of her life, despite the eventual divorce from Charles and happy marriage to Wiard Ihnen. The sexual awakening that her marriage brought greatly changed Edith from a shy little sparrow to a much more self-aware and assertive woman. She bobbed her hair, affected more fashionable clothes, and had glamorous pictures of herself taken.

It was an era when female schoolteachers usually lost their jobs when they married. While the Hollywood School for Girls was liberal enough that Edith would be allowed to continue there, the salary was low and she was beginning to realize that Charles would not be enough of a provider to allow her to quit working. She also worried about supporting her mother. Frank Spare, many years older than Anna, had accepted a low-paying office job in Los Angeles (and would die soon thereafter). The most Edith could expect at the Hollywood School for Girls was that she might become headmistress after many years. Her forays onto the Paramount lot with the students had shown her that the film business was one place where there were good opportunities for women. The fact that she had no dramatic training or experience beyond the one high school play was a problem but not an insurmountable one.

Edith was planning, when school resumed, to cultivate those parents of her students who worked at movie studios, but a better opportunity arose during the summer. Howard Greer, the new costume designer at Paramount, had placed an ad in a Los Angeles newspaper, looking for sketch artists. Various Chounard students had applied and been turned down; all were told that they were not "versatile enough." Yet, Charles Head's aggressively charming manner had had an effect on Edith, and with him as an example she went around Chounard borrowing all kinds of sketches, erasing the names of the actual artists and substituting "Head." Upon seeing such a variety of work in the portfolio, they could hardly say she wasn't versatile. While she didn't really think she would be hired, this trip to Paramount would at least help her get her foot in the door and might lead to something else.

Years later she would repeatedly say she didn't recommend this stunt as a method of getting a job. She probably never would have told anybody about it then, but Greer recounted the tale in his 1949 autobiography, *Designing Male.* Telling it to me in 1973, Edith emphasized that she didn't exactly lie when she showed Greer the sketches.

"[Greer asked,] 'Could I see some work?' And I didn't say it was mine. I said, 'This is the sort of thing we do in our school.' He said, 'Come to work tomorrow at $40 a week.' "

Since Edith had been specializing in seascapes, not figure drawing, at Chounard Greer quickly caught on to her ruse. However, his greatest fear was that one of his assistants would someday replace him (a fear Edith herself later inherited), and it seemed improbable that Edith could do that. In the first draft of the Paramount chapter of *Hollywood Costume Design,* I wrote, ". . . he kept her on because she was hardworking and bright without displaying enough tangible talent to pose a threat to him." I showed this to Edith and she laughed. "I like that," she said—and it stayed in.

2

Apprenticeship

Paramount's position as the number one studio in Hollywood was secure after the 1916 merger of two major companies, Famous Players and Lasky. Although the studio would continue to produce some features in its Astoria, Queens, studio until 1925, the majority were made in Hollywood.

Through the second decade of the century, most actors and actresses in modern-dress films were expected to provide their own wardrobes, but for historical pictures, the studios had to find or make them. The Western Costume Company was founded in 1912 to provide only wardrobe for westerns, though soon it expanded into all kinds of costumes. When D. W. Griffith produced his lavish *Intolerance* (1916), he hired Claire West to design the costumes. After graduating from college in 1910, she studied in

Paris, and after the Griffith film she was lured over to Famous Players–Lasky by its top director, Cecil B. De Mille. She would run the wardrobe department, taking care of budgets and hiring, as well as designing costumes for the top stars for the next several years. De Mille brought in the young Mitchell Leisen to design the costumes for the historical flashback in *Male and Female* (1919), and he later told me, "Claire West had been the head of wardrobe for the Lasky studio and she wasn't about to have me making anything in her workroom. She stuck me in a little room about four by six feet with six seamstresses, and I sweated the whole thing out myself."

West left Paramount in 1924 to go to the First National Studio, and Howard Greer took over as Paramount's designer. He didn't have to oversee the business end of the department as West had, for Frank Richardson was hired for the position and would stay in the job for over fifty years. Gloria Swanson was Paramount's most important female star, famous for her lavish clothes, and Greer designed for her as well as for Pola Negri, who was supposedly her rival. Cecil B. De Mille well expressed the thinking of the era when he told Greer, "I want clothes that will make people gasp when they see them. I don't want to see any clothes anybody could possibly buy in a store." However, De Mille would leave soon to start his own studio.

At first Edith sat in a little back room with other sketch artists, proposing ideas for the garments Greer needed. "He'd come in and describe a scene and say 'De Mille doesn't like this or that' and we'd all make drawings of our ideas, but I tried harder. The others would make one and I'd make three or four. He'd like it or he'd hate it, but at least I tried. I was older than the others and had more education and I think that helped."

He taught her how to draw the way he drew, and eventually

he let her make the finished sketches that would be shown to the actresses for approval. Although she would later tell reporters that she didn't know how to sew (because she didn't want to be asked to put on demonstrations), she did have a standard knowledge of dressmaking from her mother, from Mittie, and from Los Angeles High School. She also said later that she "knew fashion" when she started. At first she was not at all convinced that she wanted to stay in the wardrobe department. Having the job there was a way of getting, daily, on the Paramount lot where she planned to get to know people and scout possibilities in other departments.

The wardrobe department was far less rigidly organized in the twenties than it would become later, when the unions instituted job classifications and minimum pay scales. Every film had at least one "wardrobe man" and "wardrobe woman" (the union later changed this designation to "costumer") who put out the clothes needed every morning, kept track of what was worn in each sequence so that it would match in editing, and in the case of the minor players, actually chose what would be worn from the stock wardrobe. In the early 1920s the stock was already extensive, consisting of everything that had been bought or made for previous films, and it grew every year. By the 1960s, however, Paramount's stock wardrobe was still much smaller than MGM's, due partly to the fact that Edith would become very adept at recycling garments to avoid the expense of making new ones. If Paramount didn't have as many costumes as it needed to garb all the extras for a big period picture, it could rent from nearby Western Costume, which also handled some of the sewing if the studio workroom became overloaded.

Edith soon realized that her ability to speak Spanish was a great asset, since many of the seamstresses had just come from Mexico and neither Greer nor Richardson spoke the language. Quickly Edith assumed many responsibilities other than sketching, so that when things were slow and sketchers weren't needed, the others were laid off but Edith kept on. At that point she notified the Hollywood School for Girls she would not be coming back.

Mary Brian was sixteen years old when she first came to Paramount in 1924 to play the part of Wendy in *Peter Pan* (1924). In February 2000, she recalled to film historian Anthony Slide: "Edith used to tease me because when I first went there, I had never been on a movie set and knew nothing about the making of films. I was told to come up, they wanted to make a dressmaking skeleton of me, and Edith said to go in and take off my clothes. 'We have to do very scientific measurements here.' I took off my dress and there I was in my undershirt and panties. I wouldn't take those off! Later my husband [editor George Tomasini] worked with her on the Alfred Hitchcock pictures and she used to kid me after all those years, 'Do you still have your little undershirt?'

"She was a great gal, aside from being a good designer. We were all rather like a family. We all met in the commissary and had lunch together. She would come on the set. There was a lot more visiting around because you saw the same people again and again." Brian also saw Edith at Sunday luncheons at the beach home of Jesse Lasky, one of the founders of Paramount.

Studios then differentiated between "leading ladies" and "stars." A star was somebody whose name alone could sell a film. Paramount's greatest female stars, Gloria Swanson and Clara Bow, often complained that the studio gave them poor scripts and directors, and indifferent leading men, because it knew the public would flock to their films no matter how mediocre they were. A leading lady had the main female part in a film but would be billed under the title and get a much smaller salary than the star did.

Mary Brian would continue at Paramount until 1932, and since she became a "leading lady" rather than a "star," most of her clothes would be designed by Edith, though for some of the cheaper westerns the wardrobe ladies just used existing costumes out of the stock wardrobe. "She wasn't aggressive. I think she kidded a lot of people into doing things her way because she was easy to get along with. Not bossy, just when she knew she was right she said so. She was in on the conferences sometimes, when you talked to the producer and director and they had their input. She would supervise the fitting to make sure the seamstresses sewed it right and didn't get lazy." In *Henry Hathaway,* a collection of interviews compiled by a production designer, screenwriter, and producer Polly Platt (2001), director Henry Hathaway remembered Edith dutifully putting clothes back into stock wardrobe when the pictures finished shooting. Once he needed a shawl, but the only one she could find was bright white, and his cameraman said it couldn't be photographed successfully. Edith dipped it in coffee to tone it down and later told Hathaway this almost got her fired!

Edith quickly picked up a knowledge of what would photograph well. At first all the studios were using orthochromatic black-and-white film, which accentuated reds and yellows, making them appear unnaturally dark in black and white, while blues and greens seemed very light. Panchromatic film, which gave a more accurate representation to all colors in black and white, was introduced in 1925 and gradually took over, since it could be lit with incandescent lights rather than arc lights that needed frequent adjustment. Edith followed these developments carefully.

At that time all studios routinely worked six full days a week, and when there were problems, Edith stayed late into the night and came in on Sunday too. In 1970, when I tried to get Evelyn Brent to talk to me about being dressed by Howard Greer and

Edith and Charles Head, circa 1927

COURTESY OF THE ACADEMY OF MOTION PICTURE ARTS AND SCIENCES

Travis Banton, what she remembered most was, "You'd go out at the end of the day and pass the workroom and poor Edith would still be there." Edith was making much more money than she had as a teacher but she was also working much longer hours. This workload helped distract her from the worry that Charles was unfaithful when he was on the road. When he was in town, Edith brought him to Paramount and introduced him around. To her dismay, he started getting drunk with Banton and Greer.

Some part of Edith would always love Charles, no matter how much grief he had caused her. In the later years, however, she refused to even hear his name mentioned. When she decided that I was to be her official biographer, she told John Engstead he could talk to me about their long friendship and he did, answering all my questions. Except about Charles. When I got up the nerve to ask how Charles was employed, all he would say was, "Oh, Chuck always had some kind of job . . ." He must have been avoiding the subject on instructions from Edith. In the late 1970s some relatives of Charles came into Edith's office at Universal and presented her secretary with a portrait of Charles and Edith taken in the twenties. When Edith returned from lunch and the secretary showed her the picture, her only comment was, "I didn't know I ever wore my hair like that."

Jane Ardmore told me that Edith tried to persuade her that they should say in *The Dress Doctor* that Head was her birth name. Ardmore convinced her that too many people who had known Charles were still around. The compromise was that Edith said that they were married only for a "brief time" (actually, they were married thirteen years), though perhaps she thought that was acceptable because they were so often separated.

By the middle of the decade Paramount was becoming gradually overshadowed by Metro-Goldwyn-Mayer, and after the great success of the talking *Jazz Singer* in 1927, Warner Bros. started crowding the often lackluster Paramount product in the marketplace. Gloria Swanson departed for New York, where she made several movies at Paramount studio in Astoria, Queens. After filming *Madame Sans-Gêne* (1925) in Paris, she returned triumphantly to

Hollywood. Edith remembered many years later how Paramount shut down the day she arrived so that all the employees could join the throngs in welcoming her back through the streets of downtown Los Angeles. Swanson brought her French couturier, Rene Hubert, back with her for her subsequent American films.

Howard Greer's role at Paramount began to diminish when the studio brought out Travis Banton from New York to design *The Dressmaker from Paris* (1924). Though born in Texas, Banton had grown up in New York, studied with the famed designer and teacher Robert Kalloch, and established his talent early by working for a couturiere named Madame Frances. When Mary Pickford secretly married Douglas Fairbanks in 1919, she wore a Banton gown from Madame Frances and he probably had worked on some of the productions at Paramount's Astoria studio. Banton and Greer became the best of friends and drank together after hours. While they did not have competitive feelings towards each other, eventually Greer noticed that stars he thought he had good working relations with were beginning to request Banton. In 1927 Greer's contract was up and he decided not to renew. Saying that he was tired of always "thinking in black and white," he left to open his own couture salon in Beverly Hills. During the next three decades, he dressed society ladies as well as movie stars, did an occasional film at various studios, and became very well known for his wedding gowns.

Of Banton Edith would later say, "He was a god there. Nobody dared oppose him about anything, including the budgets." Florence Vidor had thought of herself as plain and unsuited for high fashion until Banton gowned her for *The Grand Duchess and the Waiter* in 1926. He was able to integrate the geometric motifs of the Art Deco style prevalent in architecture and furnishings into his fashions in the late twenties and yet, at the same time, his corsets and bustles for Fay Wray in *The Four Feathers* (1929) could have won raves in the 1890s.

Banton taught Edith to draw the way he did: whimsical cartoon-like figures with very round faces and oversized eyes. That was different from Greer's drawing style, which was the more typical fashion sketch of the period. She would draw Banton's way the rest of her life. When the wonderful nonsense of the Jazz Age quickly faded into more conservative lines in 1930, following the stock-market crash, Banton was able to adjust overnight. Skirts dropped to the ankle, waistlines returned, as did more defined shoulder seams. It became Banton's greatest period, and usually his ideas were graceful and less sensational than what Adrian was doing at MGM. While Adrian often used sharp contrasts of black against white and/or metallic fabrics, Banton usually kept his designs to a close range of gray tones, using instead contrasts in texture. When Paramount experimented briefly with two-color Technicolor in 1930 and 1931, he created two different styles: hard-edged modern dress for *Follow Thru* and a softer period approach for *The Vagabond King*. Edith remembered working with him on both of them.

One star Banton struck out with was Clara Bow, who had become the biggest box-office draw in the whole industry. Paramount released four Bow films per year in the late twenties, and in order to get them, theaters had to agree to book the whole Paramount schedule. Not yet suffering from the mental problems, public scandals, and indifference of studio head Ben Shulberg, which would abruptly end her career, Bow was a free spirit whom most people at Paramount found easy to work with, but she had definite (and strange) ideas about fashion.

She insisted on wearing high heels and white ankle socks with every outfit, including bathing suits and evening dresses. After

Clara Bow wearing a dress with a fitted waistline in Ladies of the Mob

Banton had finished a costume, she would add junk jewelry and, worst of all, she put belts on over the straight dresses typical of the twenties. "She said she had a waistline and she wanted to show it regardless of what the fashion was," said Edith, who designed for her after Banton gave up. Edith agreed to make fitted dresses, and Bow stopped adding belts, though she did inscribe a photo to her designer: "Edith why don't you put your belt where it belongs!"

Clara and Edith became good friends, and Edith told me, "I was invited to Clara's house when she had the whole football team from USC there. It was a lot of fun but nothing happened!"

Despite the long hours, the working climate at Paramount in the twenties was relaxed. Edith had become very outgoing and now knew literally hundreds of employees on the Paramount lot. John Engstead had gotten a job at Paramount in 1927 through the aid of journalist Adela Rogers St. John right after graduating from high school. He started as the errand boy in the publicity department. He soon became the studio's liaison with all the fan magazines, and eventually began directing all still photography. Like Edith, he had a knack for getting along with everybody, and he relied on her to get gowns out of stock for portrait sittings. (She even changed them around so they wouldn't be recognized.) Only Evelyn Brent resisted wearing other actresses' cast-off dresses for still photo sessions. She threatened to charge the studio if she wore her own. Engstead solved the problem by renting some fur coats to photograph Brent in.

With all these connections, Edith might have been able to get herself a job in another department, but her position in Wardrobe had improved so much that she no longer considered moving. Travis Banton was incredibly prolific in this period, and didn't turn to Edith for ideas as much as Greer had, but increasingly he relied on her to costume the cheaper pictures and the supporting parts in the bigger ones. Occasionally she was also assigned a big-budget film. Lupe Velez was another free spirit whom Richardson assigned to Edith although the film, Victor Fleming's *Wolf Song* (1929), was highly prestigious and expensive. Taking place around 1840, it involved a trapper (Gary Cooper) who falls in love with and marries a rich Mexican girl (Velez) only to desert her when the "Wolf Song" makes him return to the woods. Velez and Cooper were having a torrid love affair at the time, and she brought him along for her fittings. When she got restless, "she'd reach over and grab him," said Edith, indicating Cooper's genitals. Of the wedding dress, which Edith hoped would bring her some acclaim, a reviewer cracked, "If there had been less dress, there would have been more scene." I pointed out that one of Velez's gowns was made of a very anachronistic Art Deco print. "Well, Lupe liked it," said Edith.

Although they didn't meet at the time, *Wolf Song* marked the first time that Edith and Wiard Ihnen, the art director, both worked on the same film. Many years later, when Ihnen lay dying in a hospital, I tried to distract his wife from her worries by arranging a private screening. At first the silence of the film bothered her and she chattered away nervously. When she settled down she began to notice sets, particularly the ranch house Velez lived in. "It looks just like our house," she commented of Ihnen's set.

The Wall Street crash in October of 1929 hit Paramount harder than the other studios. It was already financially overextended from converting to sound and acquiring the Publix chain of movie theaters. Just months earlier the heads of the studio had given themselves big bonuses, and now they were short of operating capital to make their films. Unlike MGM, which tried to help most of its silent stars to make the transition into sound, Paramount seemed determined to get rid of most of them and use cheaper actors imported from Broadway. Founder Jesse Lasky was booted out, followed a year later by studio head Ben Shulberg, and the atmosphere around the lot became increasingly nervous. A shortage of soundstages meant that companies were forced to shoot much more quickly than in the silent days, when several productions could work side by side on the same stage.

Edith responded to these pressures by becoming even more

dedicated and gradually less outgoing. Frances Dee, who became a promising leading lady virtually overnight, recalls, "She got after me when I arrived ten minutes late for a fitting. I was working on one film in the mornings, and another in the afternoon, and at night they'd drive me over to Warners for some scenes, and it is a wonder I got to the fitting at all. The first time it happened she let it pass, but the second time I was late she made some remark and I told her right back. I didn't care." Dee's friend Marion Schilling said, "I only made one picture at Paramount but I thought Edith's designs for me were much better than what I was getting at the other studios. The dress looked good on me and it was right for the character. She was nice, but strictly business at the same time."

Years later, designer Yvonne Wood would joke, "Well, Edith must have had some talent, she didn't get where she did on the casting couch." Actually, she did have one affair which greatly helped her career. When I asked her why it took her so many years to get married to Wiard Ihnen, she very reluctantly said that during the 1930s she had been engaged to two men while still married to Charles Head, and one of these was a writer. This must have been Bayard Veiller, whose secretary, Winifred Kay Thackrey, wrote in her book *Member of the Crew* (2001), "He was a womanizer, too and there again he was generous. When he was chasing little Edith Head around his desk at Paramount, he rewarded her with her first opportunities as a dress designer on three of his pictures . . . He carried a salary increase for her on his own picture budget, gave her screen credit . . ." Veiller, who had had several hit plays on Broadway, including *Within the Law,* and had been also working on films since the 1920s, came to Paramount in 1930 as a writer and associate producer. With his sponsorship, Edith was given a modest contract in 1931. Her salary was raised to $175 a week, she no longer had to fear layoffs when things got "slow" (a

Writer-producer Bayard Veiller, Edith's one-time fiancé and mentor at Paramount

real issue, considering Paramount's financial crises in the early 1930s), and even got an occasional screen credit. That contract, signed March 17, 1931, called for a raise to $225 per week in the second year, but in light of the Depression, Edith agreed to a reduction to $150 when she signed again on February 18, 1932. In 1933, her salary returned to $175, then went up to $200 in 1934. That agreement was amended in six months to allow for a trip to

New York to study fashion trends at the studio's expense, a perk only Banton had had until then.

In 1934, the studio issued its first publicity photographs of Edith. Until that time, she had hidden her face from the camera when John Engstead tried to include her in publicity shots, but now she was photographed unsmiling, without her glasses, and carefully posed to hide the crossed eye. The blurb on the back of the photo tried to give Banton all possible credit for her rise: "Edith Head, Paramount Pictures designer, has worked as Travis Banton's able assistant for ten years and has recently signed a new contract through which she becomes a designer in her own right with due credit and several productions each month as her responsibility. An enthusiastic Travis Banton 'fan,' Miss Head declares that through her rigid training under the expert's personal supervision she has 'made the grade.' " Soon afterwards, Edith gave her first interview, apparently because Banton couldn't be bothered.

Early in 1933, Edith attended a production meeting for Mitchell Leisen's upcoming film *Cradle Song.* Although she could hardly know it at the time, this meeting would ultimately change the course of her life. Also present was Wiard Ihnen, who had been assigned to the unit as art director. Leisen had started at Paramount in 1918 as a costume designer for De Mille, graduated to art direction, and assisted De Mille and Stuart Walker with the direction of three films. *Cradle Song* was the first picture that would be wholly his, and he was determined to show the studio he could leave the costumes and sets to others and concentrate fully on the script and performances. Leisen chose Ihnen for the film because the latter was fascinated with all things Spanish and Mexican, and, of course, Edith was considered to be equally expert since she had grown up in Mexico.

Ihnen was actually of Dutch background, and some of his ancestors had been in New York City since the Peter Stuyvesant days. He was a highly talented painter and architect, and got into the movies as a way to supplement his income. (He had to support his mother and sisters.) He started his film career on the 1920 *Dr. Jekyll and Mr. Hyde,* starring John Barrymore, and worked on a few other movies, but then went back into architecture for several years. He liked film work well enough, but whenever he got a few bucks ahead, he would take off for Mexico and paint for several months. Cinematographer George Folsey, who had first worked with Ihnen at Paramount's New York studio on Fifty-sixth Street in the early twenties, later remembered him as running with a very arty crowd. "At the time I was still living at home with my father, and my sister kept house for us," Folsey remembered after Ihnen's death. "I invited Wiard over for lunch and he asked if he could bring an artist friend of his, named Faust. I said OK. Wiard and Faust got into some kind of argument at the lunch table about how to draw hands. Suddenly Faust reached into his pocket and took out the skeleton of a human hand to prove his point. My poor sister fainted dead away.

"Nobody could pronounce his name, Wiard, so he tried shortening it to Ward. Later on when I came out to Hollywood and ran into him at Paramount, he said that Ward hadn't worked out and now he was going by the name of Bill Ihnen."

Ihnen had worked in films around New York through the 1920s, but at the end of the decade he was back as an architect for a firm that specialized in public buildings. The pay wasn't enough to support him and his sisters. California had an attractive Spanish past as well as a proximity to Mexico where he longed to go and paint. He wrote a letter offering his services to Paramount and was hired in 1929.

Ihnen was not especially happy at Paramount, either with his pay or the working conditions. "I'd design a set with a certain kind of door and Hans Drier (who was the head of the art department) would say, 'Why go to the expense of making that door? Go out into the backlot and get some door out of stock.' " His attitude towards his work was less dedicated than Edith's. In a rare interview in 1978 he said, "I just wanted to get out of there in the afternoon, go home and shave and get ready for my date." When Ihnen had the chance to work on the first three-strip Technicolor featurette, *La Cucharacha,* he left Paramount and never came back. Later he designed the first Technicolor feature, *Becky Sharp* (1935), at RKO, finally settling down for many years at 20th Century–Fox.

By that time his friendship with Edith was firmly in place, though few people knew about it. Her love life was busy with Bayard Veiller and the other fiancé (whose identity I've never been able to determine) to say nothing of Charles Head, who came and went until she finally divorced him in 1938. One of the ways Bill kept in touch with Edith when they were no longer working together was to call her up, describe what his date was planning to wear that evening, and ask Edith's advice on what kind of flower to bring. Not conventionally handsome, Bill Ihnen was charming though quiet, and Natalie Visart told me, "Oh yes, Bill was quite the ladies man. He had a lot of beautiful girlfriends and could have married any one of them. Everybody was amazed when they found out he chose Edith."

In the meanwhile, Edith had a contract and a little financial security. She began to upgrade her lifestyle. Through an agency she hired a black maid named Nanny Jones who became her closest friend and confidante. Nanny's stepdaughter, Robbie Fisher, sometimes worked at Edith's as "second girl," and she now remembers, "Nanny was very small, just the same size as Edith, and when she and my father were going to go out for the evening, Edith would dress Nanny up in her own clothes. Not her old clothes but the ones she was wearing then herself."

Charles Head continued to be Edith's greatest extravagance. The Depression had slowed down his traveling-salesman jobs to a dead halt, and he returned to Los Angeles determined to get back into her good graces. She was just as determined to resist, but in the end she gave in. For several years he was seen dropping in to visit her in the wardrobe department, and even escorted her to some social affairs at Paramount. Frank Richardson's wife Ilse remembered, "Chuck was very nice and friendly, very tall. I knew him outside the studio, through Edith." With nothing to do during the day while she was working, Charles drank more than ever, much to Nanny's disgust. "I never saw him myself but Nanny told me about him," says Robbie Fisher. "He was charging liquor by the case from Jurgensons until Miss Head called them up and told them not to send any more! She bought him the most beautiful clothes. He was dragging her down." Sensing Nanny's disapproval, Edith tried to make a case for Charles, citing his education and verbal cleverness. Nanny was not convinced.

With Charles, as well as her lovers, Edith resolved not to get pregnant. She once told me quite firmly, "I never wanted children. If I had been pregnant I wouldn't have had an abortion, but I never got pregnant."

Bayard Veiller seemed to be the reason that Edith finally filed for divorce from Charles early in 1938. What became of Charles after the divorce remains a mystery. In *The Dress Doctor,* Edith states that he died (rather than admits that she had been divorced). She told people that he had been killed in World War II (but the ever-watchful Billye Fritz saw him visiting her at Paramount after the war). Bill Cook recalls working on the road in the early 1960s with a traveling salesman named Charles Head, who was tall, charming, and cultivated. "The feeling was as if a prince had been banished to a foreign land and was accepting it as best he could.

Charles had money. He had a ranch in Texas that was paid for!" Paddy Calistro writes in *Edith Head's Hollywood,* "Years later, as he lay dying, she would be at his bedside." While Miss Calistro doesn't remember where she got this information, I think it must have been from John Engstead, whom she interviewed for her book. Who else would have known this?

Bayard Veiller was a wealthy man and could have supported Edith and her mother in style. In the end, however, she didn't marry him. Perhaps it was his extravagant nature, which bothered the practical Edith, or the age difference—he had a son, Anthony, who was also a well-known screenwriter and about the same age as she. Also, Bayard Veiller's importance in the business was declining. More likely, however, she hesitated simply because she did not want to be dominated by a powerful personality. She did not want to stop working either. Not yet famous, she was nonetheless well employed, a fact that gave her much satisfaction, and Veiller expected her to quit. Jane Ardmore's take on the long-term success of the Head-Ihnen marriage was, "Bill let her be Edith. He never demanded anything of her. He knew she was very independent. That was fine because he was like that himself."

During slow periods, Edith and Banton handled everything themselves, but Frank Richardson hired two sketch artists to help out when it got busy, and both of them later became well-known designers. Renie (later known as Renie Conley) came in 1933 and Adele Balkan in 1934. There were not any unions yet, and everybody was expected to pitch in and help in whatever way Richardson wanted them to. Later, job classifications would become very specific, and designers and their assistants supervised the sewing but never actually touched it. However, Conley remembered, "Richardson told me that I would have to help with the sewing if he didn't need any sketches made. I told him I could handle it, although I really couldn't. He gave me this dress with an enormous skirt for Marlene Dietrich and told me to hem it. I sat down at the machine but I was really lost, and he could see it. She was very hard to please, so he took me off of it." Both girls learned to make sketches that looked like Banton's, as Edith had. Renie left Paramount in 1937 to accept a better job at RKO.

The pecking order at Paramount—as well as how busy the department was at any given time—determined who got which designer. In an interview with Barbara Hall of the Margaret Herrick Library of the Academy of Motion Picture Arts and Sciences, conducted just before Adele Balkan's death, Balkan explained, "If it was a Dietrich, yes they got the head designer [Banton]. If it was a B picture and a medium star, not a big star, but still a well known person, they would get Edith Head." Wardrobe ladies often handled the supporting players using stock from earlier films, but "If the designer wanted to come and put his two cents in on your B picture, he would."

Dietrich's director, Josef von Sternberg, was one of the few in that period who paid attention to the wardrobe, and, indeed, his vehicles for her, such as *Shanghai Express* (1932), *The Scarlet Empress* (1934), and *The Devil Is a Woman* (1935) gave Banton his greatest opportunities. Maria Riva, in her biography of her mother, Marlene Dietrich, wrote amusingly of Dietrich's exchanges with Banton (indeed Dietrich even told him how to dress the other stars!): "Lombard can be very funny. If she gets the right pictures, she can become a big star. You have to watch what Lombard wears. She loves to look like me; why not make her a 'Dietrich' suit out of that white flannel we found—but she will need a shorter jacket than I wear. She has an American body. Also a behind so watch the skirt line." (From *Marlene Dietrich* by her daughter Maria Riva, 1993 Alfred A. Knopf.)

Claudette Colbert was the only other star whom Banton allowed to question his judgment. Her mother had been a couturiere in New York, and Claudette had studied to follow in her footsteps, giving it up only when she found she could earn better money as an actress. She had started her film career in 1929 at Paramount's Astoria studio, where she took care of her own wardrobe. She didn't come to Hollywood or work with Banton until 1932, when the Astoria studio was shut down. She had already decided that she would never be photographed full face or from the right side, and she wasn't about to give Banton any more freedom than she gave her cameramen. Insisting that her waist and hips were too thick, she also gave Banton a long list of materials and styles she would not wear. Knowing that her neck was short (and for this reason she seldom wore shoulder-length hair or chignons), Banton devised what came to be known in the industry as the "Colbert collar." The trick was to scoop out an inch or two from the top of the back of her garment, gracefully elongating the expanse of her neck between the bottom of her coiffure and the top of her dress.

Cecil B. De Mille usually had his own staff of designers who made their costumes in the Paramount workrooms but were independent of Banton and Head. Mitchell Leisen, once again De Mille's costume designer, had designed Colbert's revealing gowns for *The Sign of the Cross* in 1932, and a whole crew of designers came in to replace him for *Cleopatra* (1934), but when Colbert insisted on Banton for her costumes, De Mille didn't argue. Banton had a highly talented cutter and fitter named Ilse Meadows, whom he assigned to execute the designs. She remembered, "I had started out as an apprentice at Howard Greer's shop, and he recommended me to Mr. Banton. He told me they were so busy he didn't know what they were going to do, so I started working there." (Without the union rules that would come later, a capable seamstress like Ilse Meadows could start at the top.)

"It wasn't the usual jealousy one finds in a workroom. We loved our work. Many times we worked all night but we did it happily. First we made a muslin pattern and the designer okayed it or added or subtracted. Then we made the dress and the designer would be present at the fitting. He would make a small change to enhance the garment. Mr. Banton was a very popular man to work for, honest and fair. Edith was wonderful. We worked together in a friendship way. Sometimes we'd stay up all night [for time-and-a-half pay] to get something finished for the next day, but we didn't mind."

Another seamstress, Sheila O'Brien, first met Edith around 1932. "I had been trying to get parts as an actress, and I got a few, but during the Depression I was desperate. When I was down to drinking one cup of coffee a day and no food, I remembered I could sew, so I applied for a job at Paramount and was hired. I made a tobacco-brown corduroy suit for Edith's personal wardrobe, and a few years ago I walked through the workroom at Paramount and they were copying it! I told Edith and she said, 'Well, I had to, it wore out!'

"Paramount was in a bad way then. They put me in charge of a group of girls sewing up a bunch of dance costumes for a chorus line. I was trying to make them look good, but the material was so cheap and they didn't give us enough time to do it right. They told me that they had just a certain amount of money for labor and that was it. Later I went to MGM and things were so much better."

Ilse Meadows remembered, "I did some modern dresses for Miss Colbert and she seemed to like me, so they put me in charge of sewing her Cleopatra gowns. When it came time to fit them, Mr. Banton and Edith Head were so scared of her, they didn't even go into the fitting room with us. They stood out in the hall, and after she left I told them she was lovely to me. She said I fitted her just like her mother did." Unfortunately for Banton, Ilse soon married Frank Richardson and retired from the studio, and Banton kept dreading the Colbert fittings. Once she ripped off a blouse with a perfectly executed Colbert collar and threw it on the floor. When the seamstress protested, "I made it the same way I always do," Colbert retorted, "Why don't you get some new ideas!"

Carole Lombard, on the other hand, was no trouble at all. She had first come to Paramount in 1930 to appear in *Safety in Numbers.* Shannon Rogers (later a prominent New York designer), observed, "Travis only needed to have lunch with a girl once and he would know what she had that he could work with. Carole Lombard was just a tootsie when she came to Paramount, but he saw things in her she didn't even know she had and his clothes transformed her." Banton persuaded her to lose weight and work on her walk. He capitalized on her stance by giving her heavily beaded evening gowns, cut on the bias and longer in back so they would cling to her thighs. She returned the favor by wearing whatever he designed, refusing to even see the sketches beforehand. When she was loaned to Columbia, the clothes were designed by Robert Kalloch who had been Banton's teacher in New York, but when she went to Universal for *My Man Godfrey* (1936), she made that studio borrow Banton. Edith Head was borrowed along with him, for Gail Patrick's gowns.

As the 1930s wore on, Banton's contributions became more and more sporadic. The establishment of the Legion of Decency in 1934 eliminated practically overnight the kind of sophisticated and exotic scripts that had given him his best opportunities. His drinking increased, and he was losing interest in his work. Many of the actresses whose beauty he had enhanced, such as Kay Francis and

Evelyn Brent, stopped starring in Paramount pictures, and slowly the idea of costumes so glamorous people couldn't possibly buy them in a store became superseded by a new rationale of attractive but not over-the-top designs, which Edith did very well. As much as she was influenced by him, she was by nature more conservative, a fact that endeared her to producers, directors (who were becoming increasingly involved in costume choices), and even some actresses. Patricia Morrison praised her to me because her designs were "not flamboyant."

Banton's contract gave him the right to visit Paris every year to scout new fashions at the studio's expense. Aside from seeing what the general trends were, he would buy some gowns from the big couture houses and integrate them as needed into the films he was designing, with nary a thought about giving the original designer any credit. While attempts were made to schedule his Paris vacations for periods when the workload would be light, big pictures that he should have designed started going to Edith. *Love Me Tonight* (1932) was intended as an expensive, highly prestigious film, but the star, Jeanette MacDonald, didn't interest Banton all that much. When script problems delayed the shooting of the film, Banton simply left town as scheduled, and Edith got the assignment. Banton had known Mae West in New York (indeed, his uncle was a judge who had once sent her to jail after an obscenity trial). Banton designed West's first film, *Night After Night* (1932), in which she had only a small part, but he was out of town when her first big starring role, in *She Done Him Wrong* (1933), came along. At first West was reluctant to use the less well-known designer, but when she saw some of Edith's sketches, she agreed. The two became lifelong friends, although Banton would design costumes for the next several West films.

Sylvia Sidney was one star who didn't want to be gowned by Edith while Banton was absent. At her request, Howard Greer was

Mae West in She Done Him Wrong; *one of the first high-budget films Edith was assigned to design*

brought back to Paramount for one picture, *Thirty Day Princess* (1934). Actually Greer only designed Sidney's glamorous gowns for the film; in the beginning, where the leading character is still a poor actress, the task of designing one simple suit for her was given to the inexperienced Balkan, though Greer certainly could have done this one as well. Edith also added a garment here or there in films credited to Banton. Later she would remember covering for him when he was off on a drunken binge. Using ideas they had already discussed, or even her own ideas, she'd make sketches in the Banton style and take them to the star, saying, "Travis wanted you to see these." Increasingly she followed his costumes through the workrooms and supervised his fittings. Banton even tried to shift some of his work onto Adele Balkan until Frank

Richardson warned him, "You're getting paid to do this picture, not Adele."

Of Banton's relationship with Edith, Balkan said, "Wonderful, wonderful. He loved her. She could play bridge with him and she would do everything." Edith later remembered going to Banton's house in Los Feliz, waking him up with strong coffee and driving him to work. When he was really on a toot, he would take daylong excursions on the Western Avenue streetcar, riding back and forth to the beach until Edith located him and dragged him to the studio. Other times he turned up in San Francisco or Chicago with no memory of how or why he had gotten there. After he was gone, and speculation was rife that Edith had somehow contrived to get him fired so she could replace him, people did remember that she had secreted a liquor bottle in the office for his use. Those defending her said it was the only way she could keep him seated at the drawing board. When everything was just right, his work was still brilliant. Edith remembered one morning near the end of his time at Paramount, when he finally got down to work and then designed one gown after another, finishing sketches for a whole film in one morning.

Although he always designed for Dietrich, Colbert, and West, and gave only one Lombard film over to Head (*Supernatural,* 1933), Banton ceased to groom the upcoming starlets, as he had with Carole Lombard. He wouldn't even bother with Barbara Stanwyck when she first reported to Paramount for *Interns Can't Take Money* (1937). She didn't have the kind of glamour he liked, and her part was that of a poor woman, but she was a major star nonetheless.

In an article in the February 1948 issue of *Movieland* magazine, titled "My Favorite Designer," Barbara Stanwyck recalled how she had dressed so severely to the premiere of her film *Stella Dallas*

One Night in Lisbon, *sketch for Madeleine Carroll by Edith Head*

COURTESY OF AUTHOR

that the guard didn't recognize her and didn't want to let her in. "For *Interns Can't Take Money* [Edith] came in bubbling with enthusiasm. She wanted the two suits that I was to wear more feminine than the current vogue. Not that Edith doesn't always consider the story first, but she wanted the suits to do something for me and they did! I acquired a thorough respect and liking for Edith Head."

Edith's sketch for a dress for Marsha Hunt to wear in College Holiday

COURTESY OF AUTHOR

Interns marked the start of a very long working relationship between the two women. Stanwyck made Goldwyn, Columbia, Universal, and Warner Bros. borrow Edith during the 1940s. Stanwyck's work, more than any other actress's, paralleled Edith's: she could be effective in any kind of role, comedy or drama, sympathetic character or not. The fact that Stanwyck was more popular in the 1940s than she had been in the 1930s is indicative of how public tastes were shifting away from the glamorous but unreal

Hunt models the finished dress, which shows several changes Edith made during the fitting

femme fatales, played so well by stars such as Dietrich and dressed so well by Banton, to smartly tailored, attractive but down-to-earth types like Stanwyck. And nobody dressed Stanwyck as well as Head did. Soon after World War II ended, Stanwyck and Robert Taylor took a trip to Paris where they viewed all the first postwar fashion collections but didn't buy a thing, because, as Stanwyck explained, "Nobody understands my figure as well as my Hollywood designer." Her Hollywood designer was, of course, Edith.

Yet actress and designer were not as close personally as has been suggested. Stanwyck did recommend a dentist who replaced Edith's missing front teeth. (Frank Richardson's sister-in-law Immy Moore, who worked at Paramount, says, "Her teeth were so bad she'd cover her mouth any time she laughed." Even with the new teeth, however, Edith remained unsmiling as much as possible.) Stanwyck's real confidante was her hairdresser and secretary Holly Barnes. It was Barnes who persuaded her to not dye her hair when it started going gray in the mid-1940s. Barnes gave Stanwyck fussy hairstyles, which Edith thought unsuitable to the roles the actress was playing, but Edith didn't feel she was close enough to Stanwyck to say anything about it. Edith believed it was Barnes's fault that Stanwyck wore her hair halfway down her back even when it turned very gray, and short styles were coming in. Barnes hinted around that she'd like Edith to design a dress for her, but Edith never did. When Stanwyck went to MGM in 1948, however, Irene, MGM's head designer, decreed that the long hair must go. Photographers were called in, Robert Taylor held his wife's hand, and the deed was done.

Paramount's management kept changing in the early and middle thirties. Marsha Hunt remembers, "We'd come in every Monday and say, 'Who's running it this week?' " Finally Stanton Griffths assumed the post of studio head in 1936 and things began to settle down. Mae West's popularity had dropped drastically after the Legion of Decency and when her contract expired it was not renewed. Marlene Dietrich was actually paid for a film she didn't make, to finish off her deal. Carole Lombard did sign a new contract with Paramount in 1937, but the salary she demanded was so high that the studio was relieved when she turned down *Midnight* in 1939. She never worked at Paramount again. Of Banton's once mighty stable of stars, only Claudette Colbert remained. Banton's last months under contract (it officially ended in March 1938) were mostly spent on loan-out. He designed *Nothing Sacred* (1937) for Lombard at Selznick International, *Fools for Scandal* (1938) for Lombard at Warners and *Tovarich* (1937) for Colbert, also at Warners. He was getting $1,200 a week, and had the studio picked up the option for another year he would get a raise. It was suggested that he continue at the same salary. He refused.

By now Natalie Visart was the only designer for the De Mille spectaculars and, as Mitchell Leisen's mistress, she became a close friend of Carole Lombard, since Leisen and Lombard were close friends. Lombard wrote to her, "About Travis—well as you know the past year he has been a very bad boy and the studio just got fed up with it. That was that. He's having a little trouble getting something else. I don't think he appreciated his soft spot."

At first, Banton was not alarmed. Edith was not immediately elevated to his job; instead, she was kept on as the number two designer while the studio tried to find a new number one.

3

Holding On

In retrospect, it would seem that Edith Head was the obvious person to succeed Travis Banton and once his contract was allowed to lapse early in 1938, all should have been smooth sailing for her. The reality was far different. The studio was not convinced that she could fill the post of head designer, and the fact that she held on to her job was proof of her tenacity and her ability to use the prevailing situation to her advantage.

Although she had designed many films by herself and accumulated some screen credits and a little publicity, Edith was still viewed by most people as Banton's assistant, and could have lost her job when he lost his. Already, late in 1937, Paramount had hired another designer, Ernest Dryden, to design a Bing Crosby musical, *Dr. Rhythm.* Dryden was a well-known illustrator and designer from New York, who had a few prestigious film credits, most notably David Selznick's *Garden of Allah* (1936). Maria Riva remembers that Marlene Dietrich hadn't liked Dryden's designs and pressured Travis Banton to make her some gowns, which were interpolated into the film. Since nobody knew this was going on, the fashions in *The Garden of Allah* impressed everybody even though the film itself wasn't a big success. *Dr. Rhythm* didn't have a female star. The leading lady, Mary Carlisle, had been dressed by Edith more often than by Banton, but nonetheless Paramount hired Dryden at a salary of $650 a week as a test, to see if he could replace Banton should the negotiations for a new contract fail.

Apparently Dryden didn't work out, for when *Dr. Rhythm* was released, his name wasn't in the credits. After Banton left the studio on March 18, 1938, Paramount approached a number of other well-known designers, including Earl Luick, all of whom turned down the job. Meanwhile, Edith and Adele Balkan remained in their little office, although they were allowed to use Banton's fitting room. Like all of the studios, Paramount was finding the box-office returns for 1938 to be below the 1937 levels, and though the front office wasn't enthusiastic about Edith, she was deemed to be economical (because of her low salary and of the way she turned in a usable product cheaply) and good enough for the time being.

Moreover, Edith had already established a good rapport with the Paramount actresses (other than Claudette Colbert). Yvonne Wood later said, "The front office told Edith that the starlets were to have absolutely nothing to say about what they wore. However, she found ways to talk to them, find out what their likes and dislikes were, what they thought looked good on them. Then she would incorporate these things into her designs and say they had been her ideas all along. When these ladies became important, naturally they were loyal to Edith."

COURTESY OF THE AUTHOR

Richard Hopper's sketch for Susan Sarandon in The Great Waldo Pepper

COURTESY OF TOM CULVER

Grace Sprague's sketch of short black cocktail dress for Lily Palmer in The Pleasure of His Company. *The final dress was somewhat different*

COURTESY OF JAY JORGENSON

Grace Sprague lavished much more time than usual on this rendering of the gown for Grace Kelly to wear at the climax of To Catch a Thief, *but even so it would not be the final version that was used: the gold roses were replaced with gold birds*

Grace Sprague's sketch of a red-and-white gown for Lucy Gallant

COURTESY OF THE AUTHOR

COURTESY OF PHOTOFEST

Barbara Stanwyck in California

One of the many sketches Bob Mackie made for the crucial evening ensemble Joanne Woodward would wear in A New Kind of Love

COURTESY OF TOM CULVER

COURTESY OF TOM CULVER

Richard Hopper's sketch of an idea for a flag-inspired dress for Mae West in Myra Breckinridge

Shirley MacLaine
in Gambit

Carroll Baker in a transparent pink gown Edith designed for the premiere of The Carpetbaggers. *(Such a revealing garment was definitely against all of Edith's standards, but she knew what producer Joseph Levine wanted. He rewarded her by borrowing her from Paramount when he started his own Embassy Pictures Company)*

COURTESY OF THE AUTHOR

Edith's own sketches, probably for Airport '77

COURTESY OF THE AUTHOR

COURTESY OF TOM CULVER

Grace Sprague's sketch for one of Edith's ideas for Judy Garland in I Could Go On Singing *(not used)*

Costume test of Lucille Ball in a Head suit for Critic's Choice. *Edith loved using this kind of rough wool and apparently so did Lucille Ball, for years later she was still wearing this outfit*

Anne Baxter and Yul Brynner in DeMille's Ten Commandments *(Baxter's gown is by Head, Brynner's costume by Dorothy Jeakins)*

Hedy Lamarr in Samson and Delilah

Marsha Hunt was a starlet during Banton's last two years and she remembers, "I know Edith designed the costumes for *College Holiday* (1936) because there was one yellow tulle evening gown that I also wore to President Roosevelt's birthday celebration in Washington. We made so many personal appearances that by the end of the evening it was quite worn out! The rest of my Paramount pictures, I never quite knew who was designing the clothes, Edith, Adele Balkan, or both of them. I wasn't given sketches to approve at Paramount like I got later at MGM. I simply came to the fitting while I was working on another picture or posing for stills, and sometimes Edith would be there, sometimes just the wardrobe lady, and I put them on and that was it.

"I do remember, however that Edith always made an effort to talk to me a little when our paths crossed on the Paramount lot. I had graduated from high school at sixteen and not gone to college; I went to a dramatic school in New York. I was always very flattered that this terribly overworked lady managed to find time to talk to me when I ran into her. In the fittings she was right to the point, she never wasted her time or mine. Years later, when my career was getting going again after a long while on the blacklist, due to an appearance I made in Washington against the House Committee on UnAmerican Activities, I happened to meet Edith on the Universal lot. She wasn't designing the show I was in but she saw me on the sidewalk and she gave me a big hug. We were just talking about things in general when suddenly she said, 'That blacklist was a terrible thing.' It really touched me that she would volunteer that. Nobody else ever mentioned it when I started getting work again."

Of the starlets Edith dressed during the late thirties, the only true star to emerge was Dorothy Lamour. Originally, Evelyn Venable had been assigned to star in *The Jungle Princess* (1936), but only because

Dorothy Lamour in Edith's sarong for The Hurricane

she had long hair. When she refused the part, it went to the unknown band singer Lamour, who not only had long black hair but also a sort of Polynesian look that was perfect for the role. Unfortunately, she also had round shoulders and massive buttocks and thighs, which Edith somehow had to hide under the skimpy sarongs.

"She literally worked it out with the cameraman scene by scene," Yvonne Wood later commented. Paramount sold *The Jungle*

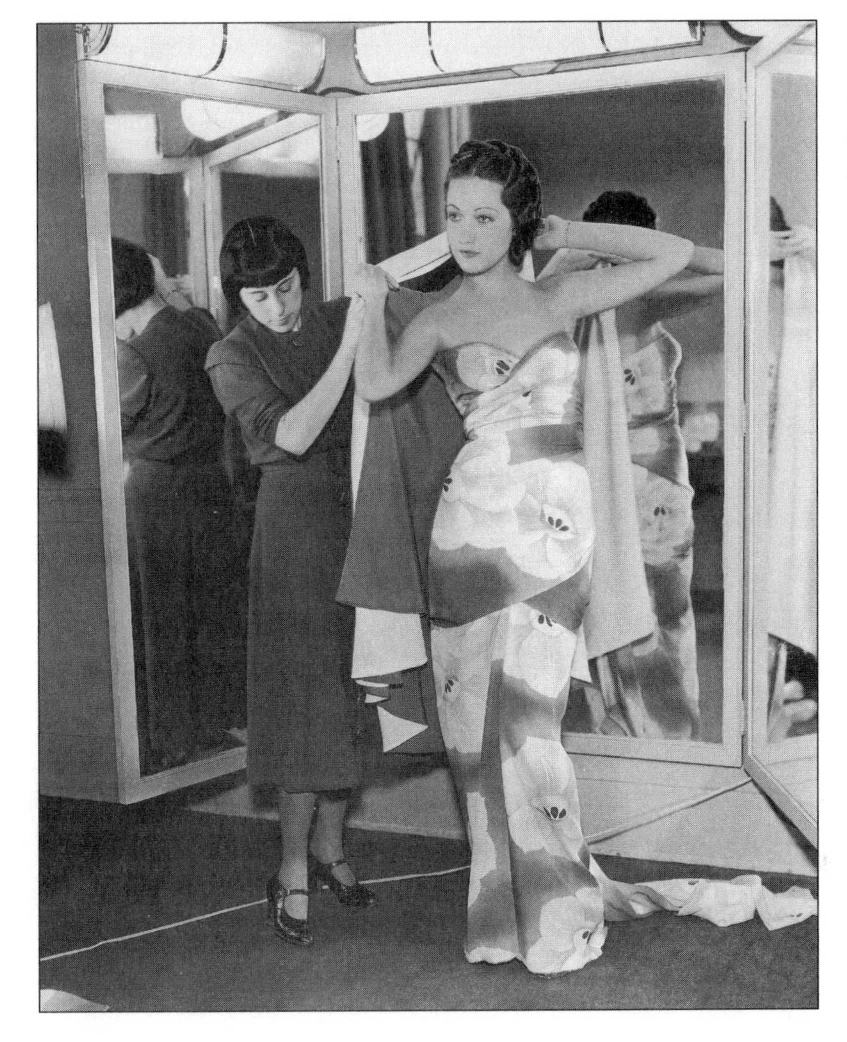

Edith fits Dorothy Lamour in a sarong-inspired evening gown (circa 1938)

Princess as a B picture, which meant that the theaters paid the studio a lower percentage of the box office for it, and when it did good business, they held it over, ultimately creating a big hit. Tropical fabrics and "sarong draping" on modern dresses became hot fashion items, the first in Edith's career. As more sarong pictures followed in the next several years, Lamour gradually put on weight, making the task of dressing her ever more difficult. Unwisely, Banton wouldn't be bothered with her in his final months at Paramount, so all of her modern-dress films were designed by Edith and the two became lifelong friends.

When Lamour married Captain William Ross Howard III in 1943, Edith designed her wedding dress. Later Edith and Bill Ihnen visited the Howards on the army base in San Bernardino, where he was stationed. The facilities were so primitive that there was no kitchen sink, and after dinner she and Lamour washed the dishes in the bathtub. About Edith, Lamour told me, "She is the kind of person that I may not see for several years and then I run into her and we start talking and it's like we had been talking just the day before." Edith remained fond of Lamour too, but later told me, "She had a terrible figure, and we were supposed to make her look so sexy."

Paramount had competent leading ladies, including Shirley Ross and Madeleine Carroll, but no female stars with real box-office clout, other than Claudette Colbert who had a contract calling for two Paramount films per year. She was the studio's biggest draw, and Edith was desperate to win her over. Colbert had often been difficult with Banton, but she now believed the rumor that Edith had somehow contrived to get Banton's job. Out of misguided loyalty, she made the one picture she did with Edith, *Zaza* (1939), a nightmare. People who only knew Colbert socially testify that she was a most charming hostess, whereas those who worked with her in the studio knew her to be a terrible control freak. Ray Milland, who costarred with her several times and had a brief affair with her, said Colbert's stubbornness was "due to her being French." Others theorized that it was a natural reaction to a lifetime of being controlled by her equally tough-minded mother.

Colbert's greatest successes were generally in light romantic comedies, but she knew that she had to vary the formula from

Costume test of Barbara Stanwyck in My Reputation. *This film, though filmed in 1943, was not released until 1946. These long delays in releasing were one of the reasons Edith avoided extreme styles which could be outmoded by the time a film finally came out*

time to time. *Zaza* had originally been planned as the American debut of the Italian import Isa Miranda, but had to be recast when Miranda had a car accident. The film was to be directed by George Cukor, from a script by Zoe Akins, and since they had just collaborated—to great critical acclaim—on *Camille* (1937), Colbert accepted the part of a turn-of-the-century cabaret singer but was highly nervous throughout the shooting. Edith later remembered, "Every sketch I made she refused. Once when we had a fitting she tore out some stiff cotton interlining and said, 'Banton would have had silk!' "

Nonetheless, Colbert didn't take Paramount up on its offer to bring Banton back for *Midnight* (1939). Like many stars, she was getting her personal clothes from Irene at the exclusive Bullock's Wilshire department store, and like several of her contemporaries, wanted to start wearing Irene clothes onscreen as well. The studio allowed this but warned her that the fittings would have to be done in the store. Colbert not only went to the store for the fittings, but also amazed everybody by picking out one dress from Irene's ready-to-wear line. Edith took care of the other women in the cast, including Hedda Hopper, Elaine Barrie, and a pregnant Mary Astor. Of her figure, Astor later wrote in her book, *Life on Film,* "Hips too wide, a waistline that could have been an inch smaller, flat-chested. It is a tie between Irene and Edith Head who did better for me. It wasn't easy." The only sewing Edith did for Colbert was in an emergency, when publicist A. C. Lyles accidentally tore the hem of the black mousseline de soie evening gown that Irene had designed. "I was visiting her on the set and I didn't realize my feet were on her dress until she stood up and the dress tore," he remembers. "They had to hold up shooting until Edith came in and fixed it."

Colbert continued to use Irene for all of her Paramount films for the next several years. When I asked Edith in 1973 about this uncomfortable arrangement, she acted like it hadn't bothered her. Some years later I asked her again, and she started to give the same answer, then suddenly she grew angry, and finally admitted what she really thought. "I really resented that," she stormed.

In 1978, when Colbert was appearing in a play in Los Angeles,

John Engstead convinced her that Edith had had no part in Banton's departure and suggested that the three of them have dinner together to bury the hatchet. Colbert agreed but Edith refused. "That woman was a bitch and a dyke to boot!" she spat, the only time I ever heard her make a homophobic remark.

Even though she wasn't dressing Colbert after *Zaza,* Paramount's one expensive non–De Mille costume picture, *If I Were King* (1938), turned out to be a surprise success for Edith. She had relatively little experience with historical epics, and had Dryden worked out, he would have designed it. The story took place in the Middle Ages and was undoubtedly a stretch for Edith, but Frances Dee recalls, "Oh, the sketches were beautiful, and when I came on the set wearing the white gown for the first time, people oohed and aahed and clapped. As far as I recall, she did Ronald Colman's costumes, and all the men too." Edith also did an interesting period recreation for Irene Dunne and Fred MacMurray in *Invitation to Happiness* (1939). Normally designers of that era were reluctant to recreate faithfully clothes of the past decade or two, for fear they would look funny to the modern eye. Also, dressing the extras in period clothes was costlier than having them wear their own. However, for this film, which began in the late 1920s, Edith gave MacMurray the funny collegiate suits of the twenties, and Dunne's dresses and hats were very retro, apart from a slight squaring of the shoulders.

By the end of 1938, Paramount was willing to announce Edith the new head designer and move her into Banton's old office. Adele Balkan remained in Edith's old office, making some of the sketches and designing more for the lesser characters, under Edith's supervision.

The first order of business was to try to make Edith more glamorous. She was still wearing the Colleen Moore Dutch boy haircut she had affected in the twenties, and it wasn't only because it was practical. Nellie Manley, Paramount's head hairdresser for many years, later remembered, "We tried to comb her hair to the side at various times but she had a very broad forehead and it didn't look good." The prevailing hairstyles of the late thirties pulled the hair up and back off the forehead and temples, but attempts to do this to Edith didn't work out either. The solution came from Anna Mae Wong, when she returned to Paramount to make a some B pictures. Athough Banton designed these films as a favor to his old friend, Edith had noticed Wong's hairstyle, combining flat bangs with a chignon at the back. Manley adapted this look for Edith, and, with very few variations, she wore it for the rest of her life.

Edith knew she had really arrived when Paramount sent her to Paris early in 1939 to scout the latest fashion trends. Howard Greer and Travis Banton (who seemed to think that they would be called back eventually) both offered her suggestions about which salons she should visit. Although the war clouds were already gathering, she dutifully attended the great couturiers' shows and even ordered a few dresses for her own wardrobe from them. (From then on, however, she designed her own clothes.) In her absence, Travis Banton, when drunk, had begun to complain that Edith had contrived to get his job, and now that she had fully assumed his responsibilities and title she sensed a new coolness towards her on the part of certain studio workers. She responded by becoming cool, distant, and utterly expressionless herself. The vivacious girl of the 1920s, the girl who had been slowly disappearing through the uncertainties of the 1930s, was now completely gone. She tried to make the department a more dignified place. Adele Balkan remembered, "We couldn't chew gum. We couldn't sing in the hallway. It didn't last . . . we reverted back . . ."

When Edith became the head designer, she began wearing her

dark glasses indoors. At the time of all black-and-white films, cinematographers and designers often would look at a set or a fabric through a blue glass in order to get an idea of how it would look in monochrome. Edith had additional reasons for the blue glasses: the glasses hid her crossed eye, and she was embarrassed at how thick the lenses were, afraid that somebody would think that she couldn't see well enough to do her job. Earlier she had worn clear glasses and taken them off as frequently as possible, but now she was so busy that she never got a chance to take them off. The main reason for the tinted lenses, however, was to make herself as inscrutable as possible. Natalie Visart said, "She actually had four different shades of blue, from clear to very dark. With the dark pair you couldn't see her eyes at all and had no way of knowing what she was thinking."

I once asked Edith how she managed to wear the blue glasses and do her work when she started designing color films. Quite proudly she replied, "Well, if I had to see a fabric, I'd look down under the glasses. If I went into the projection room to see a costume test, I'd keep the dark glasses until the lights went down, then I'd switch to my clear pair!" Gradually the blue lenses were replaced with neutral shades of gray and black. These dark glasses eventually became as much of an Edith trademark as the bangs, but eventually her eye doctor told her she must give them up. This happened during the shooting of *Myra Breckinridge* in 1969. When she came into the 20th Century–Fox wardrobe department one morning wearing the clear pair, her sympathetic codesigner Theadora Van Runkle asked her why she'd ever started wearing the dark glasses in the first place. "To hide the tears," replied Edith grimly.

The rumor that Edith had somehow plotted against Banton to get his job would haunt her for the rest of her life. Certainly the Edith Head of a few years later, the one who ruthlessly chased away any designer who tried to get a foothold at Paramount, might have been capable of such conniving, but in 1938, she would have been too scared. Had Ernest Dryden succeeded at Paramount, or had Paramount been able to attract a big "name" to replace Banton, that person would have probably brought in his own assistant. In that case, Edith's only hope would have been to become Banton's assistant wherever he worked next.

Unfortunately and much to his surprise, Banton was finding himself definitely not in demand. Dietrich, Lombard, and West all worked at various studios, making movies for which they could have requested him—but they didn't. After a quick job designing a few dresses for Olivia de Havilland to wear in *Raffles* at Goldwyn in 1940, he made a brief attempt to join Howard Greer's Beverly Hills Couture salon. His lack of discipline practically put it out of business. He then moved to New York to work for Hattie Carnegie. His assistant there was a young Pauline Trigère. "He would come in after a several-martini lunch at the Colony," Trigère recalled, "and give me a few sketches and I'd make a muslin pattern. Right after Pearl Harbor, Carnegie was sure the Japanese were going to invade the West Coast right away and she closed down the workroom." Trigère took it over and started her own business, and Banton returned to Hollywood where he got a job at 20th Century–Fox for much less salary than he had been paid at Paramount.

Edith later claimed that she was so anxious that Banton not lose his job at Fox that she would go to his house in the mornings, get him up, and drive him to Fox before she reported to Paramount. In the two years Banton worked there he did some highly memorable work, especially for Alice Faye in *Lillian Russell* (1940). Then he had a brief period at Columbia where he designed Rita Hayworth's modern fashions for *Cover Girl* (1944) and Merle Oberon's period gowns for *A Song to Remember* (1945). This job ended when the wife of studio head Harry Cohn decided to bring Jean Louis out from New York.

Aside from the drinking problem, Banton was having trouble adapting to new clothing styles and new ways of working in the film industry. His contract with Universal International went well with the period film *Letter from an Unknown Woman* (1948), but he ran into trouble working with George Cukor and writer Garson Kanin on *A Double Life* (1947). Yvonne Wood remembered, "He wasn't used to anybody telling him what to design. Signe Hasso needed a dressing gown, and Cukor and Kanin bluntly told him they wanted it up-to-the-minute, stylewise, not one of those 'Carole Lombard things with big fox-fur cuffs.' Banton designed one like that anyway and when they found he'd even ordered the fur, they took him off the picture and put me on."

"Working with Banton was the greatest training any designer could ever have," Edith often said. But as much as she learned from him what to do, she also learned very well what not to do. Aside from the obvious difference of being disciplined and dependable where Banton had been totally out of control, there was something else, equally important. Edith could work with anybody. She went beyond simply listening to everybody's point of view and somehow synthesizing it into a garment; like a psychologist, she was able to draw from her coworkers that which they often could not verbalize.

When Banton designed a gown, the major creative work was done when he was drawing it. He often just made one sketch for each scene, letting ideas develop and sort themselves out until it was just right on paper. If the gown was to be worn by Dietrich or

Colbert, he would reluctantly make changes or even a new sketch if they didn't like it, then he gave it to the workroom where he or Edith would supervise the sewing. By the time of the fitting, the gown was basically finished. He would see how it moved and might make slight adjustments. Ilse Richardson remembers, "He'd say, 'A little tighter here, a little more fullness there,' and that would be it."

Edith started out that way, but gradually, over the years, a different method developed. She would ask the star, the director, the art director, the cinematographer, and even the sound engineer for their input, and then, like a labor leader, arrive at a consensus if one was needed. When dealing with talent who were content to leave it all to her, she sometimes seemed to be having a debate within herself during the fitting. As conscious as she was of costs, she would occasionally order a drastic change or even abandon a garment and start over from scratch. "The wardrobe department was full of half-finished dresses that she'd given up on," Yvonne Wood remembered. "We'd try to find some way of using them, or she'd use them somewhere else."

The other important way in which Edith differed from Banton was that she could adapt to whatever changes took place in the industry or in fashion. Unlike the Warners designers Orry-Kelly and Milo Anderson, the latter of whom said he would "risk looking foolish to be on top of a trend," Edith was inclined to design conservatively, generally using a minimum of ornament and avoiding any fads she felt wouldn't last long. Still, she saw the value of forecasting long-range fashion trends as a means of getting publicity.

Though Banton had become increasingly unwilling to work on minor pictures or with actresses he didn't consider worth his time, Edith never took that attitude, always taking care of the B pictures and small parts on the A pictures as much as time constraints allowed. Occasionally she would be so busy that she would have to turn over a whole picture to Adele Balkan, but even then she kept a close watch on what Balkan was doing, also checking with the actresses and producer to be sure all was well. The one important picture that, as Balkan remembered, Edith had absolutely nothing to do with was Preston Sturges's *The Great McGinty* (1940). This was Sturges's first directing assignment, and it had a modest budget. Edith did submit some preliminary sketches for Muriel Angelus; they were turned down, but she had to leave for New York and so left the whole problem in Balkan's hands. When the film was released (with Edith listed as costume designer), it became an unexpected hit that did nothing for Balkan's career. Soon afterwards, Paramount laid her off during a slow time but Frank Richardson was able to get her a job next door, at RKO. She and Edith remained collegial.

Actress Kay Linaker, who played supporting roles during Edith's first years as main designer, says, "She always showed me the sketches and said, 'How do you think this would be for you?' rather than telling me what I was going to wear, like designers at the other studios did. I never had anything much to say, because the designs were so good, but there was an off-white beach robe in *Buck Benny Rides Again* (1940) that Edith had drawn, with some appliquéd black design on one side. I said, 'Is that a seahorse?' Edith said, 'It is if you say so!' When I tried it on at the fitting, it had truly become a seahorse. That scene was cut from the film, but stills of the robe were printed all over. [Edith later refitted the robe for Veronica Lake.]

"Her assistants in the department were very fond of her, loyal, always tried to help," Linaker concluded. They were also respectful of her wishes in regard to keeping her home life private. Although many of them had met Charles Head from time to time, she did not discuss her divorce in 1938 and nobody else brought it up either. The one exception was Billye Fritz. Ilse Richardson remembered, "She was my husband's assistant and she always knew everything that was going on." Over the years, she kept close tabs on Edith's private life and was only too happy to give Yvonne Wood the complete rundown when she arrived at Paramount in 1952. Billye also told Yvonne that Edith was "embarrassed to have her parents come to the office because they looked so Jewish."

Robbie Fisher, the stepdaughter of Edith's maid Nanny Jones, had a half sister, Myrtle City, who came out to Los Angeles from Texas in 1942. At first she worked as a maid in a hotel. The classic era of Central Avenue jazz clubs was in full swing and Myrtle loved it. "I thought [the corner of] Central and Santa Barbara [Avenues] was really *it.*" Since Robbie was already working occasionally at Edith's house, Myrtle met Edith, and Edith got her a better job as a personal maid to her friend Gretchen Messner. Edith had set her mother up in an apartment near the studio and when Gretchen Messner's husband was transferred to an army base in northern California, Edith hired Myrtle City as Anna's maid and driver. "Oh Miss Spare was very nice, nicer than Miss Head," Myrtle said many years later. "I always cooked all her food but she'd come into the kitchen and season it herself. When she had a bridge party, we'd get Robbie over to help, and other times I went to Miss Head's house to help Nanny. I think they were Jewish but they never said anything about it and we didn't ask them. I know I never drove her to the synagogue." When she could spare a moment, Edith would dash over to her mother's apartment, or Myrtle would bring Anna to the house in the evening, "but Miss Head never got home until late," said Myrtle many years later.

Edith's associates were utterly amazed when she announced that she had married Wiard Ihnen on September 8, 1940. Of course some of them had known Ihnen when he was at Paramount, but he had left in 1933 and never came back. Once when Edith and I were alone and she was going on and on about how happy she was with Bill, I got the courage to ask her why it had taken them so long to finally get married. After all, they had met in 1932 but didn't marry until 1940. There was a terribly long pause while she tried to find some clever way to answer, and then, in a sober tone of voice, like somebody confessing to a crime, she said, "I was engaged to two men during that time. One was a screenwriter." (It must have been Bayard Veiller.) She didn't mention the fact that she was still married to and sometimes living with Charles Head. On another occasion, when I was talking to both Edith and Bill, I asked the same question. There was another terrible pause. Finally Edith offered, "Well, Bill had another girlfriend . . ." Bill said, very, very carefully, "I had to take care of my mother and my sisters . . ."

By the time of the marriage, Edith and Bill had already achieved a strong sexual rapport as lovers, but living together on a day-to-day basis was hard on both of them at first. He moved into her house on Doheny Drive, which she had tastefully furnished with French antiques. Eventually she got rid of a lot of her things, allowing him to indulge his taste with Mexican antiques and artifacts. Not as handsome or charming as Charles, Bill had an inner strength that protected Edith from all the vicissitudes of her job. The incredibly close personal affinity Edith came to have with Bill built up slowly over the years. It became especially strong after Bill retired from films and devoted himself wholly to taking care of her. In the evenings she would tell him every little thing that had happened to her that day at the studio, while he listened as attentively as a therapist and advised her as wisely as a parent.

It was typical of Edith to often give the impression that she was in a marriage of convenience while she really loved Bill and needed his quiet strength to face her challenging life at the studio. She needed public attention and acceptance; Bill did his work and his paintings to please himself, and preferred to remain in the background. The fact that in the later years she was often seen without him at industry functions, combined with her severe manner of dress, has given rise to rumors since her death that she had been a lesbian. These would probably amuse her, since she often said, "I don't care what they print about me as long as they spell my name right." Actually she did try to include Bill more in her professional life, but met with mixed results. Once in the 1970s, when the executive board of the Costume Designers' Guild was meeting at her house, she urged Bill to stay around and meet the other designers. He said, "They don't want to meet Mr. Edith Head." However, a few weeks later, when Edith was being honored at the Masquers Club and many people spoke, when Bill's turn came, he got up very slowly and said very sweetly, "Until now my name's been Bill Ihnen. After tonight, I guess I'll be known as Mr. Edith Head."

She got along fine with his family. "His sisters would tell her where they were going and she'd tell them what to wear," remembers Robbie Fisher. Anna Spare was a much harder nut to crack. As much as she hadn't approved of Charles Head and quarrelled with him when the three tried to live together, she now understood that the strong, quiet Ihnen was a much more real threat to her close relationship with her only child. "Oh, she loved her baby," Robbie Fisher says. "Every mother feels like that, but Miss Spare made it too difficult. Some of the things I heard said about Mr. Ihnen when I was serving dinner were so unfair. After Miss Spare died, Miss Head regretted that she hadn't had her over often enough, but she sure didn't make it easy when she did."

When Edith began to realize that she could confide everything in her husband when she came home at night, she had no further need to confide in her assistants. After Balkan's departure, she made the sketches herself for a time, and when the department was busy again, she got various new sketchers but kept her distance from them. Even Richardson noticed that she was collegial and certainly never hostile, but no longer chummy as before. When there was a Paramount social event, Bill Ihnen escorted her and shook hands all around with his former colleagues, but then remained quiet for the rest of the evening as if any idle conversation might betray important secrets. When he and Edith attended social events at his studio, 20th Century–Fox, Bill was much more affable. He had no problem socializing with coworkers, and his friends at Fox became their friends as a couple, most notably producer Kenneth MacGowan and his wife and grown daughter.

In 1950, the MacGowans and Ihnens traveled to Mexico together to visit Aztec ruins. (MacGowan had retired from films in 1946 to devote himself to Mexican anthropology and founding a Theater Arts Department at UCLA, where both Edith and Bill initially taught at his request.) When MacGowan's daughter Joan Faxon had a daughter named Prudence, Edith and Bill agreed to be her godparents. "My grandmother was ten years older than Edith and my mother ten years younger, and the three were very good friends," says Prudence Faxon today. "Wherever Edith traveled on location, she'd find a doll that represented the local culture and send it to me." When Prudence was still a small child, Edith sent her a postcard from Rome with the message, "You'll be very popular here when you grow up, especially if you're [still] a blonde." Today Prudence Faxon says, "My grandparents and my parents were very close friends with the Ihnens. She was a take-charge kind of woman who got things done, yes, but nobody suspected her of being a lesbian then. If there were any truth to that, my mother would have known." The Ihnens usually spent their Christmases with the cinematographer George Folsey and his family.

Keeping her own counsel was prudent, for Edith was very aware that her position at Paramount was precarious. She received a rude shock early in 1942, when her good friend John Engstead was laid off after fifteen years of excellent (and underpaid) service in the publicity department. John was known and liked by everybody, and did his job obsessively well. Yet when there was a change in management in the studio and somebody wanted his job for a relative, he was let go. Edith realized that no matter how well one did one's job, nothing was permanent.

Frank Richardson genuinely liked Edith and thought she struck a good balance between the creative and the practical in her work, but he agreed with the studio managers that it was absurd and dangerous to have only one costume designer in such a big studio. At the time even poor little RKO next door had two, Warners had three, and Fox even more. What if she became ill or was injured? Then there were the people, most notably Mitchell Leisen, who began directing in 1933, who thought her designs were too conservative. Leisen proudly told me how he squelched Edith when she eagerly brought him a bunch of sketches to look at. "What's holding this thing up? What happens in the back? Go get some ten-cent-a-yard material and try draping it before you make a sketch!" he thundered. "We'd work for days on sketches to show him," Edith recalled, "and he'd dismiss them with a shrug and say, 'Dig deeper, Edith.' What he really wanted was to design the dresses himself, which would have been fine with me."

When Barbara Stanwyck starred in Leisen's *Remember the Night* in 1940, he leaned on Edith so heavily that for her next film, an independent made at Warner Bros. called *Meet John Doe* (1941), Stanwyck asked him to design her clothes. Leisen begged out, instead sending over his mistress, Natalie Visart, who was available at the time because Cecil B. De Mille didn't have anything in production. De Mille got Paramount to offer Visart a full-time contract so she'd be available whenever he needed her, but she refused, saying, "Between De Mille pictures Edith would have me picking up pins off of the workroom floor." Likewise, the temperamental Earl Luick refused a Paramount contract for the same reason. Omar Kiam, who had designed brilliantly for Samuel Goldwyn for several years, seems to have made a brief attempt to work at Paramount. No contract exists today as proof, but Oleg Cassini remembers hearing talk of Kiam when he arrived in 1941.

Famous today for his legendary designs for Jacqueline Kennedy, Cassini ended up at Paramount in typical Horatio Alger fashion. "I was playing tennis at the Westside Tennis Club and met the studio manager. He asked me to come down for an interview, and Frank Richardson gave me a script, which I was to break down and design costumes for as if the film were to star Claudette Colbert. I had to do it very quickly as they wanted to see if I could work under the pressures of the studio system.

"They liked my designs and I was offered a small contract, though Ray Stark, who was my agent, didn't think to get a guarantee that I would be billed. Sure enough, I went with Betty Grable to a preview of [my] first picture, some B picture, and my name was nowhere on the screen."

Unlike Adele Balkan, Cassini was not working under Edith's supervision, though she tried in vain to make it understood that he would be her "junior designer." His first big assignment was *I*

Wanted Wings (1941), with the female leads of Constance Moore and the then unknown Veronica Lake. Mitchell Leisen, who took over the picture during filming gave Cassini a lot of encouragement. "Mitchell was very precise in what he wanted but also very kind and encouraging to me," says Cassini now. "So was Frank Richardson. Nobody said I was being groomed to replace Edith exactly, but I thought I had a good chance. She was the queen of the shirtwaist dress, day or evening, with embroidery or without, all shirtmakers. I thought in time I'd get her job." Cassini represented a threat Edith never had thought she'd have to face—a handsome, heterosexual man who was dating the very actresses she thought of as "hers." "She thought I'd get them in the hay and I did," he says.

Edith, however, was taking no chances. The months before the start of World War II were very slow at the box office, and Paramount's New York office sent out an executive named Henry Ginsburg to trim the payroll. "Edith was always very friendly toward me when I ran into her in the department but she was undermining me behind my back," recalls Cassini. "She kept telling Ginsburg, 'I can handle everything, we don't need him.' I did my best to avoid Ginsburg when I saw him in the distance on the lot. Frank Richardson warned me that I was being seen out on the town and in the newspapers too often. One day I went to pick up an actress I had a date with, and knocked on her door. After a long wait the door opened, and it was Ginsburg! I resigned the next day."

Cassini joined the army, and when the war ended, he worked at 20th Century–Fox, thanks to his wife, Gene Tierney, who refused to act in *The Razor's Edge* (1946) without his costumes. "People criticized us for doing that," he recalls, "but I never would have gotten started otherwise. Talent or no, you had to have some base of power to get a job then. People now think it was so wonderful, working in the studios then. Believe me, it wasn't." He did return to Paramount briefly, a few years later, to design Tierney's clothes for *The Mating Season* (1951). On that film, Thelma Ritter was given a budget to go out and buy clothes for her part as a frumpy housewife, but it remains unclear who provided the glamorous wardrobe worn by Miriam Hopkins. When I suggested that Edith might have done it and not taken credit, Cassini laughed and said, "Oh no, I don't think Edith ever did anything without taking credit! But I had the last laugh because Edith later said that Jacqueline Kennedy was the greatest fashion influence of all time. If I had been more successful in pictures, I would never have gone to New York and none of that would have happened."

Suddenly Edith's clothes didn't seem so dowdy after all. In 1941, Preston Sturges wrote a part with a dual role (sort of) for Barbara Stanwyck in *The Lady Eve,* which gave Edith her best opportunity to date to display her high fashion skills. As the film starts, Stanwyck is Jean, a cardsharp on a cruise ship going along the South American coast. Edith gave her bare-midriff evening gowns and other glamorous outfits with a decidedly South American flavor at a time when Latin music was sweeping the radio stations and the American government was promoting good Pan-American relations. Stanwyck had broad shoulders and back, but her waist was long and her buttocks flat until they suddenly jutted out like a shelf. Earlier designers had coped with this by raising her waist slightly and giving her full skirts. Edith did this too, but she also found another trick: making Stanwyck's belts wider in the back than in the front. Most of the skirts were quite straight but in one scene, in which Jean's lover (Henry Fonda) finds out her profession and jilts her, Edith put her in a suit with a box jacket and a full, pleated skirt. When Stanwyck falls onto the

Gown for Barbara Stanwyck's personal wardrobe, made at the time of Ball of Fire

bed crying, the outfit gives her a little-girl vulnerability that is surprising and effective. In the latter part of the film, Jean transforms herself into the Lady Eve, all British and regal.

These *Lady Eve* outfits made Stanwyck feel glamorous and sexy onscreen for the first time and broadened the range of roles she would accept. She made Samuel Goldwyn borrow Edith for her next role as a nightclub performer and gangster's moll in *Ball of Fire* (1941). She later also asked that Edith be loaned to Warner

Bros., Columbia, Universal, and Hunt Stromberg for *Lady of Burlesque* (1943). Natalie Visart dressed the other strippers for that film and remembered, "Stromberg hired a bus and we all went down to the Burbank Burlesque Theatre on Main Street to do research." Edith, also along on the field trip, later laughed, "Those girls got down to a little G-string and pasties, and of course the censors wouldn't allow that. I had to keep Barbara covered up as much as ever." The *Lady of Burlesque* costumes showed that Edith had humor and imagination.

Whenever Edith was loaned to Warner Bros. for a Stanwyck picture, Milo Anderson designed for the other ladies in the cast. While most of his colleagues resented Edith's increasingly frequent incursions onto their turf, Anderson was philosophical. "I had plenty of other work to do and Stanwyck didn't interest me much. If this kept her happy, so what," he said in the 1970s. "Edith and I would have meetings and compare sketches so we wouldn't accidentally do the same thing for two actresses in a particular scene. We'd meet at the Tick Tock restaurant for lunch. Edith was very insecure. She'd say, 'Milo, don't you like my designs?' I'd say, 'No, Edith, I don't. If I liked your designs I wouldn't like my own.' "

Anderson's designs were indeed different from Edith's and he had to tone down his extreme looks a little to go along with her conservative tastes. Anderson's severely tailored suits for Jane Wyman, Ann Sheridan, and Alexis Smith in the 1944 *Doughgirls* were a case in point. They featured a wealth of ornamentation and the most heavily padded shoulders the 1940s would ever see. Edith hated padded shoulders. "Of course I did them, I had to, it was the prevailing style," she told me, "but I put the minimum of padding on Stanwyck and Ginger Rogers because their shoulders were naturally very square. Whenever I could, on a dress or a blouse, I'd use a puffed sleeve instead."

When I reminded Edith that padded shoulders make the hips seem narrower, Edith retorted triumphantly, "That's what Veronica Lake thought! You go too far with that and the neck looks scrawny!" After a sensational cover story in *Life* magazine, Lake with her "peek-a-boo" hairstyle had become a star overnight. Everything she did—and wore—was big news. She became Edith's next big fashion star. The hairstyle, which balanced her wide forehead with her thin neck (and was the only way Lake's fine hair would hold a curl) was widely copied but eventually was banned from defense factories because the dangling locks were getting caught in the machinery. Lake was photographed dutifully tucking her hair into a chignon, but without her hair she was no longer special. With her hair in braids and without the heavy makeup, the version of Lake that Edith saw around the studio looked like a ten-year-old child and that was the key to her sensational screen image as well—half femme fatale, half child. The tough girl with the heart of gold.

Lake was also a troubled person, totally unprepared for the burden of stardom, and there is a possibility that she was mentally ill (her mother later said she had been diagnosed as schizophrenic). Managing her took all of Edith's diplomacy—at times she played the sympathetic mother Lake had never had, but when Lake was being childish and petulant, Edith could become stern and authoritarian. Lake's figure and public image also required careful handling. She was very short in stature, with large breasts, a tiny waist, and wide hips. Preston Sturges's *Sullivan's Travels* (1942) was well under way when Lake revealed that she was pregnant. Fortunately she was required to wear tramp clothes through most of the film, and Edith also designed her a bulky bathrobe with darker panels below the bust to provide an optical illusion of slimness. The one dress that had a fitted waist—a black Civil War–era

Edith's slinky evening gown for Veronica Lake in This Gun for Hire

COURTESY OF THE ACADEMY OF MOTION PICTURE ARTS AND SCIENCES

Edith copied the regulation army nurse uniform for Veronica Lake to wear in So Proudly We Hail *with misgivings, since it revealed all of Lake's figure problems: the thin neck, big bust, and wide hips*

number—was disguised by Preston Sturges's decision to shoot Lake in fast motion running around Paramount.

Back at the studio for *This Gun for Hire* (1942), Lake, with her post-maternity figure, was bustier than ever, and Edith provided the requisite slinky evening gown with long sleeves to help balance the hips. Lake's part in *The Glass Key* (1942) was originally planned for Patricia Morrison. "We were fitting the dresses the night before shooting was to start when suddenly word came to stop because they'd recast the part with Veronica Lake," remembers Morrison. "Some executive tried to play studio politics with me, and I refused, so they took me out of the picture. Edith was very upset, though she tried to hide it."

Typically, Edith could remember very little about Lake, Betty Hutton, or her other 1940s stars when I asked her about them twenty-five years later. Whatever happened was all in a day's work. If she could exploit it at the time for an interview so much the better, otherwise it was always on to the next film. One Wednesday evening we were joined at dinner by film historian John Kobal, who was very proud of the fact that he had met Lake in the 1960s and pressed Edith to tell him about her. She tried and tried to remember something, anything, and finally said, "Well, one day, Veronica asked me to have lunch with her. She was shooting her last picture for Paramount. She didn't know they weren't going to renew her contract, but I did. Anyway, we sat down and she was dead drunk and it was only noon. She said, 'Edith, I've decided I need a new designer for my next picture, so I'm going to look for one in Paris.' I said, 'I think that's a great idea, you go right ahead . . .' "

Paulette Goddard was another star for whom Edith designed many costumes and whom she also disliked intensely, though she gave various unconvincing reasons. I thought at first that Edith might have caught the flirtatious Paulette making a pass at Bill Ihnen. Later I realized that it was because Goddard brought in Bernard Newman to design her clothes in the 1948 film *Hazard*.

Goddard's costar in *Hold Back the Dawn* (1941), Olivia de Havilland, was somewhat overweight when she first came to Paramount. She was recovering from an appendectomy and, as she recalls, "I had gained weight in the hospital, eating ice cream and Jell-O, which was the postoperative diet then. Edith Head made some marvelous clothes that helped a lot. She was very careful that the surfaces of the fabrics had no shine, and the lines were very good. One navy blue dress looked fine to the eye but when we watched the filmed costume tests, it had a highlight in the back that was unflattering, and she said, 'Take it out.' " For the big confrontation between de Havilland and Goddard, Edith gave de Havilland a pale blue dress, while the slimmer Goddard wore white. The slightly darker tone of de Havilland's dress created an optical illusion that made the two women seem the same size.

De Havilland returned to Paramount in 1945, after a long legal battle with Warner Bros. over *The Well-Groomed Bride* (1946). "I hated the script but my agent talked me into it. I told Edith to make the clothes as simple as possible." Making them frilly like the ones Orry-Kelly had given her for *Princess O'Rourke* would have been more appropriate. De Havilland's next part, in Mitchell Leisen's *To Each His Own* (1946), was more satisfying all around. The character of Josephine Norris was seen in three stages of her life: a small-town girl all in white ruffles in 1918 (de Havilland was under-weight after another illness when this was filmed), a hard-as-nails businesswoman in 1924, and a lonely middle-aged woman in 1945. Leisen was determined to tell the sentimental story in the most realistic terms possible, including complete period accuracy. He made sure the clothes Edith made for the 1924 sequence looked ugly to the 1945 eye. This included a smoke-blue chiffon tea gown trimmed with chinchilla. "That gave me so many little things I could do," de Havilland says, "managing the train as I went around the corner, and managing the chinchilla sleeves when I used my hands. When I put it on I just knew what Jody was feeling at that point in the story. Also it was August and blazing hot, and we didn't have a double. Mitch kept saying, 'Don't you dare perspire!' "

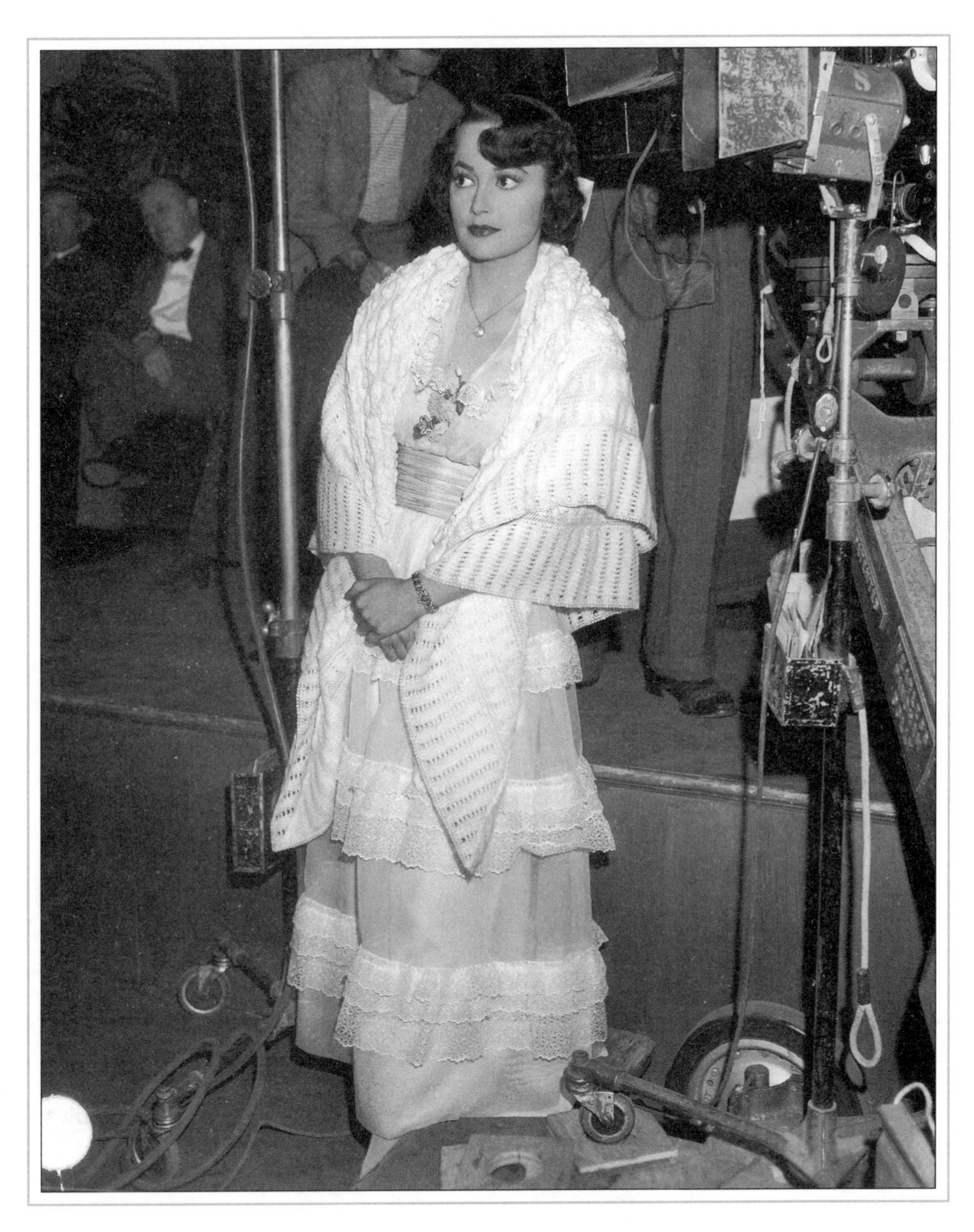

Olivia de Havilland as the younger Josephine Norris (circa 1918) in To Each His Own

Olivia de Havilland in the smoke-blue tea gown Edith designed for the middle episode (1924) of To Each His Own

As the middle-aged Josephine Norris in To Each His Own, *Olivia de Havilland wore a "frankly-forty foundation garment" stuffed with cotton under her gold lamé evening gown*

Leisen also made sure Olivia ate heavily during the shooting, but by the time they filmed the final sequence, she hadn't gained enough weight, so Edith helped out with a sagging gold-lamé evening gown over a "frankly forties" foundation garment padded out with cotton. De Havilland went on to win the Academy Award as Best Actress for this portrayal.

Designing Olivia's personal clothes proved to be more of a challenge than finding the right things for her role of Miss Norris. "When I had to appear at a function or go to New York to do interviews and I didn't have the right clothes," de Havilland says, "I'd go to Edith and ask her to design some for me. They'd be made in the Paramount workroom and I'd pay for them. Sometimes I thought she got my personality just right and I loved the clothes, but other times they were too businesslike; styles and fabrics better suited to Edith herself than to me. But I wore them, I had to, I didn't have anything else."

On and off during the 1940s, Paramount executives frequently thought about finding another head designer. In 1942, Buddy DeSylva, a songwriter who had produced a few pictures, became the head of the studio. "We knew he didn't like Edith's designs and wanted to get rid of her, but she hung on," says Willa Kim, an award-winning Broadway designer who worked for a while as a sketch artist at Paramount. DeSylva hired talent he'd worked with in New York, including Betty Hutton and costume designer Raoul Pene du Bois whose first assignment was the film version of the hit stage musical *Louisiana Purchase* (1941). When that came off well, he was given a contract with the idea that he would specialize in Technicolor musicals and historical spectaculars. His designs for Mary Martin and Betty Hutton in the Technicolor *Happy Go*

Lucky (1943) were certainly more theatrical than anything Edith would have submitted, except for a black-lace evening gown Hutton wore when she sang "He Says Murder," which seems fairly tame compared to the rest.

Mitchell Leisen, a former costume designer and art director himself, was one director who had heavily lobbied for someone to replace Edith. He had tried hard to delegate the chores of costumes and sets to others when he started directing in 1933, but after his heart attack and nervous breakdown in 1937 he slowly began to involve himself in those areas again. Leisen's *Lady in the Dark* (1944) remains, along with *Cover Girl,* the great fashion epic of the 1940s. Originally, DeSylva's plans for the clothes bypassed Edith altogether. Willa Kim remembers, "I had just graduated from Chounard and gotten a job that I wanted in the art department at the May Company. However, Al Nichol at Western Costume had my portfolio and showed it to Leisen who insisted that Paramount hire me. I didn't want to go but my boss at the May Co. said I could always go back there.

"The first thing I did at Paramount was to attend a production meeting in Leisen's office. Edith wasn't invited. DeSylva was going to have du Bois design all the fantasy production numbers, and for the book part of the film he wanted to get a different name New York designer for each of the female characters." Ginger Rogers suits were to be designed by Valentina. At first *Vogue* magazine was enlisted to help in whatever way needed, and one of the *Vogue* editors, Babs Wilomez, was hired to make sketches for smart suits for all of the young women working in the offices of the film's *Allure* magazine.

These plans started to fall apart when Rogers didn't like the Valentina designs. In the end none were used, and Edith, who had worked well with Rogers on *The Major and the Minor* in 1942, qui-

Edith used a doll to show Ginger Rogers how she would convert her fashionable outfit into a little-girl dress for a scene in The Major and the Minor. *Later they posed together for this publicity photo*

etly stepped in to fill the gap, though she was heavily supervised by Leisen. (Rogers's masculine tailored suits were actually made at Mitchell and Haigue, a shop Leisen co-owned.) The few Wilomez sketches that found their way into the final film were so heavily adapted by Edith, Leisen, and the Technicolor experts that the studio decided to give her no credit at all (her contract didn't require them to anyway). Also, relations between Paramount and *Vogue* had become strained and it was hard communicating across the continent during the war, so *Vogue* quietly dropped out of the picture too.

For the dream sequences, du Bois designed the sets and the costumes. He expected to have a totally free hand, as he did when working in the theater, and Leisen began to wish du Bois were as acquiescent as Edith. She later said, "Raoul du Bois came from the stage and he was used to doing what he wanted. He didn't like having to sit down and discuss things with Mitch. In any movie, but particularly one of Mitch's, it has to be a collaboration. Once Raoul realized this, things went more smoothly."

Du Bois brought in Madame Barbara Karinska, with whom he'd worked in New York, to execute the costumes for the musical numbers, and she sometimes took liberties with the designs. When I interviewed Ray Milland for my Leisen book in 1971, he talked of his ringmaster outfit for "The Saga of Jenny" number as though it was Leisen's design, saying, "The costume Mitch designed for me for that number was out of this world . . ." Yet, when I met him again a few years later during the filming of a *Hardy Boys* episode, he remembered that costume as Edith Head's design and said that Edith had gone with him to Madame Karinska's fitting. When she saw the changes Karinska made, Edith sighed and said, "That isn't the coat I designed . . ." but didn't make an issue of it. All of which just goes to show that Leisen and Head's work together had become so seamless that even the actors didn't really know which of them (or both) actually designed any particular item. Milland also said, "Madame Karinska was one of the few who could take one of Mitch's drawings and figure out how to make it. She corrected him too, when he was off on something. For one thing, his military uniforms were always straight out of *The Student Prince.*"

Ginger Rogers's mink dress for the "Jenny" number garnered the film enormous publicity. Virtually every newspaper and magazine featured it, and when *Lady in the Dark* opened in war-torn London, a blowup of Rogers in the mink dress several stories high was attached to the front of the theater. Actually, there were two mink dresses. The first one appears during the book part of the film. The fashion maven Liza Elliott (Rogers) and her assistant, Mary Phillips, unpack the dress, which has "just arrived from Hollywood." Liza decides to wear the dress for an evening on the town, a marked contrast to the masculine suits she has worn so far in the film. This was the "mink dress number one," with a bodice covered with red and gold jewels, which matches the lining of the mink skirt. There was also a mink jacket and a muff of mink tails. Rogers was able to wear this for the scenes in the nightclub, but when the dress reappeared in the fantasy sequence preceding the "Jenny" number, they found out that the skirt was so heavy that she couldn't dance in it, and "mink dress number two" was brought in. This one also had a mink skirt, but the jacket and stole were gone and the lining of the skirt was sequined. The top of the dress was covered with the same pattern of gold sequins against a solid background of red sequins. Willa Kim remembers that Karinska executed the sequin dress with Kim assisting, and that Head had nothing to do with it. Kim says, "I traced the design of the sequins on enormous sheets of wrapping paper and took it to the beaders in downtown Los Angeles to embroider." Kim doesn't remember working on the first (jeweled) mink dress, which Edith may have had more of a hand in.

On the first day the mink dress was filmed, Edith personally came to the set of *Lady in the Dark,* dismissed the wardrobe girl, stood behind Ginger Rogers, and held up the skirt by the hem so the weight wouldn't tire Rogers out. Actress Margaret Kerry who

Ginger Rogers rehearses "The Saga of Jenny" from Lady in the Dark *in the celebrated mink dress designed by director Mitchell Leisen and executed by Madame Karinska. Willa Kim, Karinska's assistant who supervised the making of the sequined lining, says, "Edith Head had nothing to do with it," though she may have worked more on the other mink dress, which used red and gold glass beads instead of sequins. In the background is Ray Milland wearing a ringmaster costume designed by Edith but heavily reworked by Karinska*

was visiting the set recalls that "Edith Head looked straight ahead, with no expression, like she was on trial."

In *The Dress Doctor,* Edith is very careful about how much credit she takes for any mink dress, saying only that she helped Leisen to choose the mink skins. Years later, when Edith was giving a fashion show for charity, she included the mink dress (the one with the sequins; the one with the red and gold jewels was lost). She took credit for it and made no mention of Leisen, which infuriated him since he was present that night. "With all her Academy Awards, she has to go claiming other people's designs. Our whole table practically got up and threw things at her," he later told me. She told me, "I didn't know what to do that night. He gave me credit for the picture, which was very generous since he really did more of it than either I or du Bois. He didn't want people to know how much he was working on the clothes."

Ginger Rogers now joined the ranks of stars who made the other studios borrow Edith. Returning to RKO for *Tender Comrade* (1943) for her role as a very smartly clad defense-plant worker, Ginger was gowned by Edith while Edith's former assistant Renie Conley designed for the other ladies. (Following the usual pattern with Stanwyck, RKO paid Paramount a flat sum for Edith's services and Paramount charged RKO 150 percent of the actual costs of each outfit.) Next Edith designed a turn-of-the-century wardrobe for the Technicolor musical *The Gibson Girl.* The clothes had been completed when RKO canceled the picture. Instead Rogers went to Selznick for *I'll Be Seeing You* (1944), which also had dresses by Head. Rogers insisted on Head only because she liked her designs; the two women weren't close friends. After Edith's death, Rogers commented, "I knew Edith Head personally but it took a very long time for me to gain that privilege. She was always friendly and kind, but she believed work was work, and

Edith's party dress for Ginger Rogers as a wartime plant worker in Tender Comrade

there was a particular relationship you had at work. She never discussed her home life or her husband at work, but after he died, she changed. I knew she wasn't well but she kept her illness a secret. She was still working but she was somehow more remote."

Likewise, Ingrid Bergman was so sold on Edith after *For Whom the Bell Tolls* (1943) that she made RKO borrow her for *Bells of St. Mary's* (1945) and *Notorious* (1946). *Arch of Triumph* (1948), made at the short-lived Enterprise Studio, was Edith's last film with Bergman.

Joan Fontaine, weary of playing terrified heroines in gothic romances, liked the working-girl wardrobe Edith cooked up for *The Affairs of Susan* (1945) as well as the elegant turn-of-the-century gowns for *The Emperor Waltz* (1948). She and her husband, William Dozier, signed a contract with Paramount to borrow Edith for an English-language remake of *Mayerling* but ultimately the film was not made. However, Edith did accompany Loretta Young to RKO for *The Farmer's Daughter* (1947), for which Young won the Academy Award for Best Actress. Always praised by the fan magazines for her slender figure and long, willowy neck, Young suddenly decided that her neck was too long and that she should minimize it by raising her shoulders, which could be accomplished by using a foam-rubber form under her clothes. This necessitated raising the bust accordingly, and only overnight refrigeration would keep the form from rotting. Irene Sharaff, who designed Young's clothes for *The Bishop's Wife* (1947), described the situation in her autobiography. When I tried to bring up the subject with Edith, she denied it vehemently, even though I told her that Sharaff had already spilled the beans. Young also had RKO borrow Edith for her homespun garments in *Rachel and the Stranger* (1948). While all the designers loved designing for Young's figure (the real one) and admired her grace in wearing the clothes, some of them got very annoyed with her habit of interpolating her own clothes into the modern-dress movies so she could get the various studios to pay for them. This practice led to a big blowup with Columbia's boss Harry Cohn (Young later admitted she had been wrong). Edith took it all in her stride, however.

Bette Davis was the first star to request Edith on a loan-out who had not yet worked with her on a Paramount picture. In 1947, Davis's tenure as the first lady of Warner Bros. was drawing to a close. Since 1932, her films had been designed almost exclusively by the brilliant and hot-tempered Orry-Kelly. "She didn't like him as a person but she kept using him to design her films because she knew she needed him," recalled Milo Anderson. Her figure had several serious problems: bowed legs, very round shoulders, and a long and broad neck. Worst of all were her breasts, which hung almost to her waist. She refused to wear brassieres with underwires because she thought that the wire would cause breast cancer. When strapless bras became available, Kelly bought one and tried to get her to wear it, but she threw it at him! If Kelly pulled up on the straps too much, her shoulders ached and the breasts simply doubled over. Sometimes Kelly just let the breasts fall as they would and hid them in the unfitted waistline of a dress, but usually he lifted them as much as possible and tried to find new and different ways of camouflaging the situation with optical illusions. Short sleeves on blouse or dress usually end at the middle of the upper arm but Kelly brought Davis's sleeves down to the elbow so that they would be on the same level as the bottom of her bust. He often put white handkerchiefs in her breast pockets or corsages to draw the eye up. "Oh give me some new way to break her bust," he moaned one day to his sketcher and assistant Leah Rhodes.

Director Vincent Sherman has explained how the death of Davis's husband, Arthur Farnsworth, prior to the shooting of *Mr. Skeffington* (1944) changed her behavior at the studio from challenging to utterly impossible. Although Kelly had been fired, Davis had Jack Warner bring him back, and he did perhaps his greatest work for her on this film. Unfortunately they had come to the point where the mere sight of Kelly set off her angry outbursts, just as seeing Jack Warner did. (Kelly's frequent bitchy remarks only made matters worse: Davis was always aware that she wasn't beautiful enough to be a movie star and it concerned her greatly. While Warner's makeup chief Perc Westmore made Davis up himself every morning and always had words of encouragement, Kelly could not manage to be equally diplomatic.)

Bernard Newman then designed *Deception* (1946) for Davis during his brief period at Warners but was gone by the time she returned from her maternity leave to begin *Winter Meeting* (1948). Had Milo Anderson wanted the task he could have had it but he had worked with Davis a few times and he refused.

I asked Edith several times how her work with Davis had started and she could never remember. Perhaps it was the suggestion of her MCA agent Arthur Park, who also represented Barbara Stanwyck. In any case, Milo Anderson remembered that Edith came along to advise when Davis went shopping for *Winter Meeting* at her usual department store. Childbirth had caused Davis to look stylishly thin but exceptionally haggard. Already American designers were lengthening hemlines somewhat, and Davis wholeheartedly agreed with the longer skirts Edith suggested as a way of hiding her legs. She also diplomatically told Davis, "Don't let anybody talk you into wearing a tight skirt. You're not the type."

Edith received no credit on the film as Warners hadn't officially borrowed her from Paramount (indeed, nobody was credited). However, the working relationship between the two women began at this point, continuing to Edith's death. When Davis spoke at Edith's funeral she praised her for "never imposing a costume on anybody" (meaning that Orry-Kelly had often imposed costumes on her). Moreover, Davis copied Edith's hairstyle (flat bangs and a low chignon) for her early scenes as a New England spinster poetess in *Winter Meeting.* Since she didn't want to cut her hair into the bangs, Davis had Perc Westmore make her a small hairpiece consisting only of the bangs and a few long strands behind them, which could be blended into her own hair at the back to make the chignon. Edith's own hair was starting to go gray at that point, and lacking the time to frequent beauty parlors to get her roots touched up, she had a similar hairpiece made. Rumors later abounded that she wore the obviously false bangs because she was balding or had a very high hairline from many facelifts (actually she only had two), but the truth was that she wore them because they were convenient.

Christian Dior's sensational 1947 collection (dubbed "the New Look" by the press) met with a mixed reception in Hollywood, but it couldn't have come at a better time for Bette Davis who was set to portray a fashion magazine editor in *June Bride* (1948). In every way, the New Look was the antithesis of what had come before: shoulder pads were banished, skirts fell to the ankle and were either very full or very tight, waistlines were tightened with the aid of corselets and Dior even padded the hips of his skinny models. The New Look was great for Davis with her naturally round shoulders. Without the heavy shoulder padding Orry-Kelly had been giving her, Davis's bust didn't seem quite so low, and the long, full skirts hid her legs adroitly. Edith had a field day, giving countless interviews on the subject and typically sitting on the fence. On some days, journalists found her definitely pro, calling the hourglass shapes a "return to femininity," while on other days her natural conservatism was wary of anything so drastic coming on overnight. What if it didn't last? Fashions too blatantly "New Look" might look foolish when a picture was finally released a year or more after filming. Having a big backlog of unreleased films, the studio was especially concerned, and Edith later told me that some films were reedited to eliminate long shots revealing too-short hemlines. On the other hand, she told interviewers that the dropping of Donna Reed's hemlines in *Beyond Glory* (1948) was a device she could use to signal the passage of time.

Ever practical, Edith advised readers of average means how they could convert their existing clothes to the New Look by removing shoulder pads, adding material to the hems, and even shortening passé knee-length coats to midthigh. For a *Life* magazine layout, she removed shoulder straps and boned the bodices of evening gowns in the Paramount stock wardrobe. Hollywood in general was not so enthusiastic. Only the willowy Loretta Young would wear ankle-length skirts in the daytime; producers didn't want their starlets' legs covered up that much, and a midcalf compromise became the norm. As in retail clothing design, shoulder pads didn't disappear overnight but rather faded away gradually over a period of years.

Most Paramount directors and producers were very happy to work with Edith. If Mitchell Leisen thought her ideas were unimaginative, they were just fine with Hal B. Wallis who came in as an independent producer in 1944, following a split with Warner Bros. There he had often tangled with Bette Davis, particularly on the subject of hats, to the point that she finally sent him a subscription to *Vogue*. His idea was that costumes should not be so noticeable that they would draw attention from the drama. When Warners had filmed *The Private Lives of Elizabeth and Essex* in 1939, he had felt the hoopskirts Kelly designed for Davis were so large that they would be distracting. Davis tested with smaller hoops and then wore the ones she wanted in the film. Wallis had his own stable of stars for his Paramount releases and could (but didn't have to) use the Paramount talent in other departments, so Edith was especially anxious that he not decide to bring in a designer of his own. For his first Paramount production, *Love Letters* (1945), Edith sketched what she felt was a very modest wedding dress for Jennifer Jones. Hal Wallis wanted it made even simpler, and so it was.

Edith had little or nothing to do with the men's costumes at this point.

John Anderson, longtime men's costumer at Paramount, remembered, "Edith and I used to gab a lot, but I wouldn't say she was supervising me. The only time I saw her come into the men's department was when she was looking for a cowboy hat for Jean Arthur to wear in *Shane* (1953). She was afraid of Hal Wallis and she wouldn't have dared to make any suggestions about the actors' clothes." A longtime secretary of Hal Wallis's remembered, "We tried to schedule her appointments with Mr. Wallis so she wouldn't have to wait long in the outer office, but things would come up and she'd be sitting there a long while and she'd get very nervous. Finally she'd say, 'Please tell Mr. Wallis I've gone back to the department to work on his film.' "

1946 and 1947 brought a thinning out of Edith's possible competition at Paramount. Raoul Pene du Bois had designed Mitchell Leisen's Technicolor epic *Frenchman's Creek* (1944), in which Edith had no part. Willa Kim doesn't remember Leisen working on the costumes himself, but the art director Ernst Fegté did. ". . . it was really Mitch who made most of them. Mitch was the only person who knew how many of the clothes of that era were really put together, and in making them up from du Bois' sketches, he changed them a great deal. Some of them were his designs from start to finish. Whenever I needed to consult with him about a set, I had to go to wardrobe to find him." Leisen used du Bois again for *Kitty* (1945).

Mary Kay Dodson was a competitor that Edith hadn't seen coming.

Other than du Bois and Natalie Visart (who worked only for De Mille), Edith had had the department to herself for a while after Oleg Cassini's departure. With the beginning of World War II, Irene was persuaded to become MGM's head designer. Shutting down her couture salon at Bullock's Wilshire meant letting her models go. One of them, Mary Kay Dodson, was dating the son of Paramount executive Y. Frank Freeman. Although Dodson was beautiful and glamorous, it was decided that she would not become a starlet but rather would be assigned to train as a designer. When she signed a contract as a designer in 1942, it was stated in the contract that she "had not previously designed dresses or hats." Knowing how important it was to keep on good terms with Y. Frank Freeman, Edith enthusiastically endorsed this plan, secretly sure that Dodson would never amount to anything. "Mary Kay was incredibly glamorous, as glamorous as Edith was plain," says Willa Kim. "She'd come into the department wearing the most luxurious furs and dresses."

Mary Kay Dodson

Mary Kay Dodson got her Paramount contract because of her connections but, much to Edith's dismay, she proved to be quite talented. Now busy at MGM, Irene was no longer available for Claudette Colbert's Paramount pictures, so Colbert brought Howard Greer back for *Practically Yours* in 1944, and Leisen, who was directing, chose Dodson rather than Head to dress the other women in the cast. Although she got no screen credit, Dodson's capable handling of the work (and capable handling of Leisen) was widely noticed. From then on she was given assignments fully as important as Edith's. Leisen chose her again for his *Golden Earrings* (1947) and even used her as Marlene Dietrich's double when he started shooting before Dietrich had arrived from Paris.

Mary Kay Dodson already had friendships with important Hollywood ladies dating back from her Bullock's Wilshire days. Ray Milland's wife Mal, one of the town's social leaders, recommended her wholeheartedly. Dodson was also quick to cultivate stars who would then request her. One was Joan Caulfield, who was also Bing Crosby's mistress. Caulfield got Crosby to request Dodson for *Riding High* (1950) even though she was not going to appear in it. Although the female lead, Coleen Gray, was not an important star, Edith was furious when she heard about this. Knowing that *Riding High*'s director, Frank Capra, was a good friend of Bill Ihnen's, Edith forced her reluctant husband to go see Capra and get the film reassigned to her. Production was slowing down at Paramount at this point, and when Dodson's contract expired in 1947, it was not exactly renewed. Instead she was kept available to work "as needed."

When I interviewed Lucille Ball for *Hollywood Costume Design* (an interview Edith arranged on my behalf), Ball talked of working with Dodson on the film *Fancy Pants* (1950), saying how all the hoopskirts and petticoats were so much fun. Suddenly she said, "Well, Edith couldn't design all the pictures." I replied, "She thought she could." Ball nodded glumly in agreement. Actually it was Lucille Ball who solved Edith's Dodson problem, though inadvertently. During the shooting of *Fancy Pants,* Ball and Desi Arnaz decided to get remarried by a priest, and invited Dodson to the wedding. There she met the man she would soon marry, leaving Paramount for a career as a retail designer in New York City.

The thought of how harmless Dodson had first seemed compared to how much competition she ultimately became gave Edith great pause when she was searching for assistants in the 1940s. She was beginning to be ashamed of her own style of drawing and reluctant to show her own sketches to anybody outside of the department. She also needed somebody who could give her ideas, which she would then refine and rework, when she was too busy or too tired to start the ball rolling herself. She needed somebody to bounce ideas off of as she had once done with Adele Balkan. While she was not going to confide in an assistant as she had once confided in Balkan, she wanted somebody as skillful—and at the same time as unthreatening—as Balkan had been.

Willa Kim probably seemed too talented for Edith's own good. "Edith had me do finished sketches from two of her scratchy drawings," Kim remembers. Edith allowed Kim to watch the dresses being made and fitted (apparently they were for Diana Lynn) but did not ask Richardson to make Kim her full-time assistant. "She was very sober, accommodating, really very nice except that she was dishonest. There's no need to take other people's ideas as your own. I had a couple of suits that I had had my local tailor in Echo Park make for me before I went to Paramount. One day I looked up and the same suits were on actresses. Edith had copied them exactly!

"I really wanted to get out of there. I told Frank Richardson and he said I'd better not quit because there was going to be a newsprint shortage because of the war and they would stop printing newspapers and the May Co. wouldn't need me anymore! Then I saw some of du Bois' sketches and I wanted to work with this man and Madame Karinska, and my life took a whole different turn."

It was Willa Kim who suggested Rudi Gernreich as a sketcher for Edith when the girl who had been working for her left to have a baby. When Gernreich left after about a year to start his retail business, Kim introduced Edith to Waldo Angelo. "He was working as a stock clerk at Western Costume and somebody showed me his sketches, which were marvelous. Edith hired him right away. He was very gay, so much that Raoul Pene du Bois didn't want to be seen in the commissary with him, but I loved him." His friend Nellie Carrol says, "it was very stylish to be very bitchy in those days and Waldo was very nice when he wasn't being bitchy." Edith could see at once that he complemented her perfectly as Banton had, except now she was the boss. Where she was careful and conservative in her behavior, Waldo was extravagant. He had the flair and imagination that she lacked when it came to costumes for lavish musicals, so with Waldo at her side and Buddy DeSylva no longer running the studio Edith was reasonably certain that du Bois wouldn't be brought back, though he was still vaguely under contract. Indeed Angelo seemed the perfect partner for her, assisting her so adroitly that she recommended he be given a contact in 1944 as junior designer.

Raoul Pene du Bois had taken several months off in 1944–45 to do a Broadway show for Billy Rose, but he still thought of Paramount as his main job. He had bought a house in Beverly Hills and moved his mother out to live there with him. When he began work on *Blue Skies* (1946), Mark Sandrich was directing, with a cast headed by Bing Crosby, Paul Draper, and Joan Caulfield. Sandrich died as the film was about to go into production, and filming was delayed until Stuart Heisler could take over. There were more delays when Draper quit and was replaced by Fred Astaire. Then the Broadway costume designers who were working in Hollywood were ordered to come back to New York. "I was working for Sam Goldwyn, Irene Sharaff was at MGM, and Raoul was at Paramount," Miles White remembers. "Irene and I eventually made other pictures but Raoul never did."

Du Bois had finished designing one of the musical numbers on *Blue Skies* when he was forced to leave, and he asked that the studio not give him any credit. Angelo took over the numbers, working under Edith's watchful eye while she did the book part of the film with Angelo assisting her. She could have taken credit for his work as it was done under her supervision, but she allowed the final credits to read, "Gowns by Edith Head; Musical Costumes by Waldo Angelo" because she was fond of him and also because she had her eye on the next De Mille spectacular, *Unconquered* (1947), which was in preproduction. De Mille's longtime designer Natalie Visart had retired to raise a family. (In the end, however, De Mille hired Gwen Wakeling and Madame Karinska, and Edith didn't work for him until *Samson and Delilah* in 1949.)

Paramount was passing through a strange period of very curtailed production after World War II. Like all the studios, Paramount had experienced enormous profits during the war years when the public was earning money, had a great need for recreation, and there were few material goods available to buy. When very ordinary pictures began earning surprisingly high grosses and being held over week after week in the theaters, all of the studios were faced with backlogs of unreleased films. Paramount, however, kept producing full steam ahead during the final months of the war, anticipating that there would be industry-wide strikes when the war ended and the cost of production would go up. Throughout 1946 and 1947 the studio produced far fewer films than before, although earnings remained high. Waldo Angelo left suddenly for New York. "He had just bought a house and set it up and suddenly he got ticked off about something and went back to New York where he had a lot of opportunities designing nightclubs," says Nellie Carroll. His good friend, designer Michael Travis, said, "I saw him working later with du Bois in New York and it was the same with Edith. They'd give him a basic premise and he'd do several sketches. They'd choose some and draw over them and he'd make new ones, which would be shown to the producer and the star. They'd want changes and he'd draw it again. But he wanted to be in the driver's seat when he barely had a learner's permit. He didn't have Edith's finesse in dealing with people. He said whatever he was thinking and if people didn't like it, too bad. Edith wanted to keep him and she let him do some Technicolor musical shorts by himself, but she wasn't going to give him a whole feature." Also designer Michael Woulfe remembers, "Waldo's contract was up and he could see he had no future at Paramount as long as Edith was there so he left."

Edith's generosity towards Waldo Angelo actually extended to Michael Woulfe. "He and I were both living in a boardinghouse on Highland Avenue. I made a sketch, which I was showing to him and Willa Kim, and Waldo was tearing it apart. Willa said, 'You wait, Waldo. Michael may be the first one of us to get a credit on a picture,' and sure enough I was. James Cagney and his brother William formed an independent company and I was up for a job there, but somebody was badmouthing me. Waldo told Edith and Edith told Bill Ihnen to put in a good word for me because he was the Cagney Brothers' art director. I got the job and my first picture was *Blood on the Sun* (1945) with Sylvia Sidney."

This good deed soon backfired on Edith because Hal Wallis

(who had become Paramount's biggest producer) borrowed Sylvia Sidney from the Cagneys for *The Searching Wind* (1946) and the Cagneys insisted that Woulfe be allowed to design her clothes. "Edith had already sketched the whole picture when she found out about this," says Woulfe, and "there was nothing she could do. Even if she did the rest she would have to take second billing because I was doing the main star. So she told Wallis she would have one of her assistants do it, and she did indeed supervise the girl very closely. But we never had any meetings to make sure it would all go together. The story started in the twenties, and at the time there was a Broadway show called *Million Dollar Baby* set in the twenties, and everybody thought those styles were a big laugh. This was a drama and I had to be correct and serious about it. The first day of shooting I saw what the other designer had made for Ann Richards, and it was strictly 1940s, complete with the pompadour hairdo."

In 1948 earnings took a plunge due to television and postwar social changes. Edith's position, however, remained strong. Due to an unexpected phenomenon, *Art Linkletter's House Party,* she had suddenly become more famous than most of the stars she was dressing. As early as 1940, Edith had contributed articles to *Photoplay* magazine, telling the average girl how to dress like a star on a small budget, and had also preached the same gospel in syndicated newspaper articles, a practice that her fellow designers did not admire. When Linkletter started his radio show *House Party* in 1945, he was aware of these articles and he sought her out for regular appearances because "The point of the show was to help people. Her point of view was so practical. I didn't want somebody talking about fabulous clothes that could only be worn in a movie. At first she was so shy. She wore her hats way down over her eyes and would never look anybody in the eye when she was talking to them. She had me over to dinner with Bill Ihnen at her house and at first she refused my offer because she was so afraid." Linkletter's easygoing manner and skill as an interviewer got her through the first broadcasts and gave her a confidence she had never had before. Overnight she was being asked to appear on many other radio broadcasts, even *Burns and Allen.* She stayed with *House Party* even as it moved to television and continued into the 1970s, when it went off the air so Linkletter could devote his entire time to an antidrug crusade following the death of his daughter Dianne.

Although she sometimes varied the formula by presenting fashion shows, Edith's usual format was to invite several women from the studio audience down to the front, where she would critique their clothes and offer suggestions on how to improve their looks. On one episode from the early 1960s that I'll never forget, the subject was a skinny teenage girl with a massive bouffant hairdo, wearing a blouse with a lacy V-necked décolletage. Edith refrained from talking about the hair—that was somebody else's department, but admonished the girl that the blouse was too dressy to wear to school. Rather forcefully, she then pulled up the back of the neck, shortening the opening and (hopefully) the girl's scrawny neck. "They always chose the worst people from the ones who volunteered," Edith told me, "and towards the end the sponsors told me to lighten up on them so I had to accentuate the positive more." Never smiling and wearing her severe suits and dark glasses indoors, Edith became an important television personality, as Yvonne Wood discovered when she moved to a rural area in northern California.

"I thought all the people I met would want to know about the stars, but when they found out I was a designer, all they asked me was about Edith. Was she really like that? Some people thought she was horrible and others thought she was great." When Linkletter announced she would be on the next day, sometimes even the men came home from work to see her."

Linkletter remembers, "We would show some stills or a clip from Edith's latest picture to keep Paramount happy but that was never the reason we had her on the show. From the mail we got we knew that the public really appreciated her advice. She did some really nice things in those years. When the Winter Olympics were held in Lake Arrowhead, and I was in charge of recreation for the evenings, I asked her if she could think of something to do and she suggested putting on a fashion show of her famous movie costumes. She came up with some models and great clothes from her films and put on the show. It wasn't televised and she didn't get any publicity, she just did it to contribute."

Edith began to get a lot of fan mail at Paramount too. She had standard answers to commonly asked questions, but whenever possible she read the letters and dictated individual replies. She had a stock of small photos to sign and put in the envelopes and she always signed each reply personally.

The other thing that vastly strengthened Edith's position at the studio was that she started winning Academy Awards. For several years, the Academy had been considering giving awards to costume designers but was stuck on how to decide the nominees since the other craft awards' nominees were chosen by a committee of Academy members from that particular craft. Under the leadership of Charles LeMaire of 20th Century–Fox, a plan was formulated: for the first several years, the art directors would make the nominations. Edith hoped at first that there would be separate nominations for each studio (that way she would always win the Paramount one), but that was clearly impossible, as the other crafts weren't handled that way. However, it was decided that there would be two categories: black-and-white and color films. Since Bill Ihnen was prominent among the art directors (and indeed Edith was popular with them because she bent over backwards to cooperate) she was sure of being nominated in both categories virtually every year.

The first year, 1948, she was nominated for Billy Wilder's lavish color film *The Emperor Waltz.* Also nominated for Best Color Design was *Joan of Arc.* Since *The Emperor Waltz* had been a bigger box-office success, Edith was almost sure she would win, but in the end the prize went to Dorothy Jeakins and Madame Karinska for *Joan.* Edith was crushed not to win the first Oscar to be given in her profession, particularly since Jeakins, who had an extensive academic background, was known to refer to Edith as "that little dressmaker." The next year, however, Edith did start her winning streak with William Wyler's *Heiress.* Knowing that Wyler wanted it absolutely authentic, Edith went to the Brooklyn Museum to research the clothes of the 1840s and 1850s. Olivia de Havilland portrayed a plain girl who, despite her father's wealth, lacked self-confidence. Although her clothes were of luxurious silk moire, Edith made sure that they didn't quite fit, and de Havilland felt ill at ease wearing them through most of the film. Only in the final sequence, taking place several years later, when the character had come into her own, did Edith give her star a really attractive gown, made of lavender chiffon. *The Heiress* brought de Havilland her second Academy Award and Edith her first. (Valles, a designer who specialized in men's costumes, contributed the men's costumes for the film and also got an award.)

Thereafter Edith was usually nominated in each category every year. Because she was the best known of the designers and because she was well liked by the rank-and-file of Academy members (all of whom vote once the nominations are made), she would go on to win far more often than anybody else. Such highly regarded talents as Jean Louis and Walter Plunkett won only once, and Helen Rose and Orry-Kelly twice.

4

Edith Head, Superstar

One of Edith's best assignments ever, Billy Wilder's *Sunset Boulevard*, came in early 1949. Now regarded as one of cinema's great classics, the film brought the already legendary Gloria Swanson back to the screen in a role she would make immortal: Norma Desmond.

Norma Desmond is a once-great, now-forgotten star of the silent screen living in seclusion, tended by her faithful butler and ex-husband, Max. Norma lives in an archaic 1920s mansion, but in finding a look for her, Edith, Swanson, and Wilder decided that her clothes would follow the basic contemporary lines albeit always with some bizarre touches of 1920s exoticism, which would get more pronounced as the film proceeds and Norma becomes increasingly insane. Swanson's reputation as a clotheshorse remained intact, and she would later launch her own line of budget garments, so Edith encouraged her to contribute ideas. "You don't design a picture *for* Gloria Swanson," she told me when she worked with her again three decades later. "You design it *with* Gloria Swanson." At the age of forty-nine, Swanson remained so youthful that the makeup man had to paint lines on her face for some scenes, but Edith noticed that her abdomen had become quite thick and she couldn't give her the tight-waisted New Look without a waist cincher (which Swanson didn't want). So Edith kept the lines on most of the gowns fairly straight, with the exception of the full-skirted tulle evening gown needed for the New Year's Eve party attended only by William Holden's character. To avoid starting the fullness of the skirt at the natural waist, and calling attention to this thickness, Edith lowered the waistline in the middle but kept it at the usual place on the sides.

As much as possible, Edith avoided the use of store-bought or any kind of already existing clothes in films, knowing that they could end the practice of designing and making costumes (which did indeed happen in the 1960s). However, for *Sunset Boulevard,* she did encourage the second lead, Nancy Olson, to bring in some of her own dresses to save money on a budget already strained by the Swanson creations. "I had a dark green dress, which I showed Edith, and we used it in the party scene along with a cameo pin my father had given me," says Olson. It wasn't a designer dress but it was perfect for the character of Kathy. "I didn't have much of a sense of myself then, and neither did Edith, but we just kept trying things until we found what was right. She was also the first one to throw out something when she realized it wouldn't work. For *Mr. Music* (1950) she designed an evening gown for me in blue-gray satin. It looked great in the sketch and when I tried it on, but when we looked at the filmed costume test, we realized it

Edith with Gloria Swanson during production of Sunset Boulevard

wouldn't work, and she said, 'Get rid of it.' On the other hand, she made me a dark brown silk dress with a beige lace collar and a band of the lace three quarters down the skirt for my wedding to Alan Jay Lerner, and it was just perfect for me. She also designed a butterscotch-colored velvet gown with a dropped waist and a tulle skirt for me to wear to an industry function, and that was perfect for me too."

Sunset Boulevard was too gruesome to win wide acceptance at first, but another film—also about an aging actress—proved to be

This page and opposite: Costume tests and publicity pictures of Gloria Swanson in her gowns for Sunset Boulevard

a big hit a few months later, and Edith was the only person in any department to have worked on both *Sunset* and *All About Eve* (1950). How this came about was a story that in itself could become a film.

As head of the wardrobe department at 20th Century–Fox, Charles LeMaire designed some of the pictures himself while

supervising the other designers he hired and administering all phases of the department. He was well aware of Edith's raids on Warner Bros., RKO, and Columbia, and was determined that she would never work on a Fox production, let alone *Eve,* which promised to be a very important project. With a script by Joseph L. Mankiewicz (who had just won both the Best Director and Best Screenplay Oscars for *A Letter to Three Wives* [1949], *Eve* had a cast full of Fox ladies, with Anne Baxter in the title role, Claudette Colbert as the aging theater star Margo Channing, Celeste Holm as Margo's best friend Karen, and Thelma Ritter as Margo's maid.

As all of this was being organized, Bette Davis was working at RKO, starring in *Payment on Demand* (1951), her first film after eighteen years under contract to Warner Bros. Davis had thought that she would be flooded with offers when it was announced that she was leaving Warners, but to the contrary, six months passed before Howard Hughes offered her *Payment.* When she began shooting, Davis was heavier than she had ever been on-screen, so they started with scenes in the middle of the film, where she was playing a frankly middle-aged character in a gray wig. Davis lost weight as the filming progressed, so by the time they finished the film (and shot the scenes where she needed to appear more youthful) she was back to her usual weight. Edith handled the weight fluctuations adroitly while compensating for the usual Davis problems (the long, broad neck; low bust; et cetera) more skillfully than ever before. Davis was especially fond of one white evening gown, which Edith constructed with all the support inside the front of the dress, eliminating the need for a bra.

Davis's advisors were telling her that her reputation as a troublemaker and her declining box-office popularity were the reasons she had received so few offers. She made an effort to behave, and despite the fact that she broke up with her third husband during

Bette Davis testing the evening gown for Payment on Demand. *The construction was similar to the one she would soon wear in* All About Eve

the filming of *Payment,* the production passed without incident. She was finding also that as much as it had become impossible for her to confer with Orry-Kelly without getting into a quarrel, it was equally impossible to quarrel with Edith. Even when Davis was desperate to vent her anger on somebody, anybody who happened to be near, Edith was just as determined that there would be no fireworks—and there never were.

As *Payment on Demand* was finishing on the RKO lot, a crisis was brewing over at 20th Century–Fox. *All About Eve* was set to roll, but there was one serious problem: Claudette Colbert had injured her back on the last day of shooting *Three Came Home* (1950), and after several weeks of postponement still had not sufficiently recovered to start *Eve.* Giving her up was a hard decision to make, since the story revolved around aspiring newcomer Eve's schemes to use her friendship with Margo to study and copy the aging star to benefit her own career. Joseph Mankiewicz and Charles LeMaire planned to make much use of the fact that Baxter and Colbert resembled each other physically a great deal. Margo, as originally planned, was decidedly a supporting role, and the whole question of an aging actress hit too close to home for those ladies who were approached to take it over. In desperation, Darryl Zanuck offered it to Bette Davis, who accepted even though it meant she would have to start shooting without any time off at all between films.

There's an old saying: "You don't kid a kidder." It might be rephrased: "You don't play a player," and Charles LeMaire was a player second only to Edith when it came to studio politics. He had received his job at Fox as a reward for agreeing to marry the soon-to-be-discarded wife of a Fox executive. The lady in question was willing to give her husband a divorce, provided that the studio would find her a suitable second husband, and LeMaire, a longtime Broadway designer whose assignments had been getting infrequent by the early 1940s, agreed to marry her if he were made the head of the Fox costume department. It had worked out well all around: for several years, Fox had been needing a strong hand in the job, which LeMaire supplied, and he lived happily with his new wife until her death.

At first LeMaire was only to supervise the designers, but soon

All About Eve's *female stars in the dresses they would wear in the famous party scene. Bette Davis's dress was designed by Edith Head, Anne Baxter's by Charles LeMaire (purposely similar to the one Davis wore), and Celeste Holm's (by LeMaire) is totally different*

Three tests of costumes were designed by Edith Head for Bette Davis in All About Eve. *All were changed or discarded entirely before the final film was made. This was one of them*

producers began asking him to design some of the films himself. With his excellent connections with the front office, he assigned himself some of the real plums, such as *Eve*. He desperately did not want Edith working on any Fox films (let alone this one), and he could have protested when he was told that Bette Davis wanted Edith to design her costumes. However, he knew very well how difficult Davis could get and how hard it was to make her look glamorous. It was imperative that the film start shooting the following Monday, or Fox would lose the use of the Curran Theatre in San Francisco as well as the services of George Sanders. Moreover, the only time Davis was available for fittings was in the evenings, after a long day at RKO. Even if Davis would allow LeMaire to design for her, it would mean he would have to drive across Los Angeles every night for a week, forced to ignore his other duties at Fox. Edith at Paramount, on the other hand, was conveniently located right next door to RKO. LeMaire gave in.

He even scheduled a meeting with Edith and Davis in the latter's dressing room between scenes of *Payment on Demand.* He and Edith coordinated their work so that Davis's dress for the crucial party scene greatly resembled the one LeMaire gave Anne Baxter. The famous story—that the party dress was too big when Davis put it on for the first time, and slipped off her shoulders—is true. Like the evening gown in *Payment on Demand,* Edith had designed it with support built into the front so that it would be worn without a bra. In order for this to work, the shoulders of the gown had to be firmly in place, and Edith wanted to take them in, but Davis shrugged and said she "liked it that way." Unsupported, her breasts fell to her waist, but Edith had surrounded them with distracting, full, fur-trimmed sleeves and somehow the dress still looked very good. LeMaire did design one of Davis's dresses himself: the period costume that Margo (and later Eve) wears onstage in the play within the movie, titled *Aged in Wood.* However, ultimately the film was edited in such a way that Davis was only seen for a split second in that dress.

Much has been made of how consciously Davis, Mankiewicz, and Head copied Tallulah Bankhead in creating Margo Channing. Mankiewicz said the husky Tallulah voice Davis affected was accidental: she was hoarse when she started shooting and then had to maintain that voice throughout. After the fact, Edith told interviewers that she had based Channing's clothes on Bankhead's, but I doubt it. Bankhead was largely forgotten until *All About Eve* made her a star again. Davis's long hair resembled Bankhead's, but it was an accident. Actually Davis was tired of this style and wanted to get a short "poodle cut," but there simply wasn't enough time to work it out. Short hair on Davis was always a problem, because one of her ears stuck out while the other lay flat against her head. (Eventually she had this corrected when she had her face lifted.) Edith designed various dramatic hats for her, and they tested them with upswept hairstyles, but in the end she wore the same bushy, shoulder-length style she had had in part of *Payment on Demand.* It hid the ears and the broad neck, and proved to be dramatically valid since all the other women in the film had short hair, making Margo look a little behind the times.

The clothes were all made in the Paramount workroom. When shooting began at San Francisco's Curran Theatre, Davis was wearing a gray suit with a high white collar and a big bow of the same material. This replaced a simpler blouse, which Edith had made and tested, because Davis knew ahead of time that she wanted to fiddle with the collar during an angry scene. She also instructed Edith to make the suit loose enough so Gary Merrill could push her over onto a bed on the stage of the theater. At a meeting in Edith's office, Davis suddenly ran across the room and threw herself onto a divan. When Edith protested that there was no such action in the script, Davis said, "Yes, but that's what I'm going to do."

There never was any possibility that Edith might dress anybody else: in *All About Eve* LeMaire wouldn't have allowed it. Over the years it galled him to no end that he had had to share the Academy Award for this film with Edith.

After *All About Eve,* Edith wasn't loaned to any other studio for eight years (until Billy Wilder requested her for *Witness for the Prosecution* in 1957). Possibly this was because Bette Davis, Barbara Stanwyck, and Ginger Rogers no longer wielded enough power to make the other studios borrow her, but also Paramount didn't want to share her. She did, however, make some clothes now and then for important actresses, such as Rosalind Russell when she was mistress of ceremonies for the opening of NBC's new Burbank Studio, and Bette Davis who needed some hair-hiding hats to conceal her "poodle cut" while it was growing out. Edith herself cut her hair short in 1949 but soon let it grow out again because Bill liked it long.

She remained ever vigilant against other designers encroaching onto her Paramount territory, as Michael Woulfe's experiences with Lizabeth Scott would prove. Woulfe recalls: "When RKO borrowed Lizabeth Scott for *The Company She Keeps* (1950), I didn't make any sketches because I assumed she'd bring Edith with her. When I was called to the producer's office and I didn't have anything, I told Scott this, and she said, 'But I've been trying to get away from Edith Head!' So I designed the whole film and I was trying to get her away from the severely tailored looks (she was playing a probation officer). I found out that we had to get Hal Wallis's approval on everything, even though it was an RKO film, because Scott was under contract to him and he wanted her very tailored! Anyway, after it was over, Scott went back to Paramount and told Wallis she wanted to borrow me for her next picture for him. We had a big meeting and Wallis said, 'I couldn't do that to Edith.' But Scott was determined. So, to placate her, Edith sent her shopper over to RKO to check out all my fabrics, et cetera. Still, Scott wasn't satisfied, so one day I got word from the head of the department at RKO that Edith was being forced to come over to look at the *Company* wardrobe personally. I wasn't enemies with Edith, and I thought how humiliating this must be for her. I made sure I wasn't there when she came." Edith obviously felt that humiliation was preferable to ever allowing any other designer's name on a Paramount picture.

In 1949 Edith finally got her name on a Cecil B. De Mille spectacular, *Samson and Delilah.* The only fly in the ointment was Elois Jenssen. Hedy Lamarr, who starred as Delilah, had worked with designer Jenssen at the small Eagle Lion Studio on *Let's Live a Little* (1948) and insisted that Jenssen be brought into *Samson.* Although the ever-vigilant Billye Fritz would later remark that "Edith didn't let her do anything," Jenssen nonetheless received an Academy Award along with the others for Best Costume Design in a Color Film for *Samson.* However annoyed Edith was at the time, she eventually became friends with Elois who proved very useful two decades later, by driving when Edith needed to be taken to the hospital to have her blood transfusions.

Dorothy Jeakins had designed the men's costumes on *Samson and Delilah* and also worked with Edith on the next De Mille film, *The Greatest Show on Earth* (1952). She and Edith designed the offstage wardrobe for the principals, and Jeakins went with the company to the Florida location (Edith seldom went on location at that point). Miles White designed the costumes for the actual circus acts. "John Ringling stipulated that they had to bring me in, in order to get his cooperation," White said. "Some of the pieces were already being used in the circus, others were copies of things we were using in the circus, and some were new for the film. I went to Hollywood to fit the stars, and I used Edith's office and fitting room although I didn't actually meet her at that time."

Elizabeth Taylor was borrowed from MGM for George Stevens's *Place in the Sun* (1951). Since Taylor was portraying a

Elizabeth Taylor in the white satin evening gown she wears in her first scenes of A Place in the Sun

debutante, it was not surprising that the script would call for evening gowns, and Edith designed two, both strapless with boned bodices. The first one, in white satin, was emphasized by the studio in the publicity releases, but it was the other, with an enormous white tulle skirt over pale green satin, and white violets covering the bust, that really caught on with the public and was widely copied by manufacturers. "Go to any prom this season and you'll see dozens of them," was the remark a fashion editor made, which Edith never tired of quoting. Taylor, just eighteen years old and at the peak of her youthful beauty, then returned to MGM where she would wear Helen Rose's designs in her next several films. When she was again loaned to Paramount, it was to replace Vivien Leigh, who had suffered a nervous breakdown during the filming of *Elephant Walk* (1954). Later Edith told me that working with Leigh had been a wonderful experience, that Leigh was gracious at their meetings and the suggestions she made truly enhanced the designs. The clothes had been finished, as well as all of the location work in Ceylon, when Leigh cracked. She is still visible in the long shots of the final film. If Taylor had remained as slender in 1953 as she had been in 1949, it would have been hard to tell the women apart, but by now she was much heavier after a pregnancy, and the difference clearly showed. Still, the basic lines of the 1950s were good to Taylor: the emphasis on the bust and tight waist accentuated her best points, while the long, full skirts hid her wide hips and short legs.

Pine-Thomas Productions had started as an independent unit within Paramount in the 1940s, specializing in low-budget features. Although Paramount released all these films, many of them were shot on other lots to save money, and Edith generally didn't design the costumes, as her salary would have strained the budgets. One exception was *Lucy Gallant* (1955), in which Jane Wyman portrayed the owner of a department store in Texas. Publicist A. C. Lyles, who worked with Pine-Thomas, remembers, "I got the idea of having Edith commentate her designs for the movie's fashion show." Edith would describe the experience in *The Dress Doctor* as "nerve-wracking," but Lyles remembers that "she sailed through it beautifully." (Standing on the sidelines, quietly giving his wife moral support, was Bill Ihnen.)

Eventually Lyles took over the production of low-budget features from Pine-Thomas but was never able to officially assign Edith to any of his pictures. "The rule at Paramount was that whatever productions she was working on in any given week, all of them would share the cost of her salary equally, and I didn't have the budget for that. However, she always helped me on the Q.T. I'd tell her what actresses were playing the leads and she'd go through the stock wardrobe and put aside things that would be suitable and the right size.

"When I was planning *Red Tomahawk* (1967), I told Edith I was bringing Betty Hutton back for the lead. At the time, things were so slow on the lot that she wasn't working on a single film, and I couldn't carry her full salary. She said, 'We're making some period dresses for the stock wardrobe just to keep the girls busy. I'll make them in Betty's size and then you can use them.' In the end, however, Betty didn't do the part."

Frank Caffey, the Paramount studio manager, and Frank Richardson were aware that Edith had little experience designing men's clothes so they decided to bring in Yvonne Wood for *Just for You* in 1952. "There were a couple of musical numbers with a lot of male dancers, which I did, and I also shopped at Brooks Brothers' juvenile department for the boy who played Bing Crosby's son," Woods recalled. "Crosby had a member of his staff bring in all of his personal wardrobe and I chose what I thought would look best. I wasn't allowed to talk to him, and he didn't talk to me except for one day. One of the outfits I nixed for the number was a dreadful pair of canary-yellow pants. I had put the chorus boys in pewter-gray tuxedos, and Edith did gold gowns for the girls, and Crosby wore a black tux. While we were shooting it, he came up behind me and said he really liked those pants but he could see they wouldn't have worked. He was right but I wasn't about to give him that so I said, 'Oh no, they would have looked great with the girls' gold dresses!'" (Edith was far more diplomatic with Crosby, whose power she recognized. Whenever she saw a rough-weave woolen she thought he might like for a sport coat, she bought some and gave it to him. "They looked like horse blankets," she said of his sport coats.)

Wood stayed on for a while to design the men's costumes for *Casanova's Big Night* and *Red Garters* (1954). "The producers of *Casanova* put top actors into all the supporting parts because they knew Hope would be on his toes and give a better performance that way," Wood recalled. "Mary Kay Dodson had designed *Monsieur Beaucaire* with Hope a few years earlier, which was about the same period, and she kept him in pastels, so I decided to use strong colors. One day I came back to my office after lunch and could see that somebody had been going through my sketches. Billye Fritz told me that Edith had been in there (she had keys to all the doors). I said, 'If you want to know what I'm doing, why don't you just ask me for a meeting?' but she liked the cloak-and-dagger approach better.

"When Edith and I went to see the producers with our sketches, I had one sketch for each change and they were all approved right away. Edith, however, had several sketches for each change, and the show she put on was priceless. These guys were earning four times her salary, and after she gave them so much double talk, they were so thoroughly confused it was all I could do to keep from laughing. But that way they could never come back to her when the dresses were all made up and complain about anything."

Red Garters proved to be Mitchell Leisen's last project at Paramount. The management warned him and Edith that he was to have nothing to say about the costumes, but she secretly went to see him at his apartment one evening with the sketches anyway. (After a week of shooting he was fired and replaced by George

Marshall.) Wood recalled, "The genesis of that picture was one number in *Just for You*. There was a Mexican musical number, which took place on a stage in a theater. When I saw that the art director had made a sketch for the set that was just a suggestion, an outline, I suggested to the producer, Pat Duggan, that we do the costumes the same way, going for big, broad effects. He said, 'Well, fine, if you can get Edith to design for the women that way.' This was difficult, because Edith had spent a lot of time in Mexico and she knew exactly what the native costumes really looked like. I said, 'Edith, this is supposed to be a number on a stage, not real people in a town square.' Eventually she got the idea and when it was well received, they decided to do a whole picture like that, with a western story. Edith designed for the women and I did the men."

Producer Duggan liked Wood's work so much that he tried to get permission to assign her to his next film, *Forever Female* (1953). However, this called for modern fashions for Ginger Rogers, clearly Edith's specialty, and the studio heads wouldn't allow it. "They told him, 'Edith's got four Oscars, how many has your girl won?' and Edith did it."

Wood, however, did get two other assignments at Paramount, *Botany Bay* (1953) and the supporting cast of *The Court Jester* (1956). "John Farrow was directing *Botany Bay* and he didn't want Edith, because he'd caught her in too many lies in the past. The female lead was Patricia Medina, and Edith didn't put up a fight when Richardson wanted to give me the whole picture, because Medina wasn't one of her main people.

"Edith was long overdue for a vacation, and she and Bill started driving up the coast. However, every time they came to a town, she'd stop and call up Billye Fritz to find out what was going on. When they were in Santa Barbara, Billye told her that the studio had decided to make *Botany Bay* in color instead of black and white. That was enough; she turned around and came right back. But there was nothing she could do because Farrow wouldn't have her." It proved to be a difficult film because "Even though Patricia was very small, she was still too tall for Ladd. I told Farrow that we could hide the lifts better if Ladd wore boots instead of shoes, but Ladd didn't want boots and the shoes with lifts we made for him were obvious as hell. There was nothing Farrow could do but keep his feet out of shots as much as possible."

Up to this time Edith had seldom been asked to design for men. In modern-dress pictures, the actors were still required to wear their own clothes, and for westerns and period pictures, the uncredited men's costumers took care of them. Ray Milland told me, "For *California* (1946), Barbara Stanwyck had to spend a week in the wardrobe department, fitting the gowns with Edith. I simply met the costumer over at Western Costume and we went through all their period western things. If I liked something and it fit me we'd use it, otherwise we'd have a copy made in my size. Edith checked to see that they didn't clash with Barbara's clothes and we were set."

Now, however, Edith was worried that Yvonne would become a permanent fixture, doing men's costumes at Paramount, and she insisted on designing Danny Kaye's costumes for *The Court Jester* herself. It proved to be a major headache, according to Yvonne who was assigned all of the supporting cast. "Kaye couldn't be bothered to come in to film the costume tests, so they had his stunt double do it for him. The double had much better looking legs, and to make sure Kaye's legs would match, Kaye had to wear symmetricals (leg pads)." *The Court Jester* was one of Paramount's first films in the new Vistavision process, which the studio had developed with Technicolor as an answer to 20th Century–Fox's Cinemascope. Promoted as "Motion Picture High Fidelity,"

VistaVision used a double-width negative, which indeed was capable of recording more photographic information and detail. However, to get the maximum possible clarity, it was necessary to absolutely flood the set with light, so the cameraman had to stop down his lens. The heat generated by those lights was often unbearable for the actors, especially Kaye with his hot and scratchy leg pads. "Edith caught a lot of hell from Kaye about that, but there was really nothing she could do," said Yvonne.

Always socially polite with Yvonne, Edith steadfastly resisted her efforts to become real friends for almost a decade. "I really admired her and I wasn't trying to take her place, but she couldn't see that. I wasn't that ambitious, I was just trying to make a living, and I knew there was only room for one Edith Head in the business," Wood said. "She treated Elois Jenssen the same way for a long while, though they eventually became good friends."

By now, Edith had a new and highly capable assistant named Pat Barto. "I remember Pat Barto very well," says Betty Ray, a dancer who worked in films all over Hollywood. "Pat was always right at Edith's side, hardly saying anything, and Edith didn't need to say much to her because Pat instinctively knew just what Edith wanted her to do. When I was at MGM, Helen Rose had assistants, of course, and so did Irene Sharaff at Fox, but none of them had quite the rapport that Edith had with Pat. Also Edith really knew how to make costumes we could dance in. When I was in *Call Me Madam* (1953), which Irene Sharaff designed, and we changed from our rehearsal clothes to the costumes, it took some getting used to. That wouldn't have happened with Edith."

Pat Barto painted beautiful sketches in gouache, but eventually Edith assigned the sketching to Grace Sprague and kept Barto at her side all day as an all-around assistant. "Edith had made one mistake with Mary Kay Dodson and she wasn't about to let that happen again," commented Yvonne. "She kept Pat with her at all times and even made her eat lunch with her every day. To avoid talking about anything personal, she and Pat played word games at lunch. Occasionally I was allowed to eat with them and that's what we did." Like Mary Kay, Pat was very beautiful, with brilliant red hair worn in a bun like Edith's. "Edith made her dress just like she did, in severely tailored suits and white gloves at all times."

Grace Sprague initially came to Paramount from New York to work on Hitchcock's *Rear Window* (1954). For the first time, Hitchcock decided to sketch out the whole film on storyboards, and Sprague drew them for him. When that was finished, she stayed on with Edith until her untimely death a few years later. Her work had a light, airy quality that Edith liked, and it actually had some effect on Edith's own drawings. (The illustrations for *The Dress Doctor,* for which Edith took credit, were actually Sprague's.) "Gracie could really crank them out," recalled Yvonne Wood. "Edith would give her a basic idea and she'd do all kinds of variations on it, and then Edith would pick the ones she liked, draw over them, and then have Grace do a final version to show the producer. If the producer or the star or anybody wanted changes, Grace could make another one in a few minutes, which Edith gave to the workroom."

When I asked Edith what happened to Sprague, she replied, with annoyance, "She died!" It would take her a long time to find a replacement she really liked.

Rear Window marked the true beginning of Edith's long and happy association with Alfred Hitchcock. A decade earlier, RKO had borrowed her, at Ingrid Bergman's request, for *Notorious,* and she had found the director difficult. ("Is he giving you as much trouble as he is giving me?" she asked Adele Balkan who was designing the costumes for the other women in the film.)

COURTESY OF THE ACADEMY OF MOTION PICTURE ARTS AND SCIENCES

Grace Kelly in Balenciaga-inspired suit with unfitted jacket for Rear Window. *(Alfred Hitchcock let Edith use ultra–high style for this as long as she made it in his favorite eau-de-Nile green color)*

Based on a story by Cornell Woolrich, *Rear Window* would prove to be one of Hitchcock's all-time classics. In spite of the difficulties, Edith liked working with him because his films were highly prestigious, of course, but more important, because she always had a strong sense of what he wanted and knew just how far she should go on her own. She later told an audience of students at the American Film Institute, "Hitchcock's scripts tell what color the dress is to be and whatever other details he considers important." Tony Perkins once described how Hitchcock let him use his own idea of eating candy corn throughout *Psycho* (1960), and, in the same way, once the basic parameters were decided, Edith had a lot of freedom on a Hitchcock picture. In Grace Kelly she also had the absolutely perfect subject for her clothes. Sublimely beautiful, with a perfect figure and walk, Kelly was one actress with nothing Edith needed to hide or compensate for. Edith knew enough to stay away from strong colors on her (although her first outfit for *Rear Window,* which used black against white, was highly striking) and because Kelly was playing a fashion model, Edith could use one of the latest Paris ideas, a suit with an undefined waistline in eau-de-Nile green, one of her (and Hitchcock's) favorite colors. Edith also avoided using any prints except for the fluffy beige dress in the climax of the film, in which Kelly climbs into the apartment of Raymond Burr whom she and James Stewart suspect of murder. With this dress, Kelly also wore high heels and multiple petticoats in order to seem as feminine and vulnerable as possible. In the brief epilogue, however, she's in blue jeans and a hot-pink blouse, to accentuate the inner strength Stewart has now perceived in her.

Georgine Darcy played the part of Miss Torso, whom Stewart watches from across the courtyard. Though she had no dialogue, wore shorts most of the time, and was seen only in long shots, this was a Hitchcock film, and Edith had ample budget to design and make all of her costumes. "Nowadays people keep asking me if she was a lesbian," Darcy says, "but nobody thought so at the time. She wasn't unpleasant but she was all business. She was always coming on the set to check things out."

Grace Kelly in floral print dress for climactic scenes of Rear Window. *The hat was not used*

Hitchcock's *To Catch a Thief* (1955) afforded Edith such rich opportunities that it became her all-time favorite film. When I showed Edith the first draft of *Hollywood Costume Design,* she bristled at my remark that the location trip to the French Riviera was "a tonic" for her. "It was damned hard work," she said, and I rewrote the passage. The picture was so important to Paramount that she was sent along to the location (something that had hardly ever happened before), which forced Frank Richardson to bring in Mary Grant to design *We're No Angels* (1955), a film Edith could have handled easily had she been in town. Paramount even assigned a French tutor to Edith to brush up on her French. All of the wardrobe Kelly would wear on location had already been made up at the studio, but Hitchcock wanted Edith on hand "just in case." She arrived in Cannes on June 1, 1954. She later claimed that she bought at Hermès the brief plaid bathing trunks Cary Grant wore in the film, though Grant denied she had any part in his clothes.

The first time Grant sees Kelly in the hotel lobby, Hitchcock wanted her to be a knockout, and for once Edith decided to go for broke with a black-and-white capri-pants outfit. Originally they had planned that Kelly would also wear this outfit in the previous scene in her hotel room, which was actually shot later on in Hollywood. However, on June 28, Frank Caffey wrote to Edith: "Hitch felt that the sport outfit that she wears in the lobby scene was such a startling thing that it would be well to disclose it to the audience for the first time when she steps out of the elevator. Therefore she will have to appear in some sort of dressing gown in the scene immediately preceding this." Edith had it ready for Kelly when she returned to Hollywood.

The colors increased as the tensions mounted, climaxing in a gold lamé ballgown with an enormous skirt trimmed with gold birds. The two other evening dresses, both in draped chiffon, one in various shades of pale blue, the other a strapless white, played up the supposedly glacial side of Kelly's character. While Kelly is wearing the white, Grant coolly informs her, "These diamonds are imitation," to which she replies, "I'm for real," as fireworks explode in the night sky outside. The pale blue chiffon dress had tiny spaghetti straps for support, but Edith later told me that Hitchcock wanted the white chiffon dress to be strapless so that there would be nothing on Kelly's shoulders to distract from the diamonds. Grace Kelly told Edith she didn't want to wear pants for the picnic scene because "I'm on the make for him, but it has to be subtle."

Grace Sprague helped Edith refine her ideas along the way, but the ideas were still basically Hitchcock's and Edith's. Ironically, she did not win the 1955 Academy Award for *Thief;* it went to Charles LeMaire for *Love Is a Many-Splendored Thing,* which, Edith was quick to point out, "was a big song that year. All the dresses were made from the same traditional Chinese pattern, all he did was choose the fabrics."

To Catch a Thief was not only Edith's favorite film (and, arguably, her best job ever) but it also marked her last project with Grace Kelly. During the filming on the French Riviera, Kelly had been introduced to Monaco's Prince Rainier, to whom she became engaged. Then she returned to MGM where she was under contract. Kelly lived at the Beverly Hills Hotel but was unable to enjoy the pool there because of gawkers and photographers, so Edith let her use the Casa Ladera pool every day. When it was announced that Helen Rose would design her wedding dress, Edith was livid but Kelly coolly reminded her: "MGM is paying for it. Would Paramount do that?" Edith had to admit that Paramount wouldn't, and had to settle for designing Kelly's going-away suit for her hon-

COURTESY OF THE ACADEMY OF MOTION PICTURE ARTS AND SCIENCES

Grace Kelly in startling black-and-white capri-pants outfit for To Catch a Thief

eymoon. The two women remained on such good terms that when Edith sent Nanny on a vacation trip to Europe, she arranged for Grace to receive her personally at Monaco's palace. Years later, when Grace, the prince, and their teenage children came to Los Angeles, Edith received them in her bungalow at Universal. Ruby Graf, her secretary at Universal, says, "Grace wasn't feeling well and didn't want to eat in the commissary, so Edith had lunch brought in and Grace received the people she wanted to see—Lew Wasserman and Alfred Hitchcock—right there."

Edith's relationship with Audrey Hepburn proved to be even more disappointing. Initially, nobody at Paramount had an inkling of what a sensation Hepburn would become. *Roman Holiday* (1953) had long been simmering on the back burner as a Frank Capra production. Then Capra sold the script to his friend William Wyler, who planned to borrow Jean Simmons from Howard Hughes's RKO to portray the bored young princess on a goodwill tour. When Simmons turned down Hughes's romantic overtures, he punished her by refusing to follow through with the loan-out. Paramount tried to borrow Elizabeth Taylor from MGM, but unsuccessfully. Almost in desperation, Wyler asked a friend to make some tests of actresses in England, and on that basis selected Hepburn, who was about to leave for the lead in the Broadway production of *Gigi,* which brought her some notice but did not make her a star overnight. When Edith was shown the test she thought Hepburn was pleasant but strange-looking. Checking out Hepburn's measurements, and with her usual preoccupation with camouflage, Edith made several alternate outfits and traveled to New York with Nellie Manley for meetings with Hepburn as the *Gigi* run was coming to a close.

Edith had made two evening gowns so that she'd have a choice once she met Hepburn in person and got a better sense of her. Ultimately she decided to use the white-and-silver brocade dress, although the other, a black velvet, is also seen briefly in a montage. With it she used a diamond necklace, appropriate for a princess, of course, but also to hide the prominent collarbones and sinewy neck she'd seen in the screen test. She was also worried that Hepburn's feet were too big, and her legs were shapely but a bit too heavy, she thought, reflecting her training as a ballet dancer.

Test of Audrey Hepburn in Roman Holiday *(the blouse was not used as Edith thought Hepburn's frail arms needed to be covered more)*

Compared to the legs, Hepburn's arms and shoulders seemed very frail, so Edith decided against a sleeveless blouse she had brought. Since Hepburn would be wearing the same skirt and blouse throughout most of the film, Edith made the skirt as long and as full as possible, and provided various scarves to camouflage the neck. She also suggested that Hepburn use bust pads, and Hepburn told her she already was! For the final scene, Edith dressed Hepburn in white lace.

Roman Holiday was filmed on location in the summer of 1952. When it was completed, Hepburn returned to the United States to begin a national tour of *Gigi*. This brought her to Los Angeles in the spring of 1953, and while *Gigi* played to half-full houses at the Biltmore Theater in downtown L.A., Hepburn came to Paramount afternoons to pose for publicity pictures and plan her next film, *Sabrina* (1954). Not only would she be perfect in the Cinderella role as the chauffeur's daughter who falls in love, first with William Holden, then with Humphrey Bogart, the boss's sons, but she was decidedly a bargain: Paramount paid Associated British only $9,000 for her services, compared to the six-figure salaries the men would get.

Gigi finished its tour in San Francisco, and Edith journeyed there to finalize the *Sabrina* designs. This was very gracious of her, since *Roman Holiday* had not yet been released, and Hepburn was not a star who needed to be courted. Back in Los Angeles, she was in for a rude shock: Hepburn asked Billy Wilder to propose that she be allowed to wear a "real Paris dress" for the scene in which Sabrina comes back to New York from Paris so changed that Holden doesn't recognize her. Perhaps there would be one or two other Parisian dresses as well. Edith agreed to this reluctantly, but assured herself that when Audrey came back with the dresses, she could persuade the others that they were "all wrong" or, at the very least, refit and modify them. Wilder's wife, also Audrey, a former Paramount starlet, suggested that Hepburn borrow the dresses from Balenciaga. However, when Hepburn got to Paris, Balenciaga sent her to see his friend Hubert de Givenchy, who was just starting his own business.

In the story that has been retold many times since, when Audrey arrived at Givenchy's studio, he was very busy with a new collection, and when his assistant told him that a "Miss Hepburn" was waiting, he assumed that it was *Katharine* Hepburn. However, he was so charmed with *Audrey* Hepburn that he allowed her to search through his past collections and borrow anything she wanted. The suit that she would wear in the first scene with Holden was so small that only one model in Paris could get into it, and then "just barely." Hepburn took enough outfits to dress herself virtually throughout the whole film and, acting on

Paramount's instructions, told the customs agents that they were all her own clothes when she came back to the United States so that Paramount wouldn't have to pay any duties. She also made a visit to her *Roman Holiday* makeup man to get a whole new look. Now, instead of covering her "faults" (the big ears, feet, collarbones, et cetera) she would emphasize them. If *Roman Holiday* made her a star overnight, *Sabrina* made her a fashion icon.

Much to her dismay, Edith found that the Givenchy gowns did not need to be refitted, nor could anything be done to "improve" them. All that was left for Edith to design were a few simple outfits Sabrina would wear before she became glamorous, make and fit a black dress and hat from a sketch Givenchy gave Hepburn and a blouse and a pair of shorts for a sailing scene. (She also designed a few changes for the second lead, Martha Hyer.) In a video interview with Steven Paley, conducted in the 1970s, Hepburn said that "Edith was very good about it," but if Hepburn truly believed that, then Edith was a better actress than most, for she was seething, even thirty years later when I asked her about it. Here was the rare film, in which audacious clothes would not detract from the drama, and they were somebody else's audacious clothes.

When *Roman Holiday* was released that summer, it proved to be less of a box-office success than its subsequent legendary status would indicate, but right from the start, the press loved Audrey Hepburn. When Hepburn won the Academy Award for *Roman Holiday,* it was rereleased, and *Sabrina* proved to be an enormous hit. The film's Givenchy clothes were mostly preexisting—that is to say, not designed specifically with *Sabrina* in mind—so it didn't strike anybody at Paramount as unusual that Edith would take credit for them. Givenchy was not well enough known at the time to give the gowns any publicity value. When Edith won the Academy Award for Best Costume Design in a Black-and-White

One of the costumes that Edith did design for Audrey Hepburn to wear in Sabrina

Film for *Sabrina,* she said nothing, counting on the fact that Givenchy was such a gentleman he would not make a fuss. He never did.

In *The Dress Doctor,* Edith admitted that the gray woolen suit worn by Hepburn in the train station was a "real Paris dress," but claimed the black boatnecked dress (made by Edith from Givenchy's sketch) and the black-and-white ballgown. Unknowingly I used a picture of the ballgown in *Hollywood Costume Design* and gave Edith credit for it, and she did not correct me when she reviewed my manuscript.

When I finally learned the truth, she said, with annoyance, "I lied. So what? If I bought a sweater at Bullock's Wilshire, do I have to give them credit too?" The *Sabrina* gowns were the only place where she told an outright lie in *The Dress Doctor,* and ever after she showed the black boatnecked dress and the highly unusual cocktail hat as hers in her fashion shows.

By the time Audrey Hepburn made her next high-fashion picture, *Funny Face* (1957), Givenchy was given the script, and he designed clothes specifically for the film. The credits read, "Miss Hepburn's Paris Wardrobe by Hubert de Givenchy," implying that her New York beatnik clothes had been designed by Edith. However, director Stanley Donen remembers that even those were Givenchy's. What he did was to make female versions of the drab clothes he habitually wore himself. The black slacks she wore in the "Basal Metabolism" number came from Jax in Beverly Hills, and the matter of her white socks in that number was one settled by Hepburn and Donen themselves without any input from Edith. Even Kay Thompson's camel-hair coat in the "Bonjour Paris" number (filmed before the company relocated to the Paramount soundstages) was Givenchy's. Thompson was unhappy when the studio insisted that Edith design the rest of her wardrobe, but she was not a big enough star to force the issue. Edith also designed for the secretaries in Thompson's office, and for the famous "Think Pink" number. The *Funny Face* costumes were nominated for the Academy Award but did not win.

Audrey Hepburn did not appear in another Paramount film until *Breakfast at Tiffany's* (1961). Once again she arrived from Paris with several gowns from Givenchy. However, they were not enough to dress the whole film since the character of Holly Golightly also needed some plain clothes and doubles for the Givenchy dresses, which Edith provided. (Patricia Neal's four changes came from Pauline Trigère, who says she did not read the script. "They told me it was a rich woman in New York and that's what I designed," she says.) The film carried the singular credit: "Miss Hepburn's wardrobe principally by Hubert de Givenchy, Miss Neal's wardrobe principally by Pauline Trigère, costume supervision by Edith Head."

The Givenchy sheaths seem simple to the eye, but Renie Conley found out otherwise when she saw Head and Hepburn cooking up some more phony Givenchys in other fabrics at Western Costume after *Breakfast at Tiffany's* finished shooting. "They had taken one of the dresses apart to copy it, and it was full of horsehair stuffing and lead weights to make it fall a certain way," she remembered.

The always helpful Edith had an ulterior motive in making the phony Givenchys: she knew that Hepburn was negotiating with Hal Wallis to appear in *Summer and Smoke* (1961), and since Givenchy had not before designed period costumes, Edith was sure the job would go to her. In his autobiography, Wallis says that the matter of who would design the costumes was the reason that Hepburn did not star in *Summer and Smoke.* (Others think the real problem was her salary.) In any case, the role went to Geraldine Page and Edith designed it.

Edith only saw Audrey Hepburn one more time, in the seventies. While lunching alone one day in the Universal commisary, she suddenly saw the ever-sprightly Audrey leaning over from the next banquette. "Why Edith, you haven't changed a bit," she said. Thinking that Hepburn would never make another film (in fact, she eventually made three), Edith for once said what was really on her mind. "I haven't had time to, I've been too busy working," she retorted in reference to the fact that Hepburn wasn't working.

"Audrey could have been a designer herself, she had such perfect taste," was Edith's diplomatic appraisal, but for once the diplomatic statement to the press was really true. Going to Givenchy and making the selections she made (styles Edith would never have deemed appropriate) was a rite of passage for Hepburn. She truly was the one star who instinctively knew what was best for her.

Although Joan Crawford and her designer Sheila O'Brien had always managed to patch things up after a dispute, the fight they had during the Universal production of *Female on the Beach* (1955) was so bad that they almost never spoke again. One simple nightgown remained to be designed and fitted, and Bill Thomas, a Universal staff designer, was excited when he was told to do it. However, "she was so impossible to please that we spent as much time fitting that nightgown as I would normally spend on a whole picture," he later recalled, and so he did not offer to take over O'Brien's job of making Crawford's endless private wardrobe.

Crawford next came to Paramount in 1955, for a film to be titled *Lisbon.* Edith designed and fitted the dresses, which Crawford bought when the film was canceled. Edith agreed when Crawford asked her to design some more for her private wardrobe, but was dismayed when she went to Crawford's house to discuss the sketches and Crawford poured drink after drink. Although Sheila O'Brien used to speculate that Edith and Bill occasionally "got a little tight," Edith was wary of what else Crawford might have in mind and wanted at the very least to get home for dinner without a traffic accident. She had Frank Richardson advise Crawford that having Edith design personal clothes was a privilege reserved for Paramount stars, and as Crawford never worked there again, Edith was off the hook. (She later did a couple of gowns for Crawford to wear to the Academy Awards.) Jane Ardmore, who collaborated with Crawford on her autobiography, *Portrait of Joan,* suggested a few times that she, Edith, and Crawford get together for a "hen party," but Edith declined, pleading a busy schedule.

Crawford never stopped trying, even mentioning the *Lisbon* clothes in *Portrait of Joan.* Despite persistent rumors that Crawford, Stanwyck, and Head met regularly for a Sapphic "sewing party," Jane Ardmore couldn't persuade Edith even to have lunch with Crawford once.

Edith did design for a lesbian legend, Marlene Dietrich. Mitchell Leisen's choice, Mary Kay Dodson, had designed Dietrich's first postwar Paramount film, *Golden Earrings,* but Billy Wilder wanted Edith for *A Foreign Affair* (1948). Cast as a spinsterish congresswoman, Wilder's other star, Jean Arthur, proved to be difficult to handle. She was always afraid she'd look like nothing next to the legendary Marlene. Although Edith and cinematographer Charles Lang were making her look as pretty as they could within the confines of her role, Arthur's husband, producer Frank Ross, frequently complained about how she looked in the rushes. In this period, Bill Ihnen was under contract to Ross, preparing a screen version of *The Robe,* which was not filmed. Edith had Bill explain that if Arthur were to look too attractive in the beginning of the film, her transformation at the end wouldn't be nearly as effective. Dietrich wasn't hard to work with, however, because what she wanted was right for her role as a cabaret chanteuse with a Nazi past. Dietrich was sentimental about an evening gown (designed by Irene), which she had worn while entertaining the troops during the war. When Dietrich said she wanted to use it in *A Foreign Affair,* Edith wholeheartedly agreed. She did, however, design the rest of the film, which ranged from a sleazy bathrobe to a gorgeous nude soufflé and a copy of Irene's sequin gown for the cabaret (the original had worn out).

Dietrich decided to wear a similar soufflé see-through for her own cabaret act in 1954 but chose Jean Louis of Columbia Pictures, rather than Edith, to design it, even though she hadn't yet made a film with him. Columbia's chief Harry Cohn agreed to

Edith and the wardrobe woman confer with Marlene Dietrich during production of A Foreign Affair

this because he was considering using Dietrich for *Pal Joey* in 1957 (ultimately, Rita Hayworth was cast). Jean Louis continued to make the soufflé gowns for the rest of Dietrich's cabaret and concert career. For *Witness for the Prosecution* (1957), however, a United Artists release directed by Billy Wilder, Edith got the nod, her first loan-out since *All About Eve*. All that would be needed were two simple suits and a half-male, half-female outfit for Dietrich's cabaret number. Edith talked a great deal in *The Dress Doctor* about how every fabric, when draped on Dietrich, looked glamorous, how Dietrich wanted to go to the garment district in downtown Los Angeles herself, to shop for her accessories, and how Dietrich brought back box jackets for the wardrobe department staff. On that shopping trip, she also bought one if not both of the suits, according to Dietrich's friend Albert Lord. They were chosen for utter plainness and big enough to fit Dietrich's shoulders, and Edith's only contribution was to direct the refitting. Nowadays, of course, that is how virtually all modern-dress films are costumed, but then it was still unusual for a star as big as Dietrich to wear a ready-made garment.

New starlets were coming to Paramount. Many were tried out in the Martin-and-Lewis and Elvis Presley pictures produced by Hal Wallis. Wallis was known to be tight with a buck, to the point that his contract with Paramount allowed him to inspect all sets from just-completed Paramount films and reuse them if he chose. The other producers protested that sometimes his films with the recycled sets might actually be released before theirs, and when the sets were recognized, they'd be the ones to look cheap, but Wallis prevailed. Nonetheless, he told Edith he wanted all the starlets in the Martin-and-Lewis and Presley pictures to wear original designs rather than purchased clothes. Michael Moore, assistant director on many of these pictures, remembered, "Edith would come with her sketches to the first production meeting and show them to everybody, and if the art director or the cameraman had a problem, they'd bring it up, but after that she dealt mostly with Wallis, and the directors stayed out of it." Shirley MacLaine, discovered by Hal Wallis when she went on in place of Carol Haney in the Broadway production of *The Pajama Game,* was first cast by Wallis in the Dean Martin–Jerry Lewis vehicle *Artists and Models* (1955). On stage, her part of a factory worker had called for collar-length hair, but now

Nellie Manley gave her a pixie cut, Edith dressed her in a glamorous bat costume, and she got a kind of kooky build-up from the publicity department. She would go on to play a large variety of roles, but whatever she needed she counted on Edith to deliver, and designer Michael Travis later said, "There were certain stars, including Shirley MacLaine, who were Edith's and nobody else dared to touch them." MacLaine later remembered that Edith's method of working with her was to drape actual fabrics on her body to see how they would move, and from that would come the ideas that she sketched.

When Alfred Hitchcock cast MacLaine in *The Trouble With Harry* (1955), he was experimenting with making a lower-budget picture and decided to purchase the simple clothes MacLaine would wear. However, Edith was back for his *Man Who Knew Too Much* (1956), even though Doris Day wore the same gray suit through most of the film ("Hitchcock loved those gray suits," she told me). His next picture, *Vertigo* (1958), however, promised to give Edith more opportunities, since Vera Miles was cast in a dual role—the ethereal, blonde Madeline and the brunette salesgirl Judy. Edith had designed, made, and tested all of the wardrobe on Miles when it was learned that she was pregnant and would have to be replaced in the role. Hitchcock borrowed Kim Novak from Columbia, and Edith's accounts of what happened next varied depending on when she was telling the story.

The gray suit for *Vertigo* caused some discussion. When I showed Edith the first draft of *Hollywood Costume Design,* it said that Edith had managed to find a shade of gray that had a hint of lavender—well publicized as Novak's favorite color. She exploded and said, "Whoever told you this?" I said, "I read it in your book *The Dress Doctor.*" Her reply was vintage Edith: "You should know better than to believe anything in THAT book!" She went on to tell me that

Vera Miles in test of gray wool suit for Vertigo

Novak told her that she never wore suits and expected to wear nude shoes to match her stockings. Edith went to Hitchcock with all this and he said he'd take care of it and no more was said—Novak wore the standard Hitchcockian gray suit with black pumps. She later said she realized that it would be a help in her characterization, as if she were wearing somebody else's clothes. Unusually, for this film he did allow some bright colors: most of Novak's clothes for the Judy character were some shade of green (except for one lavender dress). Madeline's wardrobe was more somber, though the first time we see her she does have a brilliant green cape over her black dress, which provides a link between the two characters. (Green was the color of impending death. Madeline also drove a green car and there was a green neon light flashing outside Judy's dismal hotel room.) The only spot of red in the whole film was a ruby necklace, the key James Stewart needs to unlock the mystery. Barbara Bel Geddes, cast as Stewart's faithful girlfriend, was cheerful, dressed to no avail in yellows and tans.

By now Hitchcock had come to rely on Edith's judgment in all things and wanted her on the set with him as much as possible, even long after the clothes were finished. When he went to MGM for *North by Northwest* (1959), he told Helen Rose he expected the same of her. When she protested that she had other films she had to work on, he said, "Well, Edith always manages somehow . . ." (Rose, who had worked well with Vincente Minnelli and many other MGM directors, could not do what Hitchcock wanted. In the end, only one of her dresses was used. Hitchcock took Eva Marie Saint shopping for the rest. "And that was not pleasant, since I had just had a baby the week before," she remembers.)

In 1953, the Academy Awards were televised for the first time. Bill Ihnen volunteered to design a set for the stage at the Pantages Theatre. "It was just one set, but I fixed it so that by changing the lighting you could make it look all different ways. The night of the Awards, they kept it fully lit the whole time and ruined the effect I wanted to get." Edith volunteered to "coordinate" the fashions that the different actresses presenting Oscars would wear. Yvonne Wood, who was in her office at the time, heard her talking to various stars when they called to discuss possible choices—"Oh hello, Greer," "Oh hello, Susan . . ." "Whatever they suggested was fine unless it was black and white together. She said that wouldn't televise properly. Then she wore black and white herself that night!" Edith was very friendly with Margaret Herrick, executive director of the Academy of Motion Picture Arts and Sciences, and she agreed to design special gowns for any ladies who didn't have anything of their own to wear. Herrick also stood next to her in the wings of the Pantages and when a presenter walked by wearing a gown Herrick deemed too low-cut, she was given a choice of either sticking a rose into the cleavage or draping the bust with tulle. "It happened quite often," says designer Michael Travis who was brought in by Herrick later to help with production numbers.

In 1951, the Ihnens moved into their famous house, Casa Ladera. It appealed to Bill because it was a real Spanish hacienda with thick adobe walls, built originally in the 1930s for actor Robert Armstrong by real laborers imported from Mexico. Bette Davis had owned it afterwards, and added a small wing off the kitchen for her mother. It was all decked out in pink and white ruffles, with rosebuds painted on the bathroom tiles and completely out of character with the rest of the house. "It was so horrible we decided that we would keep it just as it was," said Edith in her humorous way. She turned the room over to Nanny for the nights she slept in. Edith was impressed with the romantic possibilities of the house and its enormous grounds but was dismayed to realize that it had no closets. "When we came here there was nothing but armoires." Bill eventually added a dressing room for her, filled with drawers to keep her accessories, and a small bedroom for himself, which could be reached only by walking through Edith's much larger room. She kept her room furnished with her French antiques but allowed Bill to furnish the rest of the house with Spanish and Mexican artifacts he had collected. "The tragedy of my married life is that Bill snores and I can't sleep in the same room with him," Edith lamented to me. Even as elderly people, they remained physically affectionate with each other. More than once I came into Edith's bedroom and found Bill, fully dressed, lying alongside Edith in her bed, deep in conversation, with his arm around her shoulder. They slept together at least when they traveled. When one actress tried to confide in Edith about her new romance, Edith told me, "I feel so sorry for her, at her age, going around trying to have affairs." I said, "A good man is hard to find, Edith," to which she replied, "Well, I found one!" Bill even installed a kitchenette next to his room so he could rise every morning at four to make coffee for his wife and spend a quiet hour with her. It was the only time the phone didn't ring.

In this period, Bill Ihnen was working in the movies less and less. After his contract with the Cagney Brothers expired, he signed another with independent producer Frank Ross and had designed all of *The Robe* when Ross decided to sell the project to 20th Century–Fox where it was completely redesigned as the first production in Cinemascope. Bill designed *A King and Four Queens* (1956) for Scope, and when I asked him if he did things any differently he said, "Yes, I made the buildings longer and lower, to fill the screen." He hoped to work with Edith on the film but Paramount wouldn't loan her out so she suggested Renie Conley for the job. He also told me that after this he decided that he had made enough money (he no longer needed to support his mother and sisters) and devoted himself more and more to architecture and interior design. Most of all he enjoyed painting. He built a studio for himself away from the main house and painted hundreds of canvases, which he never tried to sell or exhibit. Little by little he took over the running of the house and, in his quiet way, increasingly took care of Edith.

"I never saw Mr. Ihnen angry," says Myrtle City. When I asked Myrtle if Edith ever came home in a bad mood over problems at the studio and then vented her anger on her household, Myrtle said, "Well, we all do that sometimes. But Miss Head didn't get mad that much and they done her bad at the studio every day."

Once Edith did get angry upon her return from the studio when she saw the island Bill had installed in the middle of the kitchen floor, between the sink and the stove. She was dismayed to find that it was too high for her to use comfortably. Myrtle was quite a bit taller, and Bill had assumed that she would be the one to use it most often, so he had constructed it for Myrtle's height. "I just pay for things, nobody ever asks me what I want," fumed Edith. She got used to it, however. The first time she showed me around the house, she pointed it out to me with pride.

Anna Spare died in the mid-1950s. Nanny was wearing out so Edith let her retire but continued to support her until the late 1960s. She decided to bring Myrtle City to work full-time at Casa Ladera. Myrtle's sister Robbie says, "We weren't close to her like Nanny had been. We weren't educated, and Nanny had gone to college. They could talk about things. But Miss Head was always very nice to us. Once she gave a big party and had it catered and she told us not to work, just enjoy ourselves like the guests."

The lines of 1950s fashions pleased Edith who, in interview after interview, praised the "return to femininity." Gone were the jungle prints and the ruffles she disliked, and the shoulder pads she detested. The modified New Look that she and the other designers, such as Helen Rose, created for films pleased the stars and executives alike. Skirts were either very full, worn over petticoats, or very slim and worn over girdles. She liked the roughly woven woolens that came in towards the end of the decade. Bob Mackie, who sometimes sketched for her in the early 1960s, says, "That wool photographs well and she often wore it herself. Most of her suits were beige but she did have one wool one in a persimmon shade." In general, she was using printed fabrics less, because solid colors were less likely to go out of style if a film's release was delayed. The one thing that displeased her was the increasing emphasis on cleavage and décolletage. This was nothing new; it had actually started in the early 1930s, when brassiere manufacturers started extolling the beauty of the uplifted breast. After Lana Turner's sensational appearance in a tight-fitting sweater in *They Won't Forget* (1937), actresses clamored for bust pads. Renie Conley later stated, "By the end of the thirties, we were using as many bust pads as shoulder pads."

The New Look also placed much emphasis on décolletage and cleavage, which the movie censors tried hard to discourage. Cleavage was reluctantly allowed on period films (which is how Howard Hughes got away with his display of Jane Russell in *The Outlaw* in 1943), but not in modern-dress pictures. As low-cut necklines became increasingly common in the 1950s (even for day dresses), cinematographers arranged their lights so that the line between the breasts would be washed out. All this made Edith nervous, as did any overly graphic display of sex on the screen. At least she wasn't working under the aegis of Howard Hughes at RKO. (Michael Woulfe had that job.) Sheila O'Brien commented to me, "If a girl had a 40″ bust, she could be a star at RKO; a 38″, a supporting player. Less than 36″—not even an extra."

Edith had large breasts herself, and in public wore clothes that hid the fact. Once when she and I were planning a joint public appearance, I asked her if she still had any of her classic tailored suits from the 1950s. She replied that she still did, but declined to wear one again, because "I'd have to wear a special (minimizer) bra." At home with Bill, of course, it was another matter. Once when she and I were in Bill's room, I noticed on the floor a snapshot he had taken decades earlier. It was a picture of a very busty girl in a low-cut white bathing suit and a white, hair-covering head scarf. I picked it up and asked Edith who the girl was. "That was me," she said proudly.

Some months later I was taking in fashion sketching. She needed some sketches made and wanted to see my work in case I might be able to do the job. The two drawings I brought to show her, I chose unwisely since both featured low-cut dresses with lots of cleavage. It was the only time she ever got angry with me, and I didn't get the job. I tried to remind her of similar dresses she had designed for Sophia Loren, Anita Ekberg, and even Elizabeth Taylor, and she insisted that she never did! Later I told this story to Donna Peterson when she was in the office making sketches of some of Edith's most famous dresses. She laughed and showed me a sketch she had just finished of Mae West in *She Done Him Wrong,* which revealed no cleavage at all. "That's what Edith wants," she said.

Donna had sketched for Edith briefly in the early 1960s after Grace Sprague's death, but most of her career was spent working for Edith's archrival, Helen Rose at MGM. By the 1970s Helen had long since retired and Donna worked with Burton Miller on television shows like *Dynasty.* The day she came in to help Edith make new sketches to show at personal appearances, Edith kept saying, "I just can't understand why Helen never calls me." Donna could well have replied, "Well, if you miss her so much, why don't you call her?" Instead she just shook her head diplomatically and said, "I don't know."

Actually Helen and Donna remained good friends but Helen had retired after a decade of working in retail fashion and was living in Palm Springs. As production slowed down in the late 1950s, MGM had allowed Helen to start her own business on the side. Although she hadn't won as many Oscars as Edith had, and did not have a regular forum like *Art Linkletter's House Party* on television, Helen had designed costumes for many important films (to say nothing of Grace Kelly's wedding dress). Her business started slowly but got a big push with the release of *Cat on a Hot Tin Roof* (1958). A V-necked white chiffon gown she designed for Elizabeth Taylor for that film had been a modest seller in her first collection, but she had also made copies for Taylor in many colors. When the scandal of Taylor running off with Eddie Fisher broke, the fan magazines were full of photographs of Taylor wearing variations of the "Cat" dress, and suddenly Rose's factory (and many others) were manufacturing them by the thousands.

While Edith was aware (and jealous) of Helen's success in retail, she declined offers to do the same. From time to time a pattern company would adapt one of her movie costumes for use in home sewing, and Paramount even made deals to reproduce some of them for ready-to-wear. However, Edith knew that she needed a script with characters, and a specific actress and director to inspire her creativity. If everyone had conflicting ideas, she could deal with it, but just designing pretty clothes for the average girl didn't interest her. However the movie industry changed, she could make herself adjust to it. Helen, on the other hand, could not. After Edith died, Helen told me, "I take my hat off to her. After 1960 I didn't want to work anymore in films, it had changed so much."

Debbie Reynolds once said, "I was Miss Burbank when I entered Helen's fitting room [at MGM] and a star when I came out." In 1958, Reynolds signed a contract with Paramount. Edith first worked with her when she played a tough dance-hall girl in

George Seaton's *Rat Race* (1960), which was followed by another Seaton film, *The Pleasure of His Company* (1961). Edith herself appeared in the opening scene of the latter as a wedding-dress consultant. Ever compliant, she wore her own dress and didn't charge Paramount anything for it. Reynolds was several months pregnant when they started *My Six Loves* (1963), a situation Edith tried to hide by giving her light blouses with dark and very full skirts and moving the waistline up. Sadly, Reynolds lost the child and the film was considered such a bomb that it lay on the shelf unreleased for many months. When it finally came out, A-line dresses (which would have worked better than the skirts and blouses) had become the prevalent style.

According to Helen Rose, Jane Fonda was so difficult and made so many changes in Rose's designs for *Period of Adjustment* (1962), that Helen finally asked that her name be taken off the credits. Edith, on the other hand, welcomed Fonda's input for *Barefoot in the Park* (1967). Although Fonda worked with other designers, most notably Donfeld in *They Shoot Horses, Don't They?* (1969), she continued to ask for Edith from time to time. In the early 1970s, when Fonda's politics made it hard for her to get movie roles, Edith spoke up in her defense even though Edith was politically conservative and didn't agree with Fonda. Fonda filmed a version of Ibsen's *Doll's House* (1973) at the same time as another version, starring Claire Bloom, was also being made. The Fonda version (with gowns by Edith) couldn't find a distributor and ended up premiering on television.

Cecil B. De Mille began preparation for his biggest spectacular ever, *The Ten Commandments* (1956) as early as 1954. Edith was assigned to design for the principal women, while Dorothy Jeakins, Ralph Jester, John Jensen, and Arnold Friberg handled the rest of the cast. The group had access to much archeological research, and got together frequently to compare notes. "We'd have meetings to make sure the colors didn't clash, but if De Mille liked it, then that was all that mattered," she told me.

Despite the months of preparation and endless sketches and meetings, there were always things to be done at the last minute. Dancer Betty Ray remembers, "While De Mille was setting up the scenes of the Israelites worshipping the Golden Calf, he decided he wanted a dancer at the foot of the calf and they quickly sent for me. Then they sent me over to Edith's office and she put aside everything she was doing to make a costume for me. She draped some reddish-brown silk on me and pinned it and told her staff how to sew it. It only took a few minutes."

The casting of the very Irish-looking Anne Baxter as Nefertiti, a move that surprised many (including Baxter herself), was the beginning of Edith's one real friendship with an actress. Right afterwards, they would work together again on *Three Violent People* (1956), and when Baxter's daughter Melissa Galt was born in 1961, Edith agreed to be her godmother. John Engstead was also a longtime friend of Baxter's, and he and Baxter often socialized with the Ihnens. He and Edith both urged Baxter to write a book about her experiences living on a station in the Australian outback. When she protested that she didn't have any place to work, Edith offered her the use of Myrtle's room on the days that Myrtle went home to sleep. The result was *Intermission,* published to great success in 1976.

Edith also became very active in the Costume Designers' Guild, which Sheila O'Brien organized in 1953. Since leaving Paramount for MGM in the mid-1930s, O'Brien had gotten involved in the Costumers' Union, IATSE Local 705, which was founded in 1937. At MGM she had met Joan Crawford, who asked Sheila to teach her how to sew. This proved to be impossible, so they hit upon a

Anne Baxter in Three Violent People

different plan: Sheila would come to Crawford's house every day and make her a dress. (Crawford felt that she owed it to her fans to never wear the same dress twice.) Milo Anderson designed *Mildred Pierce* (1945), Crawford's first Warner Bros. film, an experience so difficult he wouldn't work with her again. Bernard Newman started her next, *Humoresque* (1946), but when none of the Newman dresses seemed right, Crawford started bringing in O'Brien's dresses from home. She also got some styles from Adrian's shop and he got credit for *Humoresque* as well as the next one, *Possessed* (1947), but after that Crawford wore O'Brien's designs on-screen as well as off most of the time.

O'Brien believed that the costume designers needed a guild. Walter Plunkett and Helen Rose flatly opposed the plan, and Orry-Kelly said he didn't want to be in any guild that also included designers from studios like Republic. Nonetheless, O'Brien, invoking the Taft-Hartley Act, polled all the designers in the industry and the majority wanted a guild to represent them. Characteristically, in the early stages of the movement, Edith sat on the fence, but when she saw it would happen with or without her support, she joined in enthusiastically and served on the board of directors many times for the remainder of her life.

By the early 1960s, Edith was being given fewer and fewer films to do. Hitchcock made his biggest hit ever, *Psycho,* using store-bought costumes and his television staff at Revue. (Revue regular Helen Colvig handled the things that had to be made.) Nonetheless, the publicity machine churned on, and the appearances on *Art Linkletter's House Party* continued. Shirley Willson, who was a production coordinator on the Linkletter show, says, "she could go up to the toughest men and flatter them and get them to do whatever she wanted. She was a real femme fatale in her own way." She made more and more public appearances. In 1945, Edith and Waldo Angelo had prepared for *Look* magazine a book on how to dress, which was never published (probably because after V-E day *Look* knew that the war would soon end and the fashions would change). In 1957, she signed with Little, Brown to write a new book. Jane Ardmore told me, "I had just done a book with Eddie Cantor, which was on the best-seller lists and I was asked to go see her. I could see right away that she didn't want to talk much about herself so I shifted the emphasis onto her work, and came up with the title and format of *The Dress Doctor.* The book they cooked up was on the best-seller lists itself for many months after it came out it 1959. With Edith's talent for self-promotion it couldn't have failed, but even Frank Richardson was getting a little weary of her celebrity, much as he knew it helped to sell Paramount product. Art director Henry Bumstead remembers, "One time I needed to talk to Edith about something and couldn't find her anywhere. Finally I called Richardson and he said, 'That goddamned broad is giving another interview!' "

In this period, the Lerner Shops decided they wanted to create another Edith Head–like personality figure, so they hired Renie Conley to stage fashion shows and give advice. A highly articulate and beautiful woman, Conley had already been giving lectures on anthropology and her world travels, which she illustrated with slides she took herself. She dispensed advice capably for the Lerner Shops' customers but she didn't catch on the way Edith had. Perhaps it was because she was too attractive, and the masses couldn't identify with her. Edith preached a gospel that any woman could become a star by finding out what her good points were and playing them up, and she was the world's best example of what she was talking about. Also, "she always spoke with such absolute conviction you'd think she was an Old Testament prophet delivering the Holy Word," says film historian Howard Mandelbaum.

Promoters also approached Yvonne Wood with a whole range of plans, which included speaking tours and retail designing. "We were going to sign all the papers one day over lunch but an emergency came up. I had to do a fitting and the only time the actress could meet with me was during the lunch hour. When Edith had a conflict, she had her secretary call the star or the production manager and schedule another time. She could do that. But I wasn't Edith. I had to be available when they could see me. And the more I thought about it, the more I realized I didn't want to be another Edith even if I could have. I was making enough to suit me and I didn't want to work as hard as she did."

After a five-year absence, Yvonne was back at Paramount to work on the men's and women's costumes for the musical *Li'l Abner* (1959). "They wanted me to fix up and reuse Alvin Colt's costumes from the stage show, but most of them were so worn out by that time they were too ragged even for Dogpatch. I made many new things but they weren't my ideas really, I followed Al Capp's comic strip." Yvonne stayed on for the expensive western *One-Eyed Jacks* (1961). "When the film was in postproduction, somebody came to me and asked if I would mind giving up my screen credit to Edith. That way, I knew, they could get lots of publicity, but Edith had had absolutely nothing to do with it. I called up Marlon Brando's secretary, and she was so upset she went straight to Brando on the dubbing stage where he was looping lines. He made them give me almost a whole card in the titles to myself" (a larger credit than Edith ever got at Paramount).

Yvonne always believed that Edith had had nothing to do with the scheme to change the designer credit for *One-Eyed Jacks;* others were not so sure. Remarkably, however, Edith started acting much friendlier towards Yvonne away from the studio. The practice of shooting on Saturdays had ended in the mid-1950s, allowing studio workers more time for a social life, and Edith and Bill began to visit Yvonne and her husband, men's costumer Eddie Armand, on Sunday afternoons. "One day they came to see us when my mother was living with us, and Edith told Mother how nice her hair looked. Mother thanked her but said she had to admit that it was a wig. Edith lifted up her own hairpiece and said, 'Join the club, Honey.' "

The fact that Edith got an Academy Award for *The Facts of Life* (1960) showed the wisdom of never turning down any job no matter how small. Edward Stevenson had been designing for Lucille Ball on *I Love Lucy* for several years. Their relationship had started two decades earlier, when she was a model and starlet on the RKO lot. In 1972, Ball told me, "It was my first film in several years and I wanted Eddie, but the producers wanted Edith—who I enjoy working with too—so I didn't argue. Edith was very good about it, she said, 'The workrooms at Paramount are busy, so why don't you make the costumes up at Desilu and have Eddie supervise?' Eddie came to every fitting—he's a genius at tiny changes that make a big difference—and he bought all the accessories. Edith made sure he got credit." The fact that this simple film would even be nominated was proof that there were no longer enough black-and-white films for a separate Oscar category. When her name was announced, Edith had a hard time getting away from the microphone backstage, where she was commentating the proceedings for the radio audience. The virtually unknown veteran Stevenson got an Oscar even if he was riding on Edith's coattails.

Edith had not worked with director John Ford when he came to Paramount for *The Man Who Shot Liberty Valance* in 1961, and was clearly scared of him. She asked Sheila O'Brien to recommend a good designer who could handle the stark-looking Old West outfits Ford wanted, and Sheila suggested Leah Rhodes. Leah had started at Warner Bros. as Orry-Kelly's assistant and took over for him when he was fired in 1943. A quiet, gentle woman, she once told me, "I didn't think I could be a designer because I couldn't argue like Orry!" She hadn't worked much since leaving Warners in 1953 and didn't mind that Edith would be getting sole credit for the film.

Very much aware that Columbia had let Jean Louis go, that Fox was phasing out Charles LeMaire, and that Walter Plunkett and Helen Rose were needed less and less at MGM, Edith was more determined than ever not to rock the boat at Paramount. Her weekly salary in 1960 was modest (about $950, which was less than Banton had received twenty years earlier despite the fame and Oscars), and her agents at William Morris timidly reminded the studio that she hadn't had any vacation in the last two years. (They suggested she be allowed some three-day weekends to compensate, but then she got too busy to take them.) Eventually she was given an all-expense-paid trip to Japan. When she got back, she was so busy that Sheila O'Brien held an executive board meeting of the Designers' Guild at Edith's office in Western Costume. Dorothy Jeakins took issue with the way Edith pronounced the name "Kyoto," and Edith humbly apologized for her error. After she'd left, Jeakins said, "I know I was really a bitch but I just hate her so much!"

Very occasionally Edith would do something totally uncharacteristic, apparently because she felt a need to shake things up. Bob Mackie remembers, "The first time I worked for her was during *Donovan's Reef* (directed by John Ford, in 1962). Grace Sprague was out for a week, and Edith called me in and sat me down at Grace's drawing board, which was right next to her office. I don't know what went wrong between Edith and actress Elizabeth Allan when she came in for the first meeting, but all afternoon Edith was calling all the bigwigs at Paramount and telling them that they should replace Elizabeth with Vera Miles. In retrospect, it really puzzles me because Edith could find a way to get along with anybody and, besides, she was afraid of John Ford." (Elizabeth Allan stayed in the part.)

Melville Shavelson was a screenwriter who started directing with the Bob Hope vehicle *The Seven Little Foys* (1955). "Edith wanted to talk to me about the clothes but I had enough to worry about. I told her to do whatever she wanted." His *Houseboat* (1958) was Edith's first encounter with Sophia Loren, whom she liked despite her big bustline. "Sophia was very tan, so she didn't have to wear body make-up," says Shavelson, "but Martha Hyer did, and when Cary Grant was dancing with her, it got all over the tuxedo. Part of his deal with Paramount was that he could keep the clothes when we finished, and he got very angry. We told him we'd get it cleaned but he still wasn't satisfied."

Some years later, Shavelson wrapped up *The Pigeon That Took Rome* (1962) and left for vacation. Not long before that, inspired by Edith, he had written a treatment called "Samantha" (eventually released as *A New Kind of Love* in 1963) about a New York retail designer who wears severe clothes when she goes to Paris to scout the couture shows and get ideas for knockoffs. While there, she puts on a wig and a glamorous outfit, goes out on the town, and is mistaken for a prostitute by a reporter, with many humorous complications ensuing. "As soon as I got to Europe, Paramount told me to come right back. Joanne Woodward liked the treatment and thought she could get Paul Newman to appear with her in it. The only problem was that he was due to start another picture in six weeks."

Shavelson recalls, "Joanne said, 'This is the dirtiest thing I ever read and I love it.' Newman was willing but he said, 'I don't think the public likes us together in comedies,' since *Rally 'Round the Flag, Boys!* (1958) didn't do too well. Our plan was to get real

Edith fitting Sophia in a gown for Heller in Pink Tights *(Loren's hair was subsequently bleached to pale blonde for the role)*

dresses from Paris designers for the fashion shows, and Edith would design everything Joanne, Eva Gabor, and Thelma Ritter wore, and what Paul would wear in the dream sequences. At first she told me it couldn't be done in six weeks, but then she went and did it. I depended on her a great deal to stage the fashion shows with me, because I was writing the script as we went along. She chose all the clothes from what the designers sent us, and helped me choose the models and stage the shows. We had a gag that while Newman was watching the shows and got bored, he imagined strippers walking down the runways. Edith found girls that were the same size as the regular models, made the stripper outfits, and directed them so they would walk at the same pace as the other models. Then we superimposed the stripper footage over the runway in the lab."

Bob Mackie had just graduated from Chounard. He says, "Grace Sprague was like a machine, she could turn out one sketch after another, but on this picture Edith needed all the help she could get so she called both Leah Rhodes and me in. This picture needed a lot of showgirl costumes, which weren't Grace's specialty, and Edith liked the way I did them. Edith was really lovely to me. She had me making sketch after sketch. I'd draw up her ideas and then do my own. She'd say, 'Joanne needs a wedding dress for a dream sequence. I'll see you after lunch.' After lunch she came in, took up the sketches that she liked, put some pencils in her bun and went off to see the producer. No matter which of us drew the initial sketch, by the time they went through all the meetings and the fittings and reached the screen, they were Edith's. She had a look and it was consistent."

Actually, the wedding dress was one of the few that ended up fairly close to Mackie's drawing when he saw it on the screen. "I stayed at the drawing table all day and didn't follow it through the workroom, like I would now, so of course things were changed. There was some big blonde lady in charge and not only did the studio want everything faster, they wanted them cheaper, and shortcuts were taken. I saw in the stock wardrobe some of the fabulous gowns Travis Banton had made for Marlene Dietrich and we were able to use some of them in the film. The workmanship was better than what we were getting for *New Kind of Love*.

"A-line dresses were coming in and I drew up many ideas for Eva Gabor, but she wanted to stick to her tight waists and full skirts, and that's what Edith had to give her. When that film ended, I alternated between Edith and Jean Louis, who was doing *Something's Got to Give* (1962) for Marilyn Monroe. He was very strict—he'd make a drawing himself and if he thought I'd changed anything, he'd make me do it over. Edith was much more fun. One day she met some executive, for the first time, on the couch in the reception area. When he lit a cigarette, she kicked off her shoes and lit one too! I never saw her smoking before or since, but she convinced this guy she was his best buddy right away! When it was quiet, she'd say, 'Look busy! Frank Richardson's coming down the hall.' She loved her intrigues! Really, she was more important than he was but sometimes she still reverted in her mind to the old days when she was the new girl."

Soon Mackie went to work for Ray Aghayan, beginning an association that continues to this day. Grace Sprague died suddenly in a car accident. It would be several years before Edith would discover a new sketch artist who was just right in all respects: enormously talented but sufficiently self-effacing that he would stay in the background. Moss Mabry remembers, "Richard Hopper came to the Paramount lot to audition for some other sketching job. The person he talked to knew Edith needed somebody, so he sent Richard over to her. She hired him on the spot." Hopper stayed with her for the rest of her career.

Mabry himself worked well with Edith and designed the mens' wardrobe for three films for which she did the women: *The Carpetbaggers* and *What a Way to Go* (1964), and *Harlow* (1965). Although *The Carpetbaggers* had been a sensational best-seller and Paramount pulled out all stops in lining up an all-star cast, Michael Moore sent Edith and Frank Richardson a sharp note warning them that the costs were getting to be too high and she would have to economize somewhere. She did so by having Carroll Baker use a red dress out of the stock wardrobe for a scene in which her character, Rina Marlowe, is seen shooting a film. Baker says, "She made me a stunning transparent gown, pink and glitter, with a stole of pink tulle flowers, to wear for the opening of *The Carpetbaggers* and publicity for *Harlow.* When I tried it on, everyone in the wardrobe department broke into tears, including Edith, who was not terribly sentimental."

Baker gave Edith an ivory disc that had been used in a London theater as a ticket in the 1850s. She liked it so much she collected a dozen more and had a necklace made, which became another one of her trademarks. Baker says, "I found the discs in a London antique shop and gave dear friends each one on my return. I was unhappy that Edith bought every remaining one, I thought they should belong to many people and not be hoarded. However, I loved Edith and thought her work was great." It was during the production of *The Carpetbaggers* that Paramount reopened its long-locked Marathon Street gate and had a big ceremony. Charlotte Mendenhall who was filling in as Edith's secretary remembered, "They served champagne and she didn't want to drink it but she didn't want to refuse it either, so she brought it back to the department and gave it to me. 'You're the champagne type,' she said."

Harlow had an enormous budget for clothes. Though the censors had warned the studio about mentioning "Harlow's non-use of bras," the gowns were the most revealing Edith would ever design. One day, Edith said to Moss Mabry: "Come in here, I want to show you something." He recalls, "She had gotten out piles of sketches for films she'd done in the thirties and they were damn good too. Believe me, she could draw."

Moss Mabry was also around when Edith was working on *Butch Cassidy and The Sundance Kid* (1969), on loan out to 20th Century–Fox. In this case, she designed all of the men's costumes herself as well as Katharine Ross's carefully researched period underwear. "She'd send to the research department, and when she found a real suit she thought would be good, she'd have Richard Hopper make a sketch of it. She chose the fabric, supervised the tailoring and the fittings," says Mabry. He was persuaded to design an outfit for Paul Newman to wear as he rode a bicycle in the celebrated "Raindrops Keep Falling on My Head" sequence. "Edith said, 'Oh, I'm so tired, can I borrow your brain?' I offered to do the whole thing, fittings and all, and of course I didn't get credit. It bothered me at the time but not anymore." Edith was asked for the first time to design for Judy Garland for the film *I Could Go On Singing* (1963). After her sensational Carnegie Hall comeback in 1961, Garland had made two black-and-white films, *Judgment at Nuremberg* (1961) and *A Child Is Waiting* (1963). Howard Shoup, who had designed and made one of the Carnegie Hall outfits in his shop, also did the latter film, but the producers wanted Edith for *I Could Go On Singing.* The sketches were among the last Grace Sprague did for Edith, and the clothes were made at Western for the film, which would be produced in England. Garland was heavy, and Edith kept her in dark colors. A-line dresses were helpful here since Garland never had a sharply defined waistline. Once the filming in London was underway, new copies of some of the dresses had to be made when Garland's weight fluctuated. Her friends convinced her that she could wear a bright red dress for her rendition of "I'll Go My Way by Myself." Edith had made a black crepe sheath draped in black chiffon, which was reproduced in a larger size and now bright red. When the picture came out, *Time* magazine's review panned the dress as looking like a "bag of tomatoes that got squished." Edith wrote back, "What a difference a few pages can make. In the Show Business section of your April 19 issue, you credited me with helping Joan Crawford become the most photographed star at the Oscar presentations. My cup of pride ran over until I turned to Cinema, where your movie reviewer put me in the tomato-stuffing business as the result of a red chiffon dress Judy Garland wore in *I Could Go On Singing.* Of course, since I was credited as costume designer, your critic would have no way of knowing this, but please, just for the record, I designed all of Judy's costumes for the picture with the exception of that one. . . . It's always a pleasure to appear in *Time* but please, not as a tomato specialist."

Garland wanted Edith when she signed for a weekly television show in 1964. By now she had lost a considerable amount of weight but Edith still dressed her in dark colors for the first show. Noticing the sprightly clothes Ray Aghayan was designing for the guest stars and chorus, the producers decided Garland needed the same, and Edith was glad, for once, to step aside. "I was only supposed to do four gowns per week for Judy but she was calling me all night long," Edith told me. Bob Mackie says, "On a show like that, you have to be there all the time so that as the script develops you can get things designed and made literally overnight." As I mentioned before, Edith almost never wanted to say anything unpleasant about a star, claiming, "I might have to dress her again." When I asked about *The Judy Garland Show* and she didn't want to talk about it, I reminded her that she'd never have to dress Judy Garland again. She paused, dumbfounded, then came back with a "Yes, but I may get to dress Liza Minnelli!"

The biggest young star Edith managed to latch onto in the sixties was Natalie Wood. Actually, they had met a decade earlier, when Wood was cast as Bing Crosby's daughter in *Just for You.*

Already an adolescent but small for her age, Wood had to be made into a younger child than she really was. Edith made fussy little-girl dresses to hide her developing bustline. Now she was a full-fledged star with a long list of hit pictures at Warner Bros. to her credit. She was doing *Love With the Proper Stranger* (1963) for Paramount. At first it seemed reasonable that she would want one of her designers from Warner Bros., but Edith managed to get an appointment to discuss possible clothes with her. The only problem was that Martha Hyer, also an important actress and later Hal Wallis's wife, was due to come in at the same time. Bob Mackie, says, "All the ladies were saying, 'Martha always stays for hours! We won't have time to get Edith's office ready!' They helped Edith transform a small room, which had been Leah Rhodes's office, into a place to meet with Wood, installing all the Oscars and antique sewing machines." It worked—Edith designed not only *Love With the Proper Stranger* but also Wood's costumes for her next pictures at Warners: *Sex and the Single Girl* (1964), and *Inside Daisy Clover* and *The Great Race* (1965).

Wood could still be made to look like a small child. Gavin Lambert, author of *Inside Daisy Clover,* says, "At first I was afraid that Edith would be afraid to go all the way in showing Daisy's poverty at the beginning of the story, but we had a meeting and she did just what I wanted, putting holes in the sweaters, et cetera." For *Sex and the Single Girl* the task was just the opposite, making Wood into a voluptous young woman with the aid of special bras constructed at great expense at Western Costume. Jack Delaney, head of Warners wardrobe for many years, remembered, "Western sent us a bill for $1,600 for one bra! The production manager had a fit. I told him think of it this way, $800 for each side!" Years later, when Edith was claiming that she never used bust pads on actresses, I told her, "You can't tell me that, Edith. I've seen *Sex and the Single Girl!*"

Thanks to Natalie Wood Edith finally got to make a picture at MGM. Through the 1950s it was the one studio that never borrowed her. Helen Rose remembered, "Mal Kaplan, who had worked with Edith at Paramount, came to MGM and she kept calling him and asking him when he'd get her a picture at MGM. He told her he couldn't since Metro had me and Walter Plunkett under contract." Finally in the late 1960s, with both Rose and Plunkett gone, Edith got to design *Penelope* (1966) for Natalie Wood at MGM. It turned out to be a bomb at the box office, but at least she'd finally achieved her goal.

As the sixties wore on, work at Paramount got slower and slower. Edith hoped she would get to design for Barbra Streisand's *On a Clear Day You Can See Forever* (1970), until she learned that Alan Lerner insisted that Cecil Beaton be allowed to design any of his works when they were filmed. Edith gamely went to the premiere (which featured a costume ball afterwards), minus her glasses and wearing a rhinestone-covered dress she got out of the stock wardrobe. (It supposedly had been worn by Mae Murray and was shipped out from the Astoria studio in New York when it closed in 1932. Edith dressed Bill Ihnen up as an Arab sheik.) She still hoped to work with Streisand someday, and in odd moments made sketches of ideas to elongate Streisand's short waist. It never happened. When Dorothy Jeakins left halfway through *The Way We Were* (1973), Sheila O'Brien sent Streisand a list of available designers, including Edith. Streisand chose Moss Mabry instead.

Edith regretted that Elizabeth Taylor hadn't pushed to get her for *Who's Afraid of Virginia Woolf* (1966); Irene Sharaff designed it. When its director, Mike Nichols, was beginning his second film, *The Graduate* (1967), Edith had her agents at William Morris lobby for her to get the assignment—to no avail. She was, however, loaned out to the Mirisch Company for a big western, *The*

Hallelujah Trail (1965). Yvonne Wood, who had come back to Hollywood after several years away and couldn't get work as a designer, was on that film as a costumer. "The problem was there were no problems," she said. "Everybody liked what Edith was doing right away. So she started second-guessing herself. Pamela Tiffin had a lovely yellow dress. Edith kept looking and looking at it, saying there was something the matter. There was nothing the matter! Finally she decided it had to be pink. It couldn't be dyed, so she had it spray-painted!"

Edith couldn't resist writing another book after the great success of *The Dress Doctor,* but the follow-up, *How to Dress for Success* (1967), did not sell well. "When you've had a successful book, you don't write it again," said Jane Ardmore, who was sorry the new book prevented possible further editions of *The Dress Doctor.* This time Edith's collaborator was the well-known journalist Joe Hyams, who later paid tribute to her kindness towards him in a difficult period of his life (he was going through a divorce).

Whenever John Engstead came back to Los Angeles from his retirement home in Hawaii, Edith would have a little cocktail party, inviting all of John's staff and me. As successful as he had been as a glamour photographer, John never ceased to long for the days when he ran the stills department at Paramount. Again and again Edith nodded as he repeated the same stories. Then the next day she would say to me, "John is so sentimental about Paramount and I couldn't wait to get out of there!"

Gulf & Western took over Paramount in 1966 and Edith saw the handwriting on the wall. Word was going around that they didn't intend to employ anybody over the age of sixty-five and she was now pushing seventy. In the final months of her contract, however, Edith came up with a plan. Alfred Hitchcock, now relocated at Universal, had already borrowed her for *The Birds* (1963), *Marnie*

(1964), and *Torn Curtain* (1966). He had also become a major stockholder in MCA-Universal when he turned over the rights to his highly successful television show to the company in exchange for stock. Moreover, Edith had been quietly designing clothes for the wife of Lew Wasserman, head of Universal, for several years. In 1965, Universal borrowed Edith from Paramount to appear in a "Fashion Featurette" to be shown to visitors on the studio tour. When it was revealed in the trade papers that Edith would be leaving Paramount after forty-four years, Yvonne Wood said she remarked to her husband, "I'll bet somebody else picks her up. The publicity she can get is worth too much." Sure enough, a week later it was announced that Edith would relocate to Universal.

5

The Lioness in Winter

Edith Head's arrival at Universal Studio on March 27, 1967, was given enormous attention in the press. She knew that one of her main duties would be to get publicity for the studio and be an on-hand celebrity for Universal's studio tour. She played the role up to the hilt. Her first secretary there, Ruby Graf, remembers, "She'd hear the tour tram coming down the street, stick some pencils in her bun, and run to the doorway of her office so she could just 'happen' to be coming out when the tram went by. Heaven help you if you got in her way."

Larry Harmell, now head of Universal's wardrobe department says, "She softened up when she came to Universal. She wasn't as tough as she had been when she had been at Paramount." There was good reason for this.

Vincent Dee, who was then in charge of the department, didn't want her and didn't need her. Tom Bronson, now head of wardrobe at Disney, says, "He didn't like it but he didn't say so, because it was a studio decision and there was nothing he could do about it." Edith quickly sensed that she would not be able to ride herd on Dee as she had on Frank Richardson.

When MCA, the parent company of Universal, had started producing television shows in the mid-1950s (the company was then known as Revue), Dee was the head of the department and he had built up a large staff, including several designers he could work with comfortably. As head of the department, he originally took credit for costumes on all of the television shows; however, by the early 1970s the person who shopped for the actresses was credited as "Costume Designer" (and belonged to the Designers' Guild), while the men's costumer who did the same for the men (and belonged to the Costumers' Local 705) was not mentioned in the credits. In the two unions' jurisdictions, costumers could shop for clothes and reuse existing items from stock wardrobe but were not permitted to design and make new garments. Nowadays many costumers eventually also become designers and belong to both locals, but until the 1970s this was rare. *GE Theatre* was Revue's most prestigious show in the late 1950s and early 1960s, and Dee later told me how pleased he was when he found out that *GE Theatre*'s ladies' costumer, Helen Colvig, could also sketch and design beautifully. When Revue was merged with Universal, and Dee became head of the new department, Jean Louis (formerly of Columbia) was designing the high-end films Ross Hunter produced, such as *Pillow Talk* (1959) and *Thoroughly Modern Millie* (1967), but Dee assigned some smaller pictures to Colvig and she worked between times in television.

MCA envisioned Universal as an operation with both television and feature production, on as large a scale as the pre-1948 Hollywood. It was the only studio to have contract players who would start out in television and eventually be moved into features under the direction of casting director Monique James. Besides Hitchcock, many veteran producers and directors, including Howard Hawkes, Mervyn LeRoy, George Seaton, and Hal Wallis, also had been signed up, and these were people Edith had long known and worked with. Her first assignment was a Paul Newman picture, *The Secret War of Harry Frigg* (1968), and it was announced that she would design costumes for a picture to be directed by George Stevens, but it was never made.

Edith toyed with the idea of getting a new image. One costumer remembers her coming to the studio to confer with Dee before she was on the payroll, wearing a bright pink blouse and blue jeans, with her hair in a long braid down her back. She soon decided, however, that this was not the Edith Head that the tourists were paying good money to see, so it was back to the business suits, though she did stop wearing gloves every day. She also conferred with the famous wigmaker and hairstylist Ziggy, who was on the lot for a while, making hairpieces for various stars. "She had been dying her hair absolutely coal-black," he remembered, "and I persuaded her to switch to a dark brown with a few blonde streaks." June Van Dyke, who coordinated her fashion shows, adamantly opposed this change, saying, "When you've got a trademark you stick with it," but Edith had Ziggy make her some bangs in the new shade and also started putting her chignon at the crown of her head rather than the nape of the neck. (She made some appearances this way and posed for pictures with this style, but soon it was back to the old position since that was easier to sleep on.)

June was around much more these days, because Edith gave fashion shows in the tour visitors' pavillion and was doing more and more shows for charity. "At first she would just show a few gowns during a break in somebody else's fashion show," remembers Ruby Graf, "but eventually she was doing whole shows for charity. The charity would pay the models, and June for coordinating it, but Edith just did her work as a contribution. When we were first moving into the bungalow and it wasn't furnished yet, June brought in a picnic lunch and we all ate sitting on the floor. The painters were working all around us and must have thought we were mad."

When I was first getting to know Edith, she invited me to a big fashion show in the Grand Hall of the Dorothy Chandler Pavillion of the Los Angeles Music Center. I was still naïve about her departures from the truth at that point, so when I realized that some of the dresses weren't actually from the movies she was claiming, I innocently took it upon myself to try to clear things up. "Look, kid, this is a phony show!" said Edith bluntly. She then treated us to a bluesy rendition of Duke Ellington's "Sophisticated Ladies" to show the musicians the tempo she wanted to accompany a certain gown. She and June brought along several women costumers from Universal to help that day, but at smaller venues, the tireless June had to manage everything backstage herself.

Henry Bumstead decorated Edith's Universal bungalow, all in beige and yellow and featuring Edith's collection of antique sewing machines and, of course, the Oscars. It was a full block away from the main department, so Edith could not keep an eye on things as she had done at Paramount, nor did she have a spy like Billye Fritz who could tell her when other designers were getting assignments she wanted. Sheila O'Brien could be counted on to pass along some gossip, but as business agent for the Designers' Guild, Sheila was representing the competition too, and she tried to maintain an image of impartiality. Nonetheless, several times every day, Edith would grandly instruct her secretary, "Get me Sheila O'Brien," with an air of utmost urgency second only to the president calling the Kremlin on the hot line.

Sheila maintained a careful relationship with Edith, very critical of her at times and yet very much a coconspirator at others. One year she told me of how all the designers who were members of the Academy of Motion Picture Arts and Sciences met at Edith's house to determine who would be nominated for the Oscar. Without wasting any time, Edith told another designer, "I'll vote for you if you vote for me" and thus got herself nominated again, though her winning streak was now over. Another time Sheila organized a promotional trip to Canada with a number of designers, including Edith. It was a long flight and much liquor flowed, but Edith didn't drink at all. "She made sure she was the first one to get off the plane and all the reporters and photographers only paid attention to her and the rest of us need not have made the trip," said Sheila.

At first Edith was busy designing big-budget Universal films. Hitchcock's *Topaz* (1969) was a mess from the start. Henry Bumstead recalls, "Hitch had wanted to do another script, but it was too shocking and Universal wouldn't let him. So we rushed into this and Hitch kept saying it had to be finished by Christmas because he had already rented a villa in Italy for the holidays. Edith and I were in Paris, and it was about to start filming in Copenhagen, and we didn't have a cast, and she was a nervous wreck." Finally it did get cast with a group of little-known performers. It didn't make money.

Neither did most of the films produced or directed by the veterans Edith had worked with at Paramount. George Seaton's Universal debut, *What's So Bad About Feeling Good?* (1968) was filmed in New York, so Edith went there. Michael Travis later remembered, "Waldo

Angelo was living there then and when Edith invited him to visit her at her hotel, he took me along. It was the first time I met her. She was in her bathrobe with her hair down her back, and we ate breakfast together. She said, 'Can you imagine that it has come to this? I have to buy most of Mary Tyler Moore's things. But I am going to make a few when I get back to L.A. Would you boys mind making a few sketches for me?' We didn't get paid and we didn't get any credit, of course, but at least I got to meet her. Sometime later, when I was in Los Angeles and Edith was designing the clothes for some of the presenters at the Academy Awards, Margaret Herrick asked her if she would mind if I designed the production numbers for the nominated songs. She said that would be fine and she didn't interfere with me. I just got some little credit at the end and next to no money, but it was a start."

George Seaton's wife Phyllis prevailed upon Edith to give her longtime friend Natalie Visart a job as her New York shopper on *What's So Bad About Feeling Good?* Visart's daughter, Laurel Taylor, now remembers, "I was a teenager then and wearing miniskirts and Courrèges boots, and they kept asking me what the kids were wearing. We rode around to the boutiques in Edith's limousine and Mother finished it up when Edith went back to L.A. Edith treated Mother beautifully." Some years later, however, when Natalie and her husband, Dwight Taylor, had relocated to Los Angeles and were living in an apartment John Engstead owned, Edith seemed to still be afraid that Natalie might resume her long-dormant career (her last design job had been in 1945!). John kept trying to get Edith and Natalie together for a dinner party and Edith kept putting it off. When she could refuse no longer, the dinner was held at the home of John's retoucher, Franceine Watkins, and I was invited too. Edith's behavior was as cold as ice, and it was a painful experience for all involved.

Airport (1970), directed by George Seaton but produced by Ross Hunter, was a big success. Costumer Laurann Cordero recalls, "Edith told me about how she and Seaton were such good friends, and all the pictures they'd done at Paramount, like *The Country Girl* (1954). Then she took me with her to the production meeting. Seaton took one quick look at the sketches for the stewardesses' uniforms and said very coldly, 'I don't like the colors.' Edith said, 'Then we'll have to have a meeting.' The way she said it, with no expression, you couldn't tell how she felt about it but I'm sure she was hurt. I had been thinking that someday I'd like to move up to being a designer, but after that I decided I'd stay a costumer. The original sketches showed blue uniforms; the ones we finally made were gray jumpers with yellow blouses."

Henry Bumstead said, "Seaton's problem was that his producer, William Perlberg, had to retire. Perlberg had always handled the money and let George concentrate on the writing and directing. George could produce, but the constant worrying about the money really wore him down and none of his Universal films were successful other than *Airport*."

Hal Wallis was a similar case. His only successful Universal production was *Anne of the Thousand Days* (1969), filmed in England with costumes by Margaret Furse. Even *Rooster Cogburn* (1975), the sequel to the highly popular *True Grit* (1969), starring the unbeatable team of John Wayne and Katharine Hepburn, was a box-office disappointment. While Wayne's costumes were handled by his usual costumer, Luster Bayless, Edith worked long and hard on Hepburn's. Tom Bronson said, "When she took me to a production meeting on a Wallis picture, it was all, 'Hi Edith,' 'Hi Hal.' " However, I can remember being in her office one morning as she prepared to go see Wallis with her sketches. Nervously she drew over Richard Hopper's work, simplifying the lines (Wallis always liked things simple). He had the reputation of being tight with a buck and many insiders thought *Rooster Cogburn* would have succeeded if he had hired Henry Hathaway to direct. (Hathaway had done *True Grit* very successfully, but now he requested a percentage for the sequel, which Wallis wouldn't pay.) Nonetheless, when Hepburn's costumes were made up, Wallis decided to film costume tests, an extravagant practice all the studios had abandoned many years earlier.

The Los Angeles County Museum of Art was having a summer-long retrospective of Wallis's career, and the film curator Ronald Haver asked me to do an interview with Edith about her many films with him. As much as she liked publicity, she groaned at the thought. "He's just about the only one I have left! Why can't I talk about somebody nice, like George Roy Hill?" she begged. "We're not honoring him this year," I replied. Finally Edith came up with a carefully worded statement. "Mr. Wallis doesn't ever want the costumes to detract from the drama. If I have a fashion innovation, I use it somewhere else, not in a Wallis picture." (In another interview, she remembered Wallis nixing one of her clever ideas by saying, "Save it for the runway, Edith.")

The ladies' workroom at Universal was good at making alterations, but Edith didn't like the patterns they made from her sketches, so she decided to have all her production done at Western Costume. This wasn't dangerous politically, as Universal was one of the studios that then owned Western (the others were MGM, Paramount, and 20th Century–Fox). However, it was inconvenient to have to go over there with the stars for the fittings. The studio gave Edith a car, and if she was officially on the budget of a particular film, she also got a driver. A nice man named Kenny was assigned to her. Even though cataracts were dimming her sight, Edith still managed to drive herself to and from the studio (though she got so many tickets for driving too slow that we wondered when the Department of Motor Vehicles would take her license away!). Driving to Western Costume scared her though, so Bill would drive her. "He was so devoted to her," says Wilma Dunn, a cutter and fitter who was often assigned to Edith. "He'd sit in the car waiting for her for hours and wouldn't come inside the building unless it was very cold." Wilma also commented, "She wanted the fame and the glory and she was afraid of the young people coming up."

The young person coming up who troubled Edith the most was Theadora Van Runkle who became famous virtually overnight for her work on Warren Beatty's production of *Bonnie and Clyde* (1967). The most troubling thing perhaps was that Theadora didn't want to be a star designer or even a designer at all. She was simply a single mother who wanted to be a serious painter, but turned to designing to earn money to support her two children. At least Theadora's midcalf-length skirts for Faye Dunaway started a trend away from the miniskirts, which Edith hated.

Theadora recalls, "I had known Dorothy Jeakins since I was a student at Chounard and she was the librarian," says Theadora. "I thought she was very talented but a little odd. For one thing, she never washed her hair because, she said, the buildup of oil made it easier to keep in place! Eventually she left to design costumes and after some years asked me to sketch for her. One job she really wanted was *The Sand Pebbles* (1966). Robert Wise had used Dorothy for *The Sound of Music* (1965) but now he chose Renie Conley instead, which I had nothing to do with. Then Renie asked me to sketch for her, and I accepted. I was working one afternoon in a dressing room, because there weren't any free offices, and in the dressing-room mirror, I saw Dorothy approach me from behind. She had a furious expression and looked like she was going to hit me, so I ducked. Then she was very embarrassed. She had agreed to do *Bonnie and Clyde* for Warren but she got too busy, so she turned it over to me (I think because she felt guilty about trying to hit me).

"Sheila O'Brien told Warren he couldn't hire me, but he insisted, and in the end I kept my job." The film wasn't a hit at first, but it was rereleased six months later and, gradually, became an enormous success. Most troubling to Edith was the fashion press's fascination with Theadora's hippie clothes, multiple rings, and especially her name (Van Runkle was her true married name, she hadn't made it up). Theadora was interviewed again and again, and started getting big assignments. After she signed to design *Myra Breckinridge* (1970), she was told that Mae West had asked for Edith. "Mae and I were already friends, but this didn't hurt my feelings," she says. "Mae hadn't made a film in a long while, and I could see why she would want Edith. Besides, I greatly admired Edith and thought it would be an honor to work with her.

"The first time I actually talked with Edith was early one morning when I went to International Silks and Woolens to find buttons for *Bonnie and Clyde.* I was bending over, digging way in the back of the pile when Edith came in. I was introduced, and she said, 'Anybody who would dig that hard for buttons will become a great designer.' I told her my project was set in the early thirties and she said, 'Flowered chiffons, flowered chiffons!' I said no, I had been doing research and once Bonnie and Clyde had some money from robbing banks, they started wearing tailored clothes from the Marshall Fields catalogue. She went off and that was it."

Myra Breckinridge came at a very difficult time in Edith's life, for she had just been diagnosed with myelofibrosis. This is a disorder of the bone marrow: the marrow itself is replaced by fibrous scar tissue. There is no cure, and the cause is unknown. It leads to failure

Mae West and the then unknown Tom Selleck relax between takes of Myra Breckinridge

of the bone marrow, and symptoms include enlargement of the spleen, fatigue, and severe anemia. There is no specific treatment, but blood transfusions may be given to correct the anemia. The average life expectancy with this illness is five years (though Edith would live on for twelve). When she first went into the hospital to have a blood transfusion, she was registered under an assumed name hoping that nobody would find out. Mae West didn't know this and sent Edith some flowers under her real name. Ruby Graf remembers Edith shouting, "Get those flowers out of here!"

This was to be Mae's first color film. In the beginning, Mae and Edith thought she would be gowned in pink, powder blue, and lavender, the colors she wore in her private life, often in gowns Edith helped her with. Mae's longtime secretary Tim Malakowski recalls, "Miss Head would come over to the apartment and go to the garment district downtown with Miss West in the limousine to shop for fabric and beads. Then a friend of hers made the gowns." Producer Robert Fryer decided he wanted her in black and white throughout, as a reference to her films of the 1930s. Soon Raquel Welch, cast in the title role, wanted black and white as well. "She was terrible towards Mae," Edith would tell me later when Welch asked Edith to design for her television special. These tensions didn't cause any problems between Edith and Theadora, though. One day, Edith came into the 20th Century–Fox wardrobe department and Theadora told her they were shooting a scene showing fornication on an American flag. "What costumes are they wearing?" was Edith's only reply.

"I thought we were friends, and Edith always was nice to me, but every time I called her up to suggest we do something together for fun, she'd agree, but somehow we never did it. I did see her and Bill at Fox often, because one night a week the studio kept the commissary open for dinner and showed a new film afterwards. Bill was retired but he still knew a lot of people at Fox, so they'd come to that. He'd sit down, fold his hands over his cane, and go to sleep. Edith would 'work the room,' and sometimes she would approach people she knew and they'd turn away when they saw her coming. This was very painful for me to see but she felt she had to keep appearing at these industry functions."

As determined as Edith was not to "do lunch" or go shopping with Theadora, eventually Theadora extended an invitation that was too good for Edith to turn down. Theadora had been invited to give a lecture at the Barnsdale Park Festival of the Arts. "I don't enjoy public speaking so I asked Edith if she'd come too. She was dying to come! She even hired a limousine to be sure she didn't get lost driving over there."

The program was held in the historical Hollyhock House designed by Frank Lloyd Wright, and the event's producer Alan Cartnell asked me to make some slides of both ladies' designs. Edith talked and talked and it seemed to me that she had a great rapport with Theadora.

Theadora thought so too and asked me to get her and her now-husband, photographer Bruce McBroom, invited to Casa Ladera. But now Edith had another bone to pick with Theadora. When it was announced that Lucille Ball would star as Mame, she invited Edith to do her costumes but the producer, Robert Fryer, preferred Theadora. The assignment proved to be a nightmare for Theadora, because she designed clothes that were imaginative and true to the various decades (1920s through 1950s) in which the story takes place. Lucy would have much preferred what Edith would have done had she gotten the job: design outfits that were like the ones Lucy wore on her television show with a few unobtrusive period touches.

Since I didn't realize any of this initially, and since I'd seen Edith and Theadora chatting away merrily, I kept proposing a get-together, which Edith kept refusing. Finally she reluctantly agreed to receive Theadora and Bruce for an hour one Saturday afternoon. She warned me, however, that Myrtle didn't work that day and there would be nothing more than hors d'oeuvres to eat. We all had so much to say that the party went on for hours, and since she had no food, Edith kept going to the kitchen to heat up more plates of hors d'oeuvres. Thea and I wanted to see Myrtle's bedroom, a.k.a. "The Elizabeth Taylor Slept Here Room" (Bill had painted a sign to that effect outside the door). After a thorough inspection we went back downstairs and talked for several hours more.

Edith had some tickets to the industry preview of *The Man Who Would Be King* (1975), which she passed out to us (I sat next to Theadora and Bruce, and her main comment was "What cute camels"). Since we had all had such a good time that evening, I was sure these get-togethers among the five of us would become a regular thing, but Edith would never do it again. She would not permit it because she was so wary of people who had the talent she thought she lacked. Ironically, Theadora thoroughly admired her work. "So what if not every dress Edith designed was 'killer.' Sometimes the picture shouldn't have a killer dress," she says.

A few years earlier, back at Universal, there was no question of *Sweet Charity* (1969) not going to Edith, because it starred Shirley MacLaine. Edith had never designed for director Bob Fosse before but Tom Bronson, the set men's costumer, remembers that director and designer were in sync right from the start. It was an enormous production with virtually everything made from scratch, and one of the female costumers (who had known Edith at Paramount) later commented that Edith was getting forgetful, so Vincent Dee assigned that costumer to follow Edith around all day taking notes. In this period, Edith sat at a big table every day with her first Universal secretary Ruby Graf and Richard Hopper, the sketch artist, so that there was constant communication between the three. "She would come in with her rough sketches that she'd made the night before while lying in bed, hand them to Richard, and watch as he made the more finished versions. She always had an Eagle drawing pencil in her hand, and if she felt he was not getting the idea right, she'd reach over and correct it then and there," Ruby Graf now remembers. "He also kept her up to date. If she had some idea that was passé, he'd say, 'That went out with the high-button shoes,' and she'd discard it." Sometimes she would ask him for many variations on a theme (as she had done with Waldo Angelo and Grace Sprague). She also knew when she had more than she could handle, and in *Sweet Charity* there was one disco production number she let him do virtually on his own. "You know what the young people are wearing," she said. "Richard is very important to me," she told Ruby. "Don't do anything to him that might make waves." Nonetheless, she didn't like the caricatures he drew of famous people, and warned him, "If you do anything like that of me, you'll get your walking papers." Richard drew some anyway but hurriedly tore them up after he'd shown them to Ruby.

Ruby Graf helped Edith compile her syndicated newspaper column. "It was really all her ideas. She'd come in with a bunch of notes on scraps of paper and say, 'Put these together somehow.' " Eventually Ruby decided she didn't want to work with Edith anymore because "I had thought I would be a real assistant to her but she wouldn't let me do much and it was boring. Edith even brought in a television set from her house to keep me busy. She was shocked when I told her I was transferring. 'People don't leave me!' she said." The replacement, a young widow named Marion Price, was half Edith's age yet often seemed to me like a mother to her. She had a calm, quiet manner and effortlessly kept track of all the details Edith's life entailed, frequently talking to Bill Ihnen on the phone to make sure all would run smoothly.

By the early 1970s, many important films were being produced with no major female roles. Edith had occasionally designed for men at Paramount, and even when the male costumers did the bulk of the actor work on a film, she kept an eye on it and corrected what she thought wouldn't work. Still she was apprehensive when John Huston asked her to design his *Life and Times of Judge Roy Bean* which would not be made on the Universal lot. Feeling that this period western was too much of a stretch for her and Richard Hopper, she asked for Sheila O'Brien's help in seeing if Yvonne Wood would be willing to be nominally her sketch artist but in truth design the whole film. Yvonne didn't care who got the credit; indeed, "Edith just got her usual salary from Universal and I made more each week. Every day I'd give her a stack of sketches and explain to her what she needed to know, and she'd go off to the production meeting. If John Huston or Paul Newman knew what was going on, they never said anything, because they were so fond of her." Richard Hopper designed the pink 1920s dress that Ava Gardner wore in her one sequence at the end of the film, but it was Edith who supervised the fitting. Costumer Laurann Cordero remembers, "That costume actually had two period pink slips underneath. When we put it on Ava, we put the wrong one on first. It looked great but Edith immediately knew it was wrong when Ava came out of the dressing room. Ava said, 'It looks fine, let's leave it like this,' but in the end she went back and we did it right. Ava usually wasn't a problem if she had her glass of champagne."

Ava Gardner was playing the part of the celebrated actress Lily Langtry and it was necessary to take many portraits of her in fashions ranging from the 1880s to 1910s, which Paul Newman put up on his wall. Western Costume had a large collection of fragile authentic dresses and lace jabots from this period; they are usually kept only for research. So, for the portraits, Edith and Ava went to

Western, where Ava put the antique gowns on just long enough to be photographed on the spot.

It was Yvonne rather than Edith who followed the film to the location in Mexico, and Laurann Cordero remembers, "We ran out of lace collars for the women extras. Yvonne said to get her some of the white tissue paper we used for packing, and she tore all these little holes in it to make a collar. From a distance, we knew, it would work, but Huston put that extra right in front of the scene. I guess nobody knew but us."

Now that Edith was making so few films per year, she certainly had the time she had once lacked to involve herself more with the male costumes. On the other hand, it had become a very sore subject in the whole costume business that members of the Designers' Guild (now IATSE Local 892) would get prominent billing on a film and usually only design the women, while Costumers (Local 705) would generally purchase whatever was needed for the men and get small credit on a film and no mention on a television show. Vincent Dee did not see any reason to rock the boat that was sailing along very well with costumers he had worked with for years. Edith knew that he would not support any moves she made into the men's territory, so what she needed was a costumer she could build a strong rapport with, and she found Tom Bronson. "I had come into Universal under an apprentice program," he says, "and had worked my way up to being the set costumer for *Sweet Charity.* It was a musical, so everything was designed and made for it. I went on location to New York with it and she didn't, but she liked what I did. Then she started *Airport* with another key costumer who she didn't get along with, so she went to Vincent and asked for me. By this time I had enough hours in to be a key costumer. Vincent hated like anything to do favors for anybody, but she persisted and he finally gave in. *Airport* went great.

"By the time we started *Gable and Lombard* (1976), Edith was willing to turn a lot over to me. She knew she had had a good run in this business, and I knew what she would want, and when she saw what I did she was happy. One Saturday morning, James Brolin and Jill Clayburgh were going to pose for publicity pictures, and Edith and I both went to the photographer's studio [probably John Engstead's] to make sure they were all set. They were fine, so Edith said, 'What the fuck are we doing here? Would you like to play tennis at my house?' She didn't play very well, but still, I couldn't believe this was happening. I was so in awe of her."

Bronson left Universal, however, after he asked for a raise but Dee didn't give it to him. When Edith started working on *The Sting* (1973), a surefire reteaming of Paul Newman, Robert Redford, and director George Roy Hill, Peter Saldutti was the key costumer. His father, James Saldutti, was one of the main men's tailors at Western Costume, and Peter had started working at Paramount's Costume Department in the 1950s during school vacations. He had already worked as a key costumer with Edith on *Topaz*. "We had a wonderful drunken dinner together in Copenhagen. Hitchcock gave me a special credit on the film."

Every day Saldutti reported to Edith's bungalow, where they pored over old Sears Roebuck catalogues and Richard made sketches of their choices. A quite unusual maroon fabric was selected for the suit Paul Newman would wear in the beginning of the film but for the climax at the end, in the clandestine gambling joint where many major characters converge, only a narrow range of colors would be historically correct and yet each had to be distinctive. Saldutti later said that he stayed up many nights working this out. Newman and Redford approved the sketches (Edith would later recall they were easy to please) and the suits were put into work at Western Costume under the direction of Peter's father, James. Peter later told me that

Edith began to sense that she had nothing more to contribute, said less and less, and eventually stopped coming to the meetings. She did design two dresses for Eileen Brennan, however, and was on hand a lot during the shooting, talking to George Roy Hill. Nancy Dowd, who wrote a later Hill feature, *Slap Shot* (1977), says, "George had enormous faith in whatever Edith had to say about the look of a film. I remember her visiting the *Slap Shot* set several times, although she hadn't done the costumes. It was about hockey. My brother Ned was a hockey player and the technical advisor on the film, so he worked with the costumers, but still George valued whatever Edith had to say about anything."

All of the key costumers (Peter Saldutti, Andrea Weaver, and Bernie Pollack who worked with Robert Redford) understood that Edith would be given the major credit for *The Sting*. However, it was still a shock when, ignoring the usual industry practice of thanking a lot of people when accepting an Oscar, Edith mentioned only Newman and Redford and her husband. This time the uproar that followed was too big to ignore. Sheila O'Brien advised Edith to take out an ad in the Local 705 monthly newsletter thanking the costumers, and she did. By the time I went to work at Universal, Peter Saldutti had become the head of the men's department. When I asked him about *The Sting,* he told me his side of it, finishing by saying, "I hate her and I love her." Edith later admitted to me that she had "handled it badly."

After this, Edith was careful to stay out of the men's department, though one day she had to go in. There was a small room on that floor where the drivers waited to be assigned. Usually Kenny, who was Edith's driver, was very good at knowing right when she might need him, but this time he was in the waiting room and she had to go on the men's floor to find him. As she walked in, like Daniel entering the lions' den, nobody spoke, indeed most of the costumers very obviously turned their backs on her. Nonetheless, she knew just what joke to crack. Banging on the counter, she announced, "I want a costume." Seeing that a navy movie was being prepared, she added, "I'm gonna be an admiral. A rear admiral." The man she addressed retorted, "Lady, you can't play that part. Your butt's not big enough!" Everybody laughed, and Edith and Kenny left. Jack Connelly, who prepared the budgets, said, "I don't care what any of you birds say. I always liked her."

After a few years, when Edith's contract came up, Universal didn't want to renew, proposing instead to keep Edith on call "as needed." Sheila O'Brien advised her that this would be the kiss of death, that Charles LeMaire had had a similar arrangement with 20th Century–Fox and once he left, they never called him back. Instead, Edith's agents at William Morris proposed a much lower salary (about $500 a week) but Edith would keep all the perks of her job: the official position, the office, secretary, and the car. When I started as a men's costumer at Universal in 1976, I was actually taking home more pay than she was!

I had begun interviewing Mitchell Leisen and his associates in 1969 for the book that was published in 1974 as *Hollywood Director: The Career of Mitchell Leisen.* At first it didn't occur to me to talk to Edith, since Leisen frequently put her down as did various young people I knew who were trying to get established in costume work. When Leisen's health deteriorated seriously, his longtime mistress Natalie Visart suddenly arrived on the scene and she had nothing good to say about Edith either. Nonetheless, Leisen's secretary Eleanor Broder advised me to seek an interview with Edith and told me how Edith had secretly visited Mitchell with the sketches for *Red Garters* (1954) after the studio executives had warned her to not discuss them with him.

So I called up Edith's office at Universal to ask for an interview. Marion Price put me through, and though she had had no time to reflect, Edith instantly gave me a wonderful statement. Some weeks later I sat in on a discussion Edith was holding with the USC film students between screenings of *All About Eve* and *What a Way to Go.* I was amazed at what I saw and heard. Gone was the bossy lady I had so often seen on *Art Linkletter's House Party;* the version Edith presented of herself that night was highly intellectual. As I walked out with her afterwards, she told me more about working with Leisen. All of it was highly complimentary and I used it in my book.

In 1973 I received a grant from the Louis B. Mayer Oral History Program of the American Film Institute to interview four costume designers (the other three were Charles LeMaire, René Hubert, and Jean Louis). I have just reread the transcripts of the two interviews I conducted with her at her Universal office and though she was gracious, she didn't tell me much. However, at the end of the second one, she very timidly asked me if I would like to visit her at her home. A date was set up, she introduced me to Bill Ihnen and showed me around the house. I also met Myrtle City, who was busy cooking. Edith asked me if I would stay for dinner and when I had to refuse, she seemed genuinely disappointed. We made a date for the next week, however, and suddenly I was visiting them almost weekly and talking to her on the telephone almost every day. Since Edith was usually on the telephone when I arrived, I would go into the kitchen to see Myrtle and she would teach me something about cooking. Soon, even if Edith wasn't on the phone she'd say to me, "You'd better go see Myrtle before you sit down."

I was truly surprised that this world-famous woman was not sought after and seemed to have relatively few friends. Also, her behavior around the house was very different from the stoic character the world knew. At home she was gabby and animated, and she wore colorful clothing totally unlike her office outfits. (She said that she wore the bright colors to keep her husband happy.) I mostly visited the Ihnens on Wednesdays, since that was a night when Myrtle usually prepared a big meal. However, once when Edith asked me, "Are you coming over this week?" and I said, "Wednesday?" she hurriedly said, "Oh no, that's our anniversary! Come on Thursday!"

Bill Ihnen was always polite during meals and made a few comments here and there, but most of the time he said little while Edith and I chatted away. One evening when I dropped in unexpectedly, however, I got a true picture of how he and Edith related to each other when there were no guests. She was preparing *Gable and Lombard* and had told me that she needed to see some pictures of Lombard after 1937 (when Lombard made her last Paramount film.) She and Bill were eating in the kitchen when I arrived and he asked me to wait in the living room until they finished. She was going over every little thing that had happened at the studio that day (she was also working on *The Blue Bird* (1976) and there were already problems). Bill listened closely to what she was saying and offered fatherly advice that seemed to comfort her a great deal. Eventually he said he would go out to water the garden (which was enormous). Edith came into the living room carrying a platter of pork chops and potato salad for me to eat, announcing, "We were going to eat the leftovers tomorrow night because it is Myrtle's night off. Now I'm going to have to cook!" When I protested that I had just meant to drop the pictures off, she retorted, "You're too skinny! You're going to eat this and shut up!"

Bill Ihnen didn't dislike working in films but his real interest was painting. After 1956, he decided that he had enough money to live on. He stopped working as an art director and increasingly devoted himself to running the house and taking care of Edith. Myrtle City said, "I never saw Mr. Ihnen angry." Her sister Robbie, however, had a somewhat different take on him. "He liked to boss you around and give orders," she said.

Edith had a childlike need of attention from the world and from individuals, but her wariness of relationships and her reputation scared people away. Also, she wasn't as chummy with the important people in the business after working hours as many would assume. "An actress never calls you unless she wants something," she said once, sadly. Even Barbara Stanwyck was aloof. One night Edith and Bill were out at an art gallery opening when they ran into Stanwyck and Nolan Miller, who now designed all her clothes and was her good friend. Edith asked for Stanwyck's telephone number so she could invite her over. Stanwyck replied, very coldly, "If you want to reach me, you can call Nolan." Miller was pleasant under the circumstances, but he was designing important television shows Edith wished she could have been doing, so she never called. Another time, when I had just finished several weeks of working with director George Cukor on preparing a tribute to Joan Crawford, I remarked that Cukor invited many people he had never even met to dinner at his house, but he never invited me. "He's never invited me either," said Edith. "And after all the pictures I've designed for him!" The one who didn't forget was Alfred Hitchcock. When he invited Edith and Bill to dinner, she was almost breathless with anticipation.

Bette Davis was now living full-time in Los Angeles, and while she didn't socialize with Edith, she still requested her for costumes when she could. During preparation of a television movie, *Madame*

Sin, which was shot in 1971, Edith participated in a plot to get the unsuspecting Davis onto the television program *This Is Your Life.* The ruse was that Edith was supposed to be showing Bette sketches in John Engstead's studio for a "documentary." Suddenly host Ralph Edwards appeared, announcing, "This is your life, Bette Davis!" The star was "white with fury" as Edith later put it, but got into the limousine and gamely rode to the studio where an audience and old friends were waiting for the rest of the program. Nonetheless, she asked for Edith again for the Hallmark Hall of Fame show *The Disappearance of Aimee* in 1975.

In her capacity as costume designer for the Academy Awards, Edith made a V-necked gown for Elizabeth Taylor, in Taylor's favorite pale blue-violet shade, to wear to the 1972 Oscars. When auctioned off in 2000 at an AIDS fund-raiser, it brought the highest price ($167,500) in the show. Taylor was responsible for Head's only return to Paramount after her departure in 1967. For *Ash Wednesday* (1973), she was cast as a frumpy middle-aged woman who loses weight and gets her face lifted in a vain attempt to hold on to her husband, played by Henry Fonda. Virtually all of the scenes of the padded-up Taylor in the beginning of the picture ended up on the cutting-room floor, but those with the svelte one showed Edith's work at its best, understated, contemporary fashion. A close inspection of the credits revealed that one white evening gown and turban worn in a festival sequence were actually designed by Valentino. "When they were shooting in Italy, Elizabeth gained weight and they couldn't let out my dress, so they got that one," lamented Edith. She also lamented the fact that Paramount turned down her offer to tour the country promoting *Ash Wednesday* with fashion shows.

When Taylor left Richard Burton for the second time, she needed to stay in a place where she could be protected from the press and photographers, and she asked Edith to put her up at Casa Ladera. It was all arranged so quickly that Bill Ihnen, out for the day, couldn't be notified, and when he came home the guards wouldn't let him in! Taylor was installed in Myrtle's room along with her daughter Maria and new companion, Henry Wynberg. Bill set up a bed for Myrtle in the pantry, and Robbie was told she would be needed every day for the duration. "Miss Elizabeth was really very nice," Robbie remembers. "She came into the kitchen and said she was going to make herself a hamburger and would I like her to make one for me too! I said, 'No thanks.' " Robbie's husband, Edward Fisher, came around one day to visit his wife, and when the beautiful houseguest entered the kitchen, he stood, offered his hand, and said, "My name is Eddie Fisher." "Oh no, not another one," she cried laughingly as she ran back into the living room.

Some years later, after Taylor had married Senator John Warner, Edith and Bill stayed up past ten P.M. to watch them be interviewed on television. When Taylor stated that she had been married so many times because she always got married rather than have affairs, a furious Edith sputtered, "And who was that Wynberg fellow you brought into this house!" They continued to work together. Edith was planning to pad Taylor up to portray Queen Victoria in a Hallmark Hall of Fame production of *The Mudlark,* based on an earlier movie and novel, when the plans were changed and a silly modern story called *Return Engagement* (1978) was substituted.

Edith's one good friend at Universal was Yvonne Wood, who had become the manager of the women's department. Since Yvonne belonged both to Local 705 and the Designers' Guild, Dee let her choose whether she would run the department or come in as a designer, and she chose the former, because "it was steadier.

When you do a series or a picture, you get laid off when it is over. This way I worked all the time." Once I saw Edith and Yvonne returning after lunch. Edith was acting very conspiratorial and I heard her sternly tell Yvonne, "Don't you tell anybody where we were." As soon as she was gone I asked Yvonne where they had been. She said, "The Pancake House! Edith said if anybody found out she had eaten there she wouldn't be able to get any actresses to lose weight!"

I had become friendly with Yvonne when I was researching *Hollywood Costume Design,* and she was instrumental in my getting a job at Universal, a move Edith tried hard to discourage. "Don't let them know you know me," she said, referring to *The Sting* situation, "they all hate me in there."

At that time the wardrobe department occupied two buildings across the street from each other, both since torn down. On the bottom floor of the main building, the building known as the Clubhouse, was the men's department where each television show had a key costumer (who belonged to Local 705) and a rack of clothes for next week's episode. On the next floor was a similar department for the women except that their clothes were purchased or obtained by designers who belonged to Sheila O'Brien's Designer's Guild. Each had an office, and most of them were former men's costumers. They seldom were actually allowed to design and make costumes from whole cloth, however, because there simply wasn't enough time or budget. Sometimes when Sheila would protest that Vincent Dee wasn't treating them right, he'd say, "Look, none of these guys are Adrian, or Travis Banton," to which she'd reply, "Adrian, and Travis Banton, wouldn't work under these conditions."

Edith went into the main department from her bungalow almost every day and met the other designers, but at first didn't pay much attention to them. It was understood that she was only to work on big features and would never be asked to work on a television show. However, in the early 1970s, months went by with little activity beyond publicity, and she was rethinking this. (Part of her problem was that many producers didn't want to add her high salary to the budget.) She decided she would not be adverse to designing a television movie, provided it was important enough, and Olivia de Havilland provided her with an excellent opportunity. *The Screaming Woman* (1972) had been prepared as a project for Helen Hayes, but ultimately Hayes had to drop out, as the script required her to be out in a forest all day in cold weather, which her arthritis wouldn't tolerate. Olivia accepted the role with some misgivings over the shooting schedule and the title, which, she was assured, would be changed. As she later told the students at the American Film Institute, "[Producer] Bill Frye had a costume designer he wanted but I insisted on Edith! That woman is a marvel!" Not surprisingly, Edith first suggested a black suit with some white touches. Frye said, "I don't see her in black. Violet! That's it, violet!" Olivia continues, "It was a blazing hot day, but Edith met me at eight A.M. at a fabric store to select the material for the suit, and Bill Frye joined us later at an exclusive store to shop for everything else. Neither of them asked me what I thought, and I just sat there enjoying the air-conditioning, because I knew what they would choose would be right." From then on, Edith made it known that she would work on television movies, and even appeared in a *Columbo* episode (starring Anne Baxter) as herself. After carrying out a lengthy exchange with Peter Falk flawlessly, Edith exited so close to the camera that she went out of focus. This was television, so they didn't retake the scene.

Frye used Edith on some other television projects, and when he was assigned to produce the film *Airport '77,* he talked to her often during the early stages of production. For the role of the wealthy socialite, he hoped to cast his good friend Irene Dunne, but she refused to come out of retirement. Greer Garson also had to say no, because the role had many scenes in the water and she too had arthritis. Edith related these events to me with breathless enthusiasm after swearing me to secrecy. My response was, "I bet they'll ask Olivia [de Havilland] next." Edith said, "Oh, no, she'll never work on this lot after what happened on *The Screaming Woman.*" (Olivia had secured an injunction against Universal airing the program with that title and almost blocked the broadcast, settling at the last minute the day before.)

Nonetheless, she finally was cast in the role. Edith called me to relate this news, then met with the star and Bill Frye at Casa Ladera. The character would need only one outfit, and Olivia had decided it should be purple, to convey the socialite's exuberance. Edith was just as determined that it would be black, to be as flattering as possible, and that Olivia could convey the spirit through her acting alone. This was one time when Edith did not give in to the star. The first time I saw Olivia wearing what Edith had made I was amazed. It was a seemingly simple sheath, yet so perfectly executed that Olivia seemed ten pounds thinner than she did in the Dior suits she usually wore. I asked Edith if she'd given Olivia a corset, and she said, "No, just a slip." When an exhaustive search failed to turn up a pair of black suede gloves in Los Angeles, Edith loaned Olivia a pair of her own.

Edith never wanted to get dressed on Sundays. She explained, "Because if you do, you might be tempted to go out of the house and not get enough rest." Tiny, dressed in a nightgown, with her hair down her back, Edith in her garden seemed more like a child, like the one Jennifer Jones portrayed in *Portrait of Jennie* (1948), or the one Leslie Caron was in *Gigi* (1958) a year or two before the story starts. She often had me or John Engstead visit her on Sundays, to sit outside if the weather was warm, or we'd come indoors and fix something to eat. Myrtle always had Sundays off, as a dedicated member of the African Methodist and Episcopal Church. (The church would later honor her on the same day it gave a citation to civil rights pioneer Rosa Parks.)

Olivia's role in *Airport '77* was hardly demanding, compared to most she'd done, but she approached it the way she did any other, with absolute dedication and concentration. The set costumer, a friend of mine, warned me that I must never speak to her if we met by chance on the lot, as she excluded everything but the scene coming up from her mind. The weekends, however, she was her usual enthusiastic self with nowhere to direct her boundless energies. Having lived full-time in Paris for over twenty-five years, she had few friends left in Los Angeles. Because she was unhappy with the head shots the set photographer had taken, she decided to hire John Engstead to take some pictures of her in her black dress. While they were at it, she would also do some generic ones in other clothes, and since she hadn't brought much with her from home, she asked Edith to pull some dresses from the stock wardrobe for her to wear.

Edith's response to this request was most uncharacteristic. Very annoyed, she brought some pieces home, then called John and me and told us both to be at her house Sunday for the fitting. When we got there, she told us point-blank that she intended to get Olivia in and out within a few minutes and that whatever she put on we were to say looked fabulous. Then I was to drive her to her hotel, as it would take forever for a cab to find Casa Ladera.

It all happened just like that, and soon I was driving Olivia back. She was so stunned she could hardly speak. John and I often discussed this strange event afterwards. Was Edith overdue for a blood transfusion and thus weaker than usual? Was her Sunday rule that inflexible? We didn't think so; she always let us come if we wanted to. Was she so used to dealing with difficult personalities that one who was very friendly actually threatened her more? We never figured it out.

The next year Olivia made *The Swarm* (1978) for producer Irwin Allen, with dresses by Allen's usual designer, Paul Zastupnevich. Thereafter, when she needed a gown to wear to the Academy Awards or other special event, she would ask Zastupnevich to design it.

Generally, however, Edith liked receiving people at Casa Ladera. The other members of the Designers' Guild board knew they would always go there for board meetings, because Edith didn't drive at night, but she was a most gracious hostess. Moss Mabry says, "We'd go there and she'd have every kind of liquor you could imagine at the bar, and wonderful snacks. And then these same people would be bad-mouthing her two days later at Western Costume." Howard Shoup remembered one meeting where, "the arguments were getting so bitter that I finally had to interrupt and remind everyone that I had just turned seventy that day and wasn't very happy about it. Edith went into the kitchen and got out a cake, but the only candle she could find was a big red Christmas candle with holly on it. Edith came out, singing 'Happy birthday, dear Shoupie,' and with her strange little voice it was so funny, everybody had to laugh."

Anne Baxter was active on the board of the California Chamber Symphony and she persuaded the Ihnens to hold a benefit at Casa Ladera. Rosalee Sass, then production coordinator, had to deliver some food on the previous Sunday afternoon. She found them lounging by the pool in white terry-cloth bathrobes and quite happy to have company. Gabbing away, Edith led the way to the refrigerator. Normally, the Symphony would never ask the same homeowner to hold two benefits, but when Edith was away for a long while working on *The Blue Bird,* Baxter knew Bill was lonely, and prevailed upon him to hold a special soiree for only thirty donors who had given upwards of $10,000. The gimmick was that there would be only candle light, outdoors and in. Filling the pathway up the hill and the house with candles, and staging the chamber music, gave Bill a chance to put on a bravado event that he enjoyed.

Marylou Luther, fashion editor of the *Los Angeles Times,* and her husband, Arthur Imparato, publisher of the trade paper *Fabric News,* often socialized with the Ihnens and George Peppard who lived next door. The two couples went to see *A Chorus Line* together and the next day Edith was livid over the "Tits and Ass" number. She repeated the offending lyrics again and again, adding, "Marylou agreed with me completely." Whenever there was a fabric trade convention in town, the Imparatos would give a big afternoon reception in their Beverly Hills mansion and Marylou would ask me to bring Edith. Marylou also wanted to introduce Edith to the newly hot Parisian couturier Thierry Mugler. Edith didn't know if he spoke English (actually, he did) and was afraid she couldn't remember enough French, so she invited me to translate. A good time was had by all. She did remember her French, however. When I sensed she was getting bored, I invited some Parisian friends of mine to meet her. After a slow start, the French came pouring back.

Arthur Imparato did Edith a big favor when he suggested to his friends at *Vogue Patterns* that she be hired to design a line of patterns for them in 1973. Previously she had turned down Fred Hayman of the well-known Giorgio store in Beverly Hills, saying she didn't understand designing retail clothes, but she thought patterns would be different. Koko Beall, *Vogue*'s chief designer at that time, remembers, "With the Parisian couturiers, when we found a design we knew would sell, we bought it and put it out without changing it. Edith told me that, in her designing, she was always guided by the script and the actress, and this would be a challenge. I knew what would sell, so I worked up a bunch of sketches with my staff and came out to Los Angeles. She chose the ones she liked and made suggestions. If I thought it would work we changed it, otherwise I said no. She was very easy to work with." Edith's contract with Universal allowed her to keep the income from this work, and soon Edith and June Van Dyke were staging fashion shows all over the country to promote the patterns. These tours were organized for *Vogue Patterns* by Art Joanides, head of publicity. "She was so insecure," he says now. "Once my wife and I were in Los Angeles and we invited her to dinner at Spago. When we came to pick her up, she asked my wife if she thought her dress was right for that restaurant. And Edith was giving advice to women all around the world!"

June Van Dyke arranged other (non-*Vogue*) tours on her own. Mary Hopkins, then vice president of merchandising at the May Company Department Stores, remembers, "At the Annapolis Mall, we had an outdoor staging area that was capable of holding between eight and ten thousand people, and Edith filled it two nights in a row! She was professional but quiet when she arrived in town, but boy, when she took the stage it was magic! I accompanied her to Washington, D.C., to do a television show to publicize it. One of the models who was supposed to wear a cloche hat, pushed it back away from her forehead so she could show off her face more. Edith said, 'You tell that girl that if she doesn't wear the hat right, I'm not going on the show!' I made sure the girl wore the hat right!"

The biggest problem in staging these shows was getting enough "star wardrobe" to show. Edith had left Paramount in such a hurry that she didn't take enough gowns with her when she could have, and now Paramount refused to loan or rent them to her. The ones she did have were wearing out. Thus it was a blessing in disguise when a box of several weary dresses got lost in transit and the insurance company paid Western to make new copies. The expert cutter and fitter Wilma Dunn supervised this work. Moss Mabry remembers Edith telling him, "This lady in Kansas asked me if this was really the gold dress that Grace Kelly wore in *To Catch a Thief*. She looked at it as something magical. I didn't have the heart to tell her it was a copy!"

Debbie Reynolds agreed to let the Harold Lloyd Estate borrow some of her extensive costume collection when plans were being discussed to open the late actor's mansion to the public in 1973. Edith offered to help make the choices and set it up, and the manager of the estate, Woody Wise now says, "I had seen Edith many times on television and I was scared of her. But in person she was sweet and funny." In the end, however, the plans for a museum were abandoned.

The Ihnens were invited to a dinner at the White House during the Reagan presidency. At first, Edith was annoyed that they were expected to pay their own expenses but she accepted anyway. Bill had re-created the White House of the World War I era for the film *Wilson* (1944), and won an Academy Award. At the reception, he asked so many questions about the draperies et cetera that Secret Service became alarmed, until he explained his special interest, and then he was invited to return the next day for a special private tour. He learned that all the materials that seemed to be authentically old were actually fireproof. When the Los Angeles County Museum of Art showed *Wilson* as part of a summerlong tribute to

20th Century–Fox, the film curator Ronald Haver asked me to invite Bill to take a bow. Bill had already ordered tickets (which he gave to Myrtle and Robbie), so he sat with me while Haver interviewed the director Henry King onstage. King was in his nineties but still had plenty to say. "Damn long-winded bastard," said Bill. "One time he called me into his office and said, 'I want to tell you about fences, Ihnen. There are all kinds. There are picket fences . . .' and I had to listen to all this!"

Bill could see well enough to continue his painting, but he became increasingly wary of driving at night. If Edith couldn't get Elois Jenssen to drive her to some event, she'd ask me. One evening she wanted to see a screening of the Hallmark Hall of Fame television drama *Taxi* because she was working with the director on a new show. Off we went in my rattletrap Honda, but when we got to the Academy building on Wilshire Boulevard, she didn't want to be seen getting out of a car like that, so she said, "Oh David, it's such a nice evening. Why don't we park blocks away and have a nice walk." The film was quite impressive, due to the performances of its two stars, Eva Marie Saint and Peter Falk. I noticed that during the screening Edith kept clutching her throat. Afterwards I asked why. "Eva Marie's neck is so scrawny," she said. "I wanted to cover it up with a chiffon scarf." Around the same time, Edith and Bill passed a Sunday afternoon watching the film *Call Me Madam.* Knowing how emaciated Vera-Ellen was, Edith later voiced amazement that Irene Sharaff would put her in a backless dress that "showed all her vertebrae." Bill interrupted and said it was the fault of his old colleague, cinematographer Leon Shamroy. Similarly, Edith's main comment after seeing the sensationally popular *Star Wars* (1977) was that the designer should have hidden the zipper of Carrie Fisher's dress in the side seam rather than putting it down the center of the back. (Carrie Fisher, by the way, now owns Casa Ladera.)

Although both of them seemed very solemn, Edith and Bill actually had their own private humorous language that they used when writing to each other and even in the presence of guests. Their oddball sense of humor was manifested in various ways. Once Edith and Bill drove to Palm Springs to attend the funeral of a longtime friend. They hoped to get back before nightfall, but only got as far as Pasadena, a suburb of Los Angeles. Edith had recently done a fashion show at a brand-new hotel in Pasadena, and now she and Bill showed up at the front desk and asked for a room. Recognizing her, the clerk was amazed to suddenly see her again, especially since they had no reservations, no luggage, and obviously lived nearby. Feeling no responsibility to explain what was really going on, she said blithely, "Oh I was just telling my husband what a nice place this is and we decided to come here to stay." Once they were in bed, they heard a party going on in the next room, so they got up, poured stiff drinks, and settled down again. Later, when the noise started up again, they had another round. "Multimillion dollar place like that and the walls were paper-thin," said Bill Ihnen, shaking his head, a few days later.

Bill would sometimes muse about the big issues of life. When Edith was preparing *The Blue Bird* and *The Man Who Would Be King,* she was driving less and less, and she could not have Kenny drive her to her office since neither was a Universal picture. Quietly Bill filled in, and I kept him company one day while she worked. Even as an old man, Bill was still very sexual and on this day he was feeling that desire could be a burden. "Why can't we just lay eggs to reproduce, like fish do," he said. "It would be so much more humane."

Coldwater Canyon had been almost a sleepy rural space when the Ihnens moved into Casa Ladera, with the house far from the street and any other houses. Yet, the first night Edith and Bill dined there they could hear voices, for the canyon was shaped in such a way that sound from one of the other houses bounced right into theirs. Bill set about planting as much vegetation as he could to deaden this sound and also give them added privacy; they also bought more land when it became available. Theirs was the last property on the Los Angeles side of the border with Beverly Hills, and Edith often noted the irony that Los Angeles property taxes were actually higher than those of her Beverly Hills neighbors.

By the time I knew them, Coldwater Canyon Boulevard had gotten to be such a busy thoroughfare that both Edith and Bill were afraid to drive on it during the evening rush hour. The shortest way for her to drive home from Universal was through the San Fernando Valley, going west on Ventura Boulevard, then south on Coldwater, but this meant making a left turn into her driveway and she said the drivers coming the other way never gave her a chance to cut in. Instead she took the long way around, past the Beverly Hills Hotel, so she could enter on a right turn. Because of the heavy traffic, coming home one night, Edith was alarmed to find Bill not there when she arrived. "Where's Mr. Ihnen?" she asked Robbie nervously. "He realized it was your birthday and he was afraid you'd come home and he'd have no present." "He'd better be," joked Edith.

Edith was more worried about keeping Myrtle happy than she was about Bill. Cheerful and supportive as she was, Myrtle was nonetheless determined to retire when she got her Social Security at the age of sixty-five so she could devote herself full-time to church activities. The idea of breaking in somebody new terrified Edith. Finally a compromise was reached whereby Myrtle would now work three days a week instead of five, for the same salary, and would only have to cook and take care of Edith's clothes.

Robbie would be brought in more often to help, and a young man named Ralph, from the church, was hired to clean. Edith suggested that Myrtle take a full hour after lunch to rest. She got into the habit of watching a certain soap opera, and soon Bill was hooked on it too. This was in the period when soaps still used organ music to set the mood, and since Bill was hard of hearing, he played it very loud so that Edith and I could hear the organ music all around the house. It annoyed her but she was careful not to say anything.

Edith used to refer to Bill as "The Great Wall of China" and Myrtle was very heavy too, so Edith announced that all three of them would go on a diet using recipes she provided. Myrtle dutifully cooked the food as directed, but after a month, only Edith had lost any weight.

I remarked to Edith once that I had been served fish for several weeks in a row. She sighed and said, "Myrtle didn't just give up eating meat for Lent; she also gave up cooking it!" Another time she was dismayed that Myrtle had thawed a frozen cake for dessert rather than bake one herself. Using her usual diplomacy, Edith strolled into the kitchen after dinner and remarked, "Myrtle dear, I can't believe any company would sell such a cake." Myrtle just smiled and I wondered if she got the point.

Edith always referred to her husband as "Bill" when talking to others, and often called him that too, though when she couldn't find him quickly and became anxious, she called out, "Wiard, Wiard." When she felt affectionate and wanted a hug, she called him "Willie." Other times she called him "My Lord and Master." Whatever we were talking about, she tried hard to include him in the conversation. Once I was telling her about seeing Lena Horne in a concert. She said, "Bill always loved Lena Horne." He had been quiet but now he suddenly said, "When we went to see her at the Coconut Grove, our friend said, 'Don't look now but Bill Ihnen is having an orgasm!' " Then he was quiet again.

Nothing would have made Bill Ihnen happier than to have Edith retire and stay home all day long as he did, but he was wise enough to know it could never be. During the many weeks she was gone in 1974, working first in the Soviet Union on *The Blue Bird,* then in the Middle East on *The Man Who Would Be King,* I called him from time to time. He would say, "She's not coming back yet." Finally he admitted, "It gets so lonely here."

Edith had started working on both films at the same time, in Hollywood. There had been an earlier version of *The Blue Bird* in 1940, for which Bill had done the sets. Now Edith planned one kind of headdress for Ava Gardner, who was playing the part of Luxury, which would not have completely covered her hair. The famed hairdresser Sidney Guilaroff, who was on hand to reassure his friend Gardner, told Edith that he was planning to tape Ava's face to lift up her wrinkles and that Edith would have to design another headdress, which would cover his appliances. Edith did so. Cicely Tyson also had problems when she had her Cat costume on, for it covered her hands with built-in gloves, and when she had it on, Tyson couldn't put on or take off her green contact lenses.

At the same time these costumes were being made up at Western, Edith was already working on *The Man Who Would Be King,* which was due to start shooting later, in a most remote place. With her experience as a world traveler and anthropologist, Renie Conley would have seemed a more logical designer for this film, but John Huston stuck with Edith. I remember a man from the production who came to her office every day with a stack of *National Geographics,* patiently waiting until she finished her *Blue Bird* business so she could start making sketches with Richard for

King. I warned her that Michael Caine's shoulders would look narrow, considering his height and next to Sean Connery's broad shoulders. She said, "Oh, they're going to be in uniforms and with all those epaulets and things nobody will notice!"

When she finally got back from both films, Edith had me and Roddy McDowell to dinner and had plenty to say about both pictures. Even with the major star wardrobe for *The Blue Bird* completed at Western Costume, much remained to be made in Moscow, and there the language barrier was almost insurmountable. She was given a translator, but this lady only had a diplomatic vocabulary, not couture terms. When Edith asked for sequins, they had no idea what she was talking about. She tried the French word "paillette"—to no avail. Finally she found one sewn to another costume and they understood, but they didn't have any. They ended up by taking them off the other costume. As a good friend of director George Cukor (who was also quite elderly by then), Roddy wondered how he was managing. Edith said, "He is incredibly patient. I don't know anybody else who could put up with what George has to suffer."

The Man Who Would Be King, however, was going much better once Edith got to the location. She thought Caine and Connery were lovable rogues, and the only real problem occurred when the leading lady had to be replaced. Caine's wife, Shakira, a beautiful woman who had not previously acted, was drafted for the part. Edith improvised a costume for her out of some magenta silk and all was well.

After dinner we moved into the living room, and Roddy asked Edith what she knew about Mae West's forthcoming appearance on a television interview with Dick Cavett. "Paul Novak (West's longtime companion) called me," she said, "and asked me if I would help. I asked him if he could still get her into any of the costumes from *Myra Breckinridge.* He said he thought he could still get her into one of the corsets and one of the dresses."

The show had rented a soundstage at Paramount to tape the "interview," which would really be nothing more than Cavett asking questions that cued West's famous one-liners. The production was so low-budget that they hadn't hired a makeup man for West. Edith said, "They sent somebody to the stage next door to ask the makeup man on the TV series shooting there would he please come over and tape Miss West's face? And he did. Mae sat silently in the makeup chair, alternately falling asleep, waking up, and falling asleep again. Finally she asked Paul Novak for an orange."

After all this, Edith was astounded to read sometime later that West had signed to make a film of one of her old plays, *Sextette.* Edith agreed to design the costumes, thinking that Mae might "need a friend." She thought it would at least be a chance to carry out what had been the original concept for *Myra Breckinridge:* all pastels, like Mae wore in real life. The budget was too small to hire Richard Hopper, so Edith did dozens of little sketches herself while lying in bed. A few of them were made up but mostly Mae wore her own clothes (which had been designed at various times by Edith anyway). Marvin Paige, casting director on the film, says, "they just opened them up and added several inches of material down the back. They had to make sure she didn't turn her back to the camera but then she didn't move much in most of the scenes anyway."

I lived near Western Costume and Edith sometimes invited me to keep her company when she was there working. One day I sat with her for several hours while the cutter and fitter Lily Fonda tore strips of muslin to make a pattern for a dress Susan Sarandon would wear in *The Great Waldo Pepper* (1975). Edith answered any questions Lily had, but didn't offer suggestions while Lily worked. When it was all pinned together, Edith examined it gravely, then approved it. Lily asked what they should do for buttons, dye some plastic ones to match or cover some with the fabric. Edith asked me what I thought, and I suggested they use covered buttons. I also got to be good friends with Tzetzi Ganev, another cutter and fitter who still works for Western. Recently she remembered, "Edith loved controversy. When the actress didn't make a problem, Edith would. She'd come in and say, 'Why did you do it this way? I wanted that way.' And when we changed it, then she wanted it changed back. She had no scruples. But she had charisma. She could really talk those actresses into wearing things they didn't like at first."

Tzetzi and her crew made all the dresses for an elaborate wedding for a friend of Natalie Wood. (Edith designed them as a favor to Wood.) Soon after, Wood started a new film at Universal, *The Last Married Couple in America* (1980). She approved all of Edith's sketches but in the end actually wore only one of the finished dresses in the film. June Van Dyke said, "Natalie wanted a younger look." Edith said that Wood was a compulsive shopper and saw the film as a good chance to go on a shopping spree. "She took all these pairs of solid-gold earrings and said she'd return the ones she didn't use, but of course she didn't. The studio had to pay for them all," Edith scolded. It was the end of a long friendship.

After this, Edith was working mainly in television, and was terrified of being laid off. The way she went after TV movies she formerly would have disdained reminded me of Scarlett O'Hara marrying her sister's beau. It alarmed Sheila O'Brien, who also represented the other Universal designers who usually got these assignments. One such project was a mini-series of Louisa May Alcott's *Little Women* (1978), starring Dorothy McGuire as

Marmee. I saw the aged dresses checked out of Western and shuddered. Judging from the floral prints, most of them had been made in the thirties and used endlessly ever since. After I saw Meredith Baxter come in for a fitting, I remarked to Edith how beautiful she was. "Yes, but she's thirty if she's a day," said Edith. When the mini-series got respectable ratings, NBC decided to make a weekly series of *Little Women,* and Edith agreed to work on it. It was the first (and last) time she would be involved with a weekly series.

Edith herself was looking younger than she had in years, thanks to a face-lift. I knew something was afoot when I called the house several times and Bill would only say that she was "out of town, visiting friends." I thought this sounded very strange since she never would have gone anywhere without him unless it was work-related. When I next saw her at the studio, I was alarmed by the bruises on her face. "Aren't you going to tell me how great I look?" she asked. The doctor in Santa Barbara had indeed done a good job, even the scars along her ears from her first face-lift were gone, but I told her it was too soon to be out in public unless she wore heavier makeup and a chignon behind each ear rather than a single one in the back (all of which she did for the next several weeks). She went on to say that she had planned to leave town for a while to get her cataracts removed, but at the last minute the eye surgeon decided that they weren't ready yet so she had the face-lift instead. She did indeed have the cataracts removed soon thereafter and was then more confident about both her driving and her drawing.

Edith's general health was declining in the late 1970s but she never admitted it to anyone. Rather than acknowledge her real problem (which was incurable), she said she had anemia, which didn't sound too bad. Suddenly, however, Bill Ihnen's condition became critical. In late 1978, I began to notice that he was losing weight quickly and moved around the house with great effort. One evening she told me that he was going in for a check-up, and I never saw him again. I kept coming to dinner, and sometimes when I called Edith up, Bill still answered the phone. Myrtle and Robbie told me that he had nurses in the house taking care of him, but I never saw them. Edith tried to act as if nothing was wrong.

Eventually, however, he was hospitalized with cancer of the prostate and died on June 22, 1979. Marylou Luther and I attended the funeral together at Forest Lawn. She told me that once when she and Arthur were visiting the Ihnens and Edith stepped out of the room, Bill had said that he was determined that Edith would not have a Catholic funeral for him. Nonetheless, that day, though the service was essentially Protestant, Edith also had a Catholic priest on hand to participate a little. George Folsey and his wife had driven her to Forest Lawn and looked after her that day.

Edith was never the same after Bill's death. She kept herself as busy as she could with her *Vogue* patterns, fashion shows that June Van Dyke booked and staged for her, and the occasional television movie, but I sensed she was getting bored. When my aunt Doris Leapard came to town from Tuscaloosa, Alabama, I took her up to Casa Ladera and she and Edith hit it off right away. Doris lost no time in inviting Edith to visit her and her husband, Bill, and give a little fashion show at the local Bama Theater to raise money for the arts council. June Van Dyke wasn't happy about this at all. She usually got good fees for Edith's appearances and now Edith was giving it away for free. But Edith was restless and bored, and off to Alabama she went.

Edith loved the attention she got from Doris and Bill. They put her to sleep in a bed with hand-embroidered sheets, and fed her gourmet food. When Edith said she'd never seen a dogwood tree in bloom, Bill drove all over town until he found one to show her. Her appearance at the theater was a smash hit.

Back in Los Angeles, Edith grew increasingly restless. "Oh, it was terrible when she stayed home all day," recalls Robbie. "She'd look around the house and say things like 'I'm paying three people to work for me and you can't even water the geraniums.' " Robbie and Myrtle were the only ones who knew the true nature of Edith's illness. "She said, 'Here I am dying of cancer and you women can't lift a finger.' Myrtle said, 'Miss Head, I'm old too.' "

By this time I was working at the Warner Bros. wardrobe department. One evening, as I was closing up, I decided to give Edith a call. Anne Baxter, who was staying at Casa Ladera, answered the phone. She told me she had seen Edith eating cream of wheat with white sugar for breakfast, and was sure that if only Edith improved her diet she would feel just fine. John Engstead, who was Baxter's good friend as well as Edith's, suffered greatly from arthritis, which he attacked with a rigorous regime of diet and exercise. He was sure that if Edith stopped spending whole days in bed and got on an exercise program, all would be fine. Neither he nor Baxter knew that what Edith had was incurable, and the painful blood transfusions she was undergoing were just buying time.

Once I went to see her in the hospital near downtown Los Angeles, where she had been for several days. In a nightgown, with her hair down her back and IVs taped to the backs of her hands, Edith was fit to be tied. She kept pacing around the room nervously and suddenly she'd hit the limit of how far the IV cords could stretch. But then, a few days later, she was back at her house. Then she was off on another tour to promote her *Vogue* patterns. Somehow I felt that Edith was so strong-willed, somehow she'd always manage to get just a little more time.

Rosemary Clooney called unexpectedly one day and asked if Edith would help on a television special starring her daughter-in-law, Debby Boone. Edith made some new costumes and recycled others from stock at Western Costume. The grateful Boone sent her a painted trunk, which is now in the Margaret Herrick Library of the Academy of Motion Picture Arts and Sciences. Some years later, when I was working on a benefit for the American Film Institute and Rosemary Clooney was rehearsing her songs, I took her aside and told her much Edith had enjoyed doing the special. "I'm so glad to hear that," said Clooney. "At the time we were afraid we were imposing on her."

Edith's greatest fear was that Universal would not pick up her option each time it came up for renewal. Joanne Reeves, then secretary to Universal's head of publicity, says, "As an executive, she was allowed a certain number of guests on the private tour around the studio. Towards the end, she was afraid of making waves. When she wanted to have somebody as her guest on the tour, she'd call me and ask to arrange it but she said, 'Please, can you fix it so it doesn't look like I asked.' "Whether or not she had anything that needed doing in the studio, virtually every day she managed to get to her office and be seen lunching in the commissary. I began to notice a new respect for her, even among those whose careers had suffered the most in Edith's relentless drive to keep hers going forever.

Suddenly, when she'd despaired of getting any new assignments, Universal asked her to do a small job. Carl Reiner and Steve Martin were planning an unusual film, to be called *Dead Men Don't Wear Plaid* (1982). A spoof of 1940s private-eye movies, it would use a lot of footage from real 1940s films, intercut with new black-and-white footage of Martin as a private eye. At first Edith was only to design four dresses for the leading lady, Rachel Ward, but then she was asked to design Martin's clothes too. Finally

Reiner realized he would need to replicate some of the costumes that appeared in the vintage clips. "Can you do a dress like Ingrid Bergman wore in *Notorious?*" he asked. "I designed *Notorious,*" replied Edith proudly.

The biggest problem was the budget. Although the film would be a Universal release, it was actually filmed at the Laird International Studio in Culver City. Shirley Strom, who had become Edith's last Universal secretary when Marian Price went to work in Alfred Hitchcock's office, says, "She was so weak but she came into the office every day." Peter Saldutti, who had become the head of the Universal wardrobe upon the retirement of Vincent Dee, told Edith they could afford to give her either a sketch artist or a driver, but not both. She could manage to drive to the studio but not an unknown place in Culver City, so Edith would have to make her own sketches, and the drawing board terrified her.

One Saturday morning, at seven A.M., I got a call from Edith, whose voice had become so hoarse I hardly recognized it. "Kid, do you have any forties research?" she asked. I told her I had albums of clippings from fashion magazines but added, "What would you need those for? You wrote the book." "Bring them over here," she commanded.

I arrived to find her pacing her bedroom in near hysteria. She started looking through the albums and calmed down. The photographs were making her brain percolate with ideas and she talked, half to me, half to the pictures. "Oh what a terrible jungle print . . . that sleeve isn't too bad . . ." Soon she was ignoring the books altogether. She sat down at the drafting table in her room and began to draw. One idea after another flowed from her mind, and we worked in silence all morning. As she finished a sketch, she'd hand it to me and tell me to clean up the stray marks or to blacken the background with a felt pen, but mostly I watched her.

I had never seen such virtuosity. At that moment, I knew what she had never known: Edith Head was a great designer.

Around noon, when she had a pile of about fifty sketches, Edith, still in her nightgown, announced that she was finished, and we went into the kitchen to make lunch. I remember that she cooked lamb chops on her special indoor barbecue.

In the same period, I was asked by James Waterson of the May Company to produce a special promotion for the new Muppet movie. The idea was that we would ask several prominent Hollywood designers to reinterpret one of their most famous dresses as worn by Miss Piggy. Helen Rose had Donna Peterson make a sketch of Miss Piggy wearing Lana Turner's white chiffon-and-fur number from *The Bad and the Beautiful* (1952), Elois Jenssen did her up in Lucille Ball's black velvet pants from *I Love Lucy,* and, of course, Edith chose to make Miss Piggy into Mae West in *She Done Him Wrong.* When I told Edith that we would need a 16″ × 20″ sketch rather than the 11″ × 14″ she was used to doing, she measured out the proportions on the board using her hand and forearm and drew the sketch herself.

Part of the promotion was a documentary film made by the May Company staffers. I went to interview each of the designers about his or her career. The day we interviewed Edith, she was just coming back from the *Dead Men Don't Wear Plaid* set. She was coughing throughout but managed to do her usual professional job. A few days later, I joined the filmmakers at the Los Angeles County Museum of Art where they were filming Edith putting together an exhibit of her dresses. Each one she would describe, but she had trouble remembering who had worn them and the circumstances of the film, so I prompted her before each vignette was filmed. As it turned out, this would be the last time I saw her.

Sheila O'Brien told me Edith was back in the hospital, and a

Edith's own 1981 sketch of Miss Piggy as Mae West

few days later she called to tell me when Edith had come home. I called the house and the nurse said, "She wants to talk to you." It was a long time before Edith got to the telephone and when she did, we talked at great length and about serious subjects, like what was I going to do with the rest of my life. I said I thought I'd go on doing wardrobe work. Edith's advice was: "Get out of this business, kid. You don't lie well enough." The same day she also talked to Yvonne Wood. At first the conversation was just the usual—plans to get together when the movie was finished—but at the end, Edith said, "I love you, Yvonne. I really do." Yvonne later told me, "That was how she said good-bye to me."

That night Edith started coughing so violently that she ruptured her esophagus. Preparing to take her to the hospital, the nurse told

Robbie, "She's not coming back." Edith died soon thereafter, on October 24, 1981.

June Van Dyke arranged a beautiful funeral at the Church of the Good Shepherd in Beverly Hills. I sat there quietly with my mother, as Bette Davis, Janet Leigh, and Elizabeth Taylor filed in. Howard Shoup and his longtime companion Sascha Brastoff passed me. Ever mischievious, Shoupie said to me, "Be sure you come to *mine!*" Within the year, he would be gone too.

Epilogue

"You gotta give 'em what they want, kid. If you don't, they'll find somebody who will." That was Edith's advice to me when, during my brief career as a costumer, I was having trouble with an actor. Most observers would say that is a summation of her career, but I think a more accurate one might have been, "You gotta make them think you're giving them what they want." While she was famous for giving in, she didn't always, but almost always she managed to create something that pleased most, if not all of the people involved.

The Hitchcock pictures gave Edith her best opportunities, of course, because of their top-grade scripts and casts but also because in this case she had only to please Hitchcock, not a whole array of coworkers. Still, she got another kind of satisfaction out of the tough pictures when finding solutions where all of the parties were at odds.

Though the specific case of Edith taking credit for the Givenchy dresses in *Sabrina* was not yet well known in the early 1970s, there was widespread belief in film and fashion-industry circles that Edith couldn't draw at all and never actually designed anything. Once her cataracts were fixed, I did see her draw in her own, unique style, and I had ample proof that she could design almost anything. So where did she stand in terms of actual design talent? I left show business eventually, to become a teacher, first in public schools, then college. If I had to grade her, I'd say she rates a strong B+, and I think she'd agree.

Compared to the other designers of the various periods she worked in, most of her gowns were almost as innovative as Adrian's, Irene's, and Helen Rose's, but not quite, but then Paramount producers and directors usually wanted simpler looks than their counterparts at MGM did. Edith handled many period assignments well even if she never had the extraordinary knowledge of fine detail and construction that Walter Plunkett came to have. Her work on westerns was quite acceptable but not as precise and accurate as Yvonne Wood's, and she didn't know as much about anthropology as Renie Conley and Dorothy Jeakins did. She certainly didn't quite have the flair and humor that personified the work of Orry-Kelly and later Bob Mackie. All these designers were enormously talented and deserve biographies of their own.

Edith has been criticized for relying heavily on her staff. Having a staff of associate designers is very common in retail work, and virtually all the designers of Hollywood's Golden Era at least used sketch artists. Walter Plunkett insisted that he never allowed his sketch artists to give him any input. Helen Rose said the same thing, though Moss Mabry, who came to help Helen at MGM on *Butterfield 8* (1960) when she was losing interest, says that she'd also ask Donna Peterson for more than just sketching. "Just give me some pure vanilla, Donna," she'd say. Edward Stevenson at RKO would occasionally dry up and allow Yvonne Wood to submit ideas, and even the great Orry-Kelly pleaded with Leah Rhodes, "Give me some new way to break [Bette Davis's] bust!" It was true that Edith used her assistants more than the others, but *Dead Men Don't Wear Plaid* proved to me that she could do all phases of the work by herself. In her heyday at Paramount she also turned out more pictures per year than any of the designers at the other studios, and considering her modest salary combined with the even smaller ones her assistants got, she was a bargain too good for Paramount to give up.

The fact that Edith eventually became more famous for being famous than for her talent was proof to some that she had no talent. Not so. When fate put her in the fashion game, she grabbed the ball, ran with it, and never looked back. I think she would have succeeded just as well at any profession she might have fallen into and had she come along a generation later, it probably would have been politics or diplomacy. When Madeleine Albright was secretary of state, I often saw her on television, and I was reminded of Edith. Like Edith, Albright had a long-undisclosed Jewish background. Not conventionally beautiful, she, like Edith, found her own style, was charismatic and attractive, and, most important, always knew just the right thing to say, something which would satisfy everybody in a tricky situation. Edith could have done that job, but ultimately it wouldn't have suited her as well as the one she did. The close scrutiny under which public figures find themselves these days would have severely limited Edith's intrigues and she wouldn't have enjoyed the decades of attention the movie business gave her.

In a 1955 interview, Edith candidly said, "Within the limitations set by the story, the actress's figure, the censor, good taste, the budget, the color expert, the set decorator, the sound technician, the cameraman, the director, and my own creativeness, I simply give the actress what she wants. And I don't try to cram anything down her throat.

"In any one building on New York's Seventh Avenue, there are twenty designers better than I, but they wouldn't last a day in Hollywood." That was Edith's triumph. She lasted.

Film Credits

1925

The Wanderer

1926

Mantrap

1927

Wings

1928

Red Hair

Ladies of the Mob

1929

The Saturday Night Kid

The Virginian

Wolf Song

1930

Along Came Youth

Only the Brave

The Santa Fe Trail

Shadow of the Law

1932

The Big Broadcast of 1932

Love Me Tonight

Undercover Man

1933

She Done Him Wrong

Cradle Song

Hello Everybody

Sitting Pretty

Strictly Personal

1934

Little Miss Marker

1935

The Big Broadcast of 1936

Lives of a Bengal Lancer

Mississippi

Ruggles of Red Gap

Peter Ibbetson

Wings in the Dark

1936

The Big Broadcast of 1937

The Jungle Princess

The Milky Way

Poppy

Woman Trap

College Holiday

1937

The Barrier

Blond Trouble

Blossoms on Broadway

Borderland

Bulldog Drummond Comes Back

Bulldog Drummond Escapes

Bulldog Drummond's Revenge

Clarence

The Crime Nobody Saw

A Doctor's Diary

Double or Nothing

Ebb Tide

Exclusive

Forlorn River

Girl from Scotland Yard

Murder Goes to College

The Great Gambini

Hideaway Girl

Hills of Old Wyoming

Hold 'Em Navy

Hotel Haywire

Her Husband Lies

Interns Can't Take Money

John Meade's Woman

Last Train from Madrid

Let's Make a Million

Make Way for Tomorrow

Midnight Madonna

Mind Your Own Business

Mountain Music

Souls at Sea

Night Club Scandal

A Night of Mystery

North of the Rio Grande

On Such a Night

Outcast

Partners in Crime

Partners of the Plains

She Asked for It

She's No Lady

Sophie Lang Goes West

Texas Trail

This Way Please

Thrill of a Lifetime

True Confession

Wild Money

Turn Off the Moon

Waikiki Wedding

Wells Fargo

1938

Artists and Models Abroad

The Arkansas Traveler

Bar 20 Justice

Booloo

Born to the West

Bulldog Drummond in Africa

Bulldog Drummond's Peril

Campus Confessions

Coconut Grove

Professor Beware

Prison Farm

Pride of the West

Men With Wings

Love on Toast

Little Orphan Annie

King of Alcatraz

In Old Mexico

Illegal Traffic

Hunted Men

Her Jungle Love

Heart of Arizona

Give Me a Sailor

The Frontiersman

College Swing

Ride a Crooked Mile

Say It in French

Scandal Street

Sing You Sinners

Tropic Holiday

Touchdown, Army

Tom Sawyer Detective

Tip-off Girls

Thanks for the Memory

The Texans

Sons of the Legion

Spawn of the North

Stolen Heaven

1939

Arrest Bulldog Drummond

All Women Have Secrets

Honeymoon in Bali

Heritage of the Desert

Back Door to Heaven

Beau Geste

Boy Trouble

The Great Victor Herbert

Grand Jury Secrets

The Gracie Allen Murder Case

Geronimo

Disputed Passage

Disbarred

Death of a Champion

The Cat and the Canary

Café Society

Bulldog Drummond's Secret Police

Bulldog Drummond's Bride

Night Work

The Night of Nights

Hotel Imperial

I'm From Missouri

Invitation to Happiness

Island of Lost Men

The Lady's From Kentucky

Law of the Pampas

The Light that Failed

The Llano Kid

The Magnificent Fraud

Man About Town

Million Dollar Legs

Never Say Die

$1,000 a Touchdown

Undercover Doctor

This Man in News

Television Spy

Sudden Money

St Louis Blues

Some Like It Hot

The Star Maker

Rulers of the Sea

Our Leading Citizen

Our Neighbors, the Carners

Paris Honeymoon

Persons in Hiding

What a Life

Unmarried

Zaza

1940

Adventure in Diamonds

Buck Benny Rides Again

Cherokee Strip

Christmas in July

Comin' Round the Mountain

Dancing on a Dime

Doctor Cyclops

Emergency Squad

The Farmer's Daughter

French Without Tears

Geronimo

The Ghost Breakers

Rhythm on the River

Remember the Night

Rangers of Fortune

Queen of the Mod

Quarterback

A Parole Fixer

Opened by Mistake

A Night at Earl Carrol's

Golden Gloves

The Great McGinty

I Want a Divorce

Love Thy Neighbor

Moon Over Burma

Mystery Sea Raider

Road to Singapore

Safari

Seventeen

The Show Down

Stagecoach War

Those Were the Days

Women Without Names

The Way of all Flesh

Untamed

Typhoon

Three Men From Texas

1941

Aloma of the South Seas
Among the Living
Life With Henry
Las Vegas Nights
The Lady Eve
Kiss the Boys Goodbye
I Wanted Wings
Hold Back the Dawn
Bahama Passage
Birth of the Blues
Buy Me That Town
Caught in the Draft
Doomed Caravan
Flying Blind
Forced Landing
Glamour Boy
Henry Aldrich for President
West Point Widow
World Premier
You're the One
You Belong to Me
Ball of Fire
Skylark (with Irene)
Sullivan's Travels
Road to Zanzibar
Here Comes Mr. Jordan
There's Magic in Music
Virginia
I Wanted Wings
Shepherd of the Hills
Reaching for the Sun
New York Town
One Night in Lisbon

1942

The Gay Sisters (with Anderson)
The Great Man's Lady
I Married a Witch
The Major and the Minor
The Road to Morocco
This Gun for Hire
Beyond the Blue Horizon
The Remarkable Andre
The Fleet's In
Young and Willing
My Favourite Blonde
Are Husbands Necessary?
Holiday Inn
The Glass Key
Star Spangled Rhythm
Lucky Jordan

1943

Flesh and Fantasy (with West)
True to Life
Lady of Burlesque (with Natalie Visart)
No Time for Love (with Irene)
The Crystal Ball
China
Salute for Three
Five Graves to Cairo
Riding High
Let's Face It
Hostages
Tender Comrade (with Renie)

1944

And Now Tomorrow
Going My Way
Here Come the Waves
I Love a Soldier
I'll Be Seeing You
Our Hearts Were Young and Gay
The Uninvited
Standing Room Only
Lady in the Dark (with Du Bois, Leisen)
Rainbow Island
Double Indemnity
Ministry of Fear
And the Angels Sing
Hour Before Dawn

1945

The Affairs of Susan
The Bells of St. Mary's
Christmas in Connecticut (with Anderson)
Duffy's Tavern (with Dodson)
Incendiary Blonde

The Lost Weekend
Love Letters
Masquerade in Mexico
A Medal for Benny
Miss Susie Slagle's (with Dodson)
Out of this World
The Road to Utopia
The Stork Club

1946

The Blue Dahlia
My Reputation (with Rhodes)
Notorious
The Strange Love of Martha Ivers
To Each His Own
The Virginian
The Well-Groomed Bride
Blue Skies (with Waldo Angelo)
The Perfect Marriage
Cross My Heart
The Bride Wore Boots
California

1947

The Road to Rio
The Two Mrs Carrolls (with Anderson)
Welcome Stranger
My Favorite Brunette
Desert Fury
I Walk Alone
Where There's Life
Wild Harvest
Perils of Pauline
Variety Girl
Blaze of Noon
Ramrod

1948

The Big Clock
The Emperor's Waltz
A Foreign Affair
Miss Tatlock's Millions
The Night Has a Thousand Eyes
Rachel and the Stranger
Sorry Wrong Number
Arch of Triumph
Dream Girl
My Own True Love
Beyond Glory
Sainted Sisters
So Evil My Love
Isn't It Romantic
June Bride (with Rhodes)

1949

The Heiress (with Steele)
Red, Hot and Blue
Rope of Sand
My Friend Irma
The Great Lover
The Great Gatsby
Beyond the Forest
Sunset Boulevard

1950

Copper Canyon (with Steele)
Mr. Music
My Foolish Heart (with Wills)
My Friend Irma Goes West
Riding High
Samson and Delilah (with Steele, Jeakins, Wakeling, Elois Jenssen)
Paid in Full
September Affair
All About Eve (with LeMaire)

1951

The Big Carnival
Branded
Detective Story
Here Comes the Groom
The Lemon Drop Kid
Payment on Demand
A Place in the Sun
That's My Boy

1952

Carrie

The Greatest Show on Earth (with Jeakins, White)

Jumping Jacks

Just for You (with Wood)

My Favorite Spy

Sailor Beware

Son of Paleface

Something to Live for

1953

The Caddy

Come Back Little Sheba

Off Limits

Road to Bali

Roman Holiday

Sangaree

Scared Stiff

Shane

The Stooge

Red Garters (with Wood)

The Stars Are Singing

1954

Elephant Walk

Here Come the Girls

Knock on Wood

Living It Up

Money from Home

The Naked Jungle

Rear Window

Sabrina

White Christmas

The Country Girl

About Mrs. Leslie

1955

Artists and Models

The Bridges at Toko-Ri

The Desperate Hours

The Far Horizon

The Girl Rush

Hell's Island

Lucy Gallant

The Rose Tattoo

Run for Cover

The Seven Little Foys

Strategic Air Command

Three Ring Circus

To Catch a Thief

The Trouble with Harry

You're Never Too Young

1956

Anything Goes

The Birds and the Bees

The Court Jester (with Wood)

Hollywood or Bust

The Leather Saint

The Man Who Knew Too Much

The Mountain

Pardners

The Proud and the Profane

The Rainmaker

The Scarlet Hour

The Search for Bridey Murphey

That Certain Feeling

The Lonely Man

1957

Beau James

The Buster Keaton Story

The Delicate Delinquent

The Devil's Hairpin

Fear Strikes Out

Funny Face (with Hubert de Givenchy)

Gunfight at the O.K. Corral

Hear Me Good

The Joker Is Wild

Loving You

The Sad Sack

Short Cut to Hell

The Ten Commandments (with Jeakins, Jester John Jensen, Arnold Friberg)

The Tin Star

Three Violent People

Wild Is the Wind

1958

As Young as We Are

The Buccaneer (with Jester)

The Geisha Boy

Hot Spell

Houseboat

Macaibo

The Matchmaker

Rock-A-Bye Baby

Separate Tables (with Grant)

St Louis Blues

Teacher's Pet

Vertigo

Witness for the Prosecution

1959

Alias Jesse James

The Black Orchid

Career

A Hole in the Head

The Jayhawkers

That Kind of Woman

The Five Pennies

1960

The Facts of Life (with Stevenson)

Cinderfella

Heller in Pink Tights

Pepe

The Rat Race

A Visit to a Small Planet

1961

All in a Night's Work

Breakfast at Tiffany's (with Hubert de Givenchy, Pauline Trigère)

The Errand Boy

The Ladies' Man

Man-Trap

On the Double

The Pleasure of His Company

Pocketful of Miracles (with Plunkett)

Summer and Smoke

1962

The Counterfeit Traitor

Hatari

It's Only Money

My Geisha

Too Late Blues

Who's Got the Action?

The Man Who Shot Liberty Valance

1963

The Birds

Come Blow Your Horn

Critic's Choice

Donovan's Reef

Fun in Acapulco

A Girl Named Tamiko

Hud

I Could Go on Singing

My Six Loves

A New Kind of Love

The Nutty Professor

Papa's Delicate Condition

Who's Minding the Store?

Wives and Lovers

1964

The Carpetbaggers

The Disorderly Orderly

A House Is not a Home

Love with the Proper Stranger

Man's Favorite Sport

Marnie

The Patsy

Roustabout

Sex and the Single Girl (with Norman Norell)

What a Way to Go! (with Mabry)

Where Love Has Gone

1965

Boeing, Boeing

The Family Jewels

The Hallelujah Trail
Harlow (with Mabry)
John Goldfarb, Please Come Home (with Balkan)
Love Has Many Faces
The Sons of Katie Elder
Sylvia
The Yellow Rolls-Royce (with Castello, Pierre Cardin)
The Slender Thread

1966
Assault on a Queen
The Last of the Secret Agents
Not With My Wife You Don't!
The Oscar
Paradise, Hawaiian Style
Penelope
The Swinger
This Property Is Condemned
Torn Curtain
Waco
Inside Daisy Clover (with Thomas)

1967
Barefoot in the Park
The Caper of the Golden Bulls
Chuck
Easy Come, Easy Go
Warning Shot
Hotel (with Shoup)

1968
In Enemy Country
The Pink Jungle
The Secret War of Harry Frigg
What's So Bad About Feeling Good?

1969
Topaz
Story of a Woman
Eye of the Cat
The Lost Man
Butch Cassidy and the Sundance Kid
Airport

1970
Sweet Charity
Madame Sin

1971
Red Sky at Morning
Hammersmith Is Out

1972
The Screaming Woman

1973
Judge Roy Bean
Pete 'n Tillie
A Doll's House

1974
The Don Is Dead
Ash Wednesday

1975
Airport '75
Rooster Cogburn
The Man Who Would Be King
The Great Waldo Pepper
Gable and Lombard

1976
W.C. Fields and Me (with Bill Jobe)

1977
Airport '77 (with Burton Miller)

1978
The Big Fix
Olly Olly Oxen Free
Sextette

1979

The Last Married Couple in America

Little Women

1980

Women in White

The Disappearance of Aimee

1982

Dead Men Don't Wear Plaid

OSCAR NOMINATIONS/AWARDS

(* Indicates that Head Won the Academy Award)

1948
The Emperor Waltz (color) with Gile Steele

1949
**The Heiress* (b/w) with Gile Steele

1950
**All About Eve* (b/w) with Charles LeMaire
**Samson and Delilah* (color) with Dorothy Jeakins, Elois Jenssen, Gile Steele, Gwen Wakeling

1951
**A Place in the Sun* (b/w)

1952
Carrie

1953
**Roman Holiday*

1954
**Sabrina*

1955
The Rose Tattoo (b/w)
To Catch a Thief (color)

1956
The Proud and the Profane (b/w)
The Ten Commandments (color) with Ralph Jester, John Jensen, Dorothy Jeakins, Arnold Friberg

1957
Funny Face (color) with Hubert de Givenchy

1958
The Buccaneer (color) with Ralph Jester, John Jensen

1959
Career (b/w)
The Five Pennies (color)

1960
**The Facts of Life* (b/w) with Edward Stevenson

1961

Pocketful of Miracles (color) with Walter Plunkett

1962

The Man Who Shot Liberty Valance (b/w)

1963

Love With the Proper Stranger (b/w)

Wives and Lovers (b/w)

A New Kind of Love (color)

1964

A House Is not a Home (b/w)

What a Way to Go (color) with Moss Mabry

1965

The Slender Thread (b/w)

Inside Daisy Clover (color) with Bill Thomas

1966

The Oscar (color)

1969

Sweet Charity

1970

Airport

1973

**The Sting*

1975

The Man Who Would Be King

1977

Airport '77

Index

Page numbers of illustrations and photos appear in italics. EH refers to Edith Head